OTTO PENZLER PRESENTS
AMERICAN MYSTERY CLASSICS

THE GREAT HOTEL MURDER

VINCENT STARRETT (1886–1974) was a Chicago journalist who became one of the world's foremost experts on Sherlock Holmes. A books columnist for the *Chicago Tribune*, he also wrote biographies of authors such as Robert Louis Stevenson and Ambrose Bierce, various books on books and book collecting, plus Sherlockian pastiches and numerous short stories and novels. A founding member of the Baker Street Irregulars, he is perhaps known best today for *The Private Life of Sherlock Holmes*, an imaginative biography of the great detective.

LYNDSAY FAYE is the author of six critically acclaimed books: *The Paragon Hotel; Jane Steele*, which was nominated for an Edgar for Best Novel; *Dust and Shadow*, a Sherlock Holmes pastiche; *The Gods of Gotham*, also Edgar-nominated; *Seven for a Secret*; and *The Fatal Flame*. She has also published numerous short stories featuring the Holmes character, several of which were collected in 2017's *The Whole Art of Detection*. She lives in Queens.

THE GREAT HOTEL MURDER

VINCENT STARRETT

Introduction by
LYNDSAY FAYE

AMERICAN MYSTERY CLASSICS

Penzler Publishers
New York

Published in 2020 by Penzler Publishers
58 Warren Street, New York, NY 10007
penzlerpublishers.com

Distributed by W. W. Norton

Cover image: Andy Ross
Cover design: Mauricio Diaz

Paperback ISBN 9781613161883
Hardcover ISBN 9781613161876
eBook ISBN 9781613161890

Library of Congress Control Number: 2020912208

Printed in the United States of America

9 8 7 6 5 4 3 2

THE GREAT HOTEL
MURDER

INTRODUCTION

AMONG THE REASONS to love Charles Vincent Emerson Starrett (of which there are multitudes) is that, notwithstanding his status as a passionate bibliophile, critic, poet, essayist, novelist, and *bon vivant*, the man never graduated high school. This always rang a bell with me.

I may have my bachelors in theatre and literature, but I can claim no graduate experience whatsoever. (I've been roundly booted from academic journals when this scholarly deficiency was discovered and asked politely whether I wouldn't like to write the introduction instead; I'm swell at those.) To boot, I've never taken a creative writing class in my life, and have always looked at elite programs in which venerable literary gods break the egos of their students until Pulitzer material gushes from the piñata with a kind of fascinated queasiness. I don't know whether Starrett would have remotely liked me, but I know for a fact I'd have taken a mighty shine to Starrett. Like me, he wrote books because he grew up marinating in them. These might not be lofty beginnings, but they're highly egalitarian ones.

Vincent Starrett was raised above his father's Toronto bookstore and he lived in the children's literature section. I was raised in a paper mill town in Washington State and I lived in the public library's carpet-lined bathtubs in the children's literature section. Starrett never lost his unabashed enthusiasm for all things adventurous, mysterious, piratical, alien, thrilling, or fantastical. He likewise never misplaced his affection for soothing comforts: *The Boxcar Children, Treasure Island, Little Lord Fauntleroy.*

His tastes were never sullied by pseudo-intellectual elitism, and if he were alive today, I'd bet a Benjamin Franklin that he would own first editions of *The Hunger Games* series, but possibly not *Infinite Jest.* There's nothing wrong with enjoying David Foster Wallace, mind—I'd just lay my money on Suzanne Collins as a sure thing.

Malcolm Gladwell in his now-iconic book regarding extraordinary success, *Outliers,* makes a lot of hay about being born in the right place at the right time. Starrett was undoubtedly born in the right locale—he had hundreds of fictional worlds at his fingertips the instant he descended a staircase. But in a way, the timing of his birth was likewise fortuitous. 1934, the year *Recipe for Murder* was published in *Redbook Magazine* (later to spread its wings and expand into *The Great Hotel Murder* when published the next year by Doubleday's imprint, the Crime Club), was a darkly troubled one.

When Franklin Delano Roosevelt arrived in office in 1932, a quarter of America's wage earners were unemployed. Nine thousand banks had closed by the next year, between them magically disappearing two-and-a-half billion dollars' worth of deposits. It's hardly surprising, therefore, that by far the most popular entertainment was unrepentantly escapist: radio serials, screwball comedies, sports rivalries, sci-fi fantasias. Whodunits slotted nicely into this groove and, thankfully, Starrett of all people knew his way around mystery novels.

He'd been writing his PI sleuth Jimmie Lavender in short story format for around two decades by the mid-thirties, racking up fifty or so published cases, and had started experimenting with novels helmed by Walter Ghost in 1929. His utterly and endlessly beloved essay collection *The Private Life of Sherlock Holmes* was released in October of 1933. He had experience as a reporter for the *Chicago Tribune*, then as their book critic, and by the time he sat down to write what would become *The Great Hotel Murder*, let's just say there was a pretty solid built-in audience queuing up for this sort of material. Clearly it was high time for Starrett to write his own avatar as a gentleman detective.

Don't imagine that I say this in any pejorative fashion. On the contrary. That would be hypocritical, as the vast majority of the major characters in my novels possess various striking similarities to yours truly. And I'm not saying *definitively* that Riley Blackwood, the theatre-critic-cum-amateur-sleuth who stars in *The Great Hotel Murder*, was *intended* to be just a smidge autobiographical. It may well have an accident. Certainly, Blackwood positively glows with appreciation for his Chicago habitat. "Out on the lake an excursion steamer was plodding into port, outlined in colored lights against the purple sky. The endless line of motorcars was coughing past, as always, in the street below. All the world was wagging merrily," he gushes after recovering from a conk on the head, "appalled by his own isolation."

Starrett was equally in love with his chosen Windy City, from its powerhouse publishing industry to its wild atmosphere to naming Jimmie Lavender after a pitcher for the Chicago Cubs. Indeed, by the time Blackwood finds himself in the Wisconsin woods attempting to locate a key suspect gone missing, his preference for Chicago grows downright humorous.

"He was ardently sick of trees, in spite of an early-morning notion that dwellers in the city were oafs and half-wits. Trees hemmed one in. They weighed mysteriously on the senses. He hoped that he would never *see* another adjectival *tree*. The poet who could sing of *trees* was full of bats and mice and *fleas*. Riley Blackwood, jiggling along a country road in northern

Wisconsin, would have given up a dollar and a half for just one glimpse of a sputtering white electric sign in Clark Street."

But this observation regarding love of one's metropolis is surely inconclusive—who is Philip Marlowe without Los Angeles or Sherlock Holmes without London? It may also be happenstance that Blackwood, like Starrett, is bony and satirical and bespectacled, with a genial disposition and a penchant for irony. It's possibly pure chance that both men are newspaper critics, both men started off as journalists, and both men collect mysteries (Blackwood rather more aggressively than Starrett himself, I grant, since to my knowledge Starrett never held any villains at gunpoint). Both men have an eye for the fair sex—Blackwood as a roving bachelor and Starrett both in and out of wedlock on occasion—but what of that? Of Blackwood we further learn, "The number of [his] books was legion… He liked to idle there among them, in certain moods, and feel himself a part of that great company of crime savants who stalked and blustered in so many of their pages." This passage could equally well describe Starrett, but maybe my own love of detective stories is causing me to hatch ludicrous conspiracy theories.

In any event Riley Blackwood, for some inexplicable reason, is allowed to traipse all over his friend Widdowson's lavish downtown hotspot, the Hotel Granada, solving crimes. (Or rather, attempting to solve crimes.) Briefly, a man named Dr. Trample has switched rooms with a man named Jordan Chambers (an alias, we later learn), and Chambers the next morning is found tangled in his sheets, quite dead. Who better to consult than an arts critic?

We know the drill here; the police will be flummoxed and the amateur will capture the flag with a flash in his eye and a whistle on his lips. But as I said, in the mid-1930s, when Chicago was booming and the Southern Plains were turning into the Dust

Bowl, *why not* consult an arts critic? Blackwood makes keen observations, draws astute inferences, knows the prettiest actresses, trades barbs handily, and is good at card tricks. All admirable qualities. And qualities that perfectly suit this sort of mystery—we're not solving the travails of destitute America here, and we're not avenging a lynching or looking for a missing child. There's a swank hotel dealing with an apparent suicide that Blackwood insists is a murder, and a lot of varyingly attractive people whirl about through the lobby's revolving doors. *The Great Hotel Murder* is *fun*, and Starrett knew better than to stick his nose in the air when enjoying the book in front of it.

And so do I. It would take a tremendous effort and churlishness of spirit *not* to like *The Great Hotel Murder*. The varyingly attractive people I mentioned are tropes, yes, but in Starrett's deft hands, they are much more. Sleazy PI antagonist Gene Cross is thuggish, but he's also cunning. Our somewhat-heroine Blaine Oliver is beautiful and witty, but she's refreshingly insightful and short-fused, too. Harry Prentiss, her dashing young friend, toes the line between ally and suspect until the final pages, and the elusive but affable Dr. Trample is either the obvious murderer or else the victim of astonishingly vexing coincidences. Kitty Mock—actress, occasional dope addict, and wife of the dead man—might be a bit empty between the ears, but she's shockingly practical and such a very *talented* actress that she can get away with all manner of mischief without a degree in rocket science, thank you very much. Yes, Riley Blackwood is a well-off young intellectual, but he isn't above diving into the notoriously inhospitable waters of Lake Michigan to save a man overboard.

It must be noted that Starrett would have been well aware of the character types he was toying with; he was too much of a literary critic not to have done it deliberately. And as familiar a name as Starrett's is to any admirer of the Great Detective, Mr. Sherlock Holmes of Baker Street, another legendary Sherlockian contemporary of his ought to be mentioned here, and that is Monsignor Ronald Knox—priest, radio personality, translator, essayist, satirist, lecturer, and fellow shameless peddler of original detective fiction. In 1929, Knox codified the Golden Age of Detective Fiction into a Decalogue of ten hard and fast rules. Starrett follows most of them, and that's a satisfying and familiar blanket to snuggle inside. The criminal is mentioned early on, for example—no ghosts need apply—we aren't infested with secret chambers, and twins fail to plague us.

But equally satisfying are the aspects of this rulebook Starrett flirts with breaking or outright ignores. No "Chinaman" (with all apologies for even mentioning this regrettable edict) is meant to figure in the story according to Knox; Starrett, however, who lived for a year and a half in Peking, promptly and with a certain flair announces that Blackwood's beloved Aunt Julie employs a Chinese servant. I can't help but think he knew exactly what he was doing. And Father Knox's Rule Six, that "no accident must ever help the detective, nor must he ever have an unaccountable intuition which proves to be right," is altogether run over by a roadster in *The Great Hotel Murder*. Blackwood knows the exact cut of Dr. Trample's jib from the beginning; it only remains to understand what the devil is going on.

He's also helped by a frankly hilarious number of accidents, which only adds to Blackwood's charm. One gets the feeling (and again, here we veer into territory that may ever so slightly resemble Starrett himself) that Blackwood would absolutely love to be Sherlock Holmes if he could, but is plagued by that pesky ailment so many of us suffer from: being a mere mortal.

Not everyone can be expert in boxing and chemistry, dirt types and dialects, ninja skills and legal arguments. It's exhausting just to contemplate being Sherlock Holmes for a day, let alone an entire lifetime. That's not to say the heroes don't share marvelous similarities. Regarding Gene Cross, Blackwood mentions, in the most casually Sherlockian fashion to his friend Blackwood, "He's a key piece in this puzzle. He has a very irregular outline, and God knows where he fits." Like Holmes, Blackwood is well aware we are each starring in our own drama, that life imitates art and art life, and he has a tendency to wax philosophical about it. Also like Holmes, for a character about whom we are being told a story, he is weirdly self-aware of his own existence. Holmes knew about Watson's *Strand Magazine* chronicles; many a riposte was aimed at them. As the plot gains momentum, we learn of Blackwood, "He had set out to solve the mystery in his own way; and his own way had been, of course, the way of the cerebral story-book and stage detective." When he finally does crack the case, a still more meta-fictional inner monologue pours forth.

"And what a simple explanation, if that were all of it! Simple and natural—and surprising. The good old formula. The sort of thing that lay concealed beneath the red-herring trickery of all good fictional problems, then bobbed up at the end to knock the cock-eyed reader cold with astonishment. And with dismay that he had not guessed it earlier."

"'Elementary, my dear fellow! It has all been obvious from the beginning. It was the butler, of course!'"

Unfortunately for Blackwood (and perhaps for Starrett, too), he isn't Sherlock Holmes and never will be. Regarding his own foibles and failures, he's both understandably tetchy yet endearingly philosophical. *The Great Hotel Murder* isn't the knot of Euclidean problem-solving that Sherlock Holmes wistfully thought all cases ought to look like; it's a romp, much more to Watson's tastes than Holmes's refined sensibilities. Blackwood finds himself drinking his breakfast, snaking an arm around alluring women, making outright errors in judgment, tripping over his own feet, getting whacked in the noggin, and sneaking around the woods on tippy-toe like an adolescent heading for a forbidden bonfire in a way Holmes would have found downright embarrassing.

Watson would have loved it, however. And so do I. And so did the public. *The Great Hotel Murder* hadn't even cooled off from its printing when Fox Films snapped up the movie rights. By 1935, lo and behold, it was already a flick starring Edmond Lowe and Victor McLaglen. Although Starrett liked to quip that the film differed enough from his novel that he was as surprised by the ending as anyone else, he must have been proud to see his efforts reap so much success so quickly, and bring so many people pleasure during remarkably difficult times.

It's highly gratifying to see it back in print, and again, I experience that joy on a personal level. Sherlock Holmes says (very rightly, too) that when a doctor goes wrong, he is the first of criminals—he has the training, intelligence, and foresight to plot all sorts of dastardly deeds. Well, I will go so far as to say that when a *reader* goes rogue, he or she can potentially become the best of *writers*. Starrett penned what he did for love of a ripping yarn, without blushing or prevaricating or gatekeeping of any sort, wanting only to give his audience a chance to escape the reality of their lives for a little while. What a lovely goal. What a timeless one.

It would be completely hubristic to fantasize that we might have been pals if Vincent Starrett were around today. But it's perfectly safe for me to admit that I want to be him when I grow up.

—LYNDSAY FAYE

THE GREAT HOTEL
MURDER

1.

THE BROWN-EYED BELLHOP, in regimentals than which the uniform of a major general was not more magnificent, shrilled his way across the crowded lobby and vanished along the corridor leading to the dining rooms. For a time his voice continued to be heard, *diminuendo,* in the passage; then it passed beyond the hearing of chattering idlers in the lounge, only to return mysteriously, a little later—muffled by distance and in varying keys—from the lower levels occupied by barber shop and grill. It trickled up the stairways in little blobs and trills of fragmentary sound.

"Dr. Trample . . . Dr. H. C. Trample . . . Dr. Trample . . ."

The girl in the red raincoat sat tensely forward on the edge of her chair, beside a cluster of potted palms, and waited. Her ridiculously small umbrella dripped slowly at her side; her small foot impatiently tapped the rug beneath it. Between the anxious eyes a little frown had settled. Dr. Trample, she told herself—Dr. H. C. Trample—was taking his time about keeping his appointment. And Miss Blaine Oliver, she inwardly added, was beginning to wish that she had breakfasted at home.

She viewed the humming lobby with humorous distaste. Pompous, strutting little boulevardiers, driven to refuge by the rain, continued their solemn promenades; they strolled in and out among the chairs as if they were playing "Going to Jerusalem." Furtive-looking citizens, who had neglected to turn down the collars of their overcoats, stood about in twos and threes, and talked out of the corners of their mouths. Bustling carpet merchants tossed boisterous greetings to their confrères, arriving for a convention of their kind. At the cigar stand a flashy youth exchanged audacious compliments with the salesgirl. Here and there a woman snuggled into the corner of a love seat and endeavored to look virtuous; but her sex, at this hour, was outnumbered by the thronging men. Brokers, bond salesmen, cattle buyers, gangsters; rich man, poor man, beggar man, thief. Was it possible really to tell them apart?

Outside, the rain still fell wearily. It was a melancholy morning to drive into the city for breakfast with a stranger! Well, *almost* a stranger. She had been a little girl when Horace Trample had seen her last—barely out of pinafores. Would he remember her? She was certain enough that she would remember *him*.

Her wrist watch told her that it was well past nine-thirty. Ordinarily she had breakfasted by nine, which had been the hour set for the appointment. Men were that way, of course. And their excuses were so funny! He had met a friend from South America, no doubt—or Portland, Oregon—and the boy would find them at the bar. Like all other men that she had met, Dr. Trample—Dr. H. C. Trample—probably believed that women were notoriously tardy in their trysts.

Suddenly she was aware that the boy was in the lobby again. His voice, keyed to a more temperate pitch after its circumambulatory exercises, was emerging from the glittering corridor. On the edges of the concourse it was making a final plea for Dr. H. C. Trample to reveal himself.

Then it was at her elbow.

"I'm sorry, miss, but he doesn't answer. I've been everywhere. Are you sure he isn't in his room?"

Miss Oliver nodded. "I've telephoned twice," she said; "but I'll try again. There's nothing else to do." She fumbled in her purse. . . . "Thank you!"

"Thank *you*," said the boy. "I'll go round again, if you like."

"No, don't bother. I'll keep on telephoning until he comes in. Something must have kept him," she added apologetically, and hated herself for the remark. It was her pride she was defending, not Horace Trample.

It occurred to the obliging bellhop that he would not himself have kept a girl like that waiting. He made a suggestion: "Tell the operator to keep on ringing, miss. Sometimes they oversleep."

She smiled faintly. "Thank you! I'll—I'll tell the operator to keep on ringing." She was anxious now only to be rid of this witness, as it were, to her humiliation.

How much longer, she wondered, as she moved toward the telephones, would her militant pride permit her to wait? Physicians, after all, were important human beings. They had duties in the world that set them apart, somewhat, from their neighbors. But they were inclined, she fancied, to presume a trifle on the fact of their profession—to demand a tolerance on the part of others that their vagaries did not always deserve. She had known young doctors before.

However, it was to be remembered that this one was no longer precisely young. And he was really rather important, she believed. A specialist of some kind.

It was conceivable, of course, that something had happened to him—some illness or injury; but somehow it seemed unlikely. Of all men, surely, physicians were best able to look after themselves. That Horace Trample was a New Yorker, only recently returned to the city of his birth, had no bearing on the case. He had grown up in Chicago; it was as familiar to him as the palm of his hand. It was not as if he had just arrived from some Arkansas village.

But the main thing was that she was hungry—damn him! Possibly the thing to do was go in to breakfast by herself, after leaving word at the desk.

She lifted the receiver and, after a moment, said, "Room nine-four-o, please." Thereafter there were sounds of strident ringing which continued intermittently for thirty seconds. Then the voice of the operator cut in. "I am ringing room nine-four-o," it recited with mechanical lifelessness, and vanished before retort could be made.

At length there was something final. "Room nine-four-o does not answer," said the operator; and in the little empty silence that followed Blaine Oliver replaced the receiver upon its hook and turned her troubled gaze upon the lobby. Over a door, the hands of a great clock stood at nine forty-five.

For an instant she paused in indecision; then with compressed lips started for the desk.

She had not taken a dozen steps, however, when a quick hand was laid on her arm. She whirled breathlessly, half smiling and half scolding. Her face fell.

"Blaine!" cried the young man at her elbow. "What brings *you* downtown at this hour of the morning?" One would have thought it was not yet sunrise.

"I could kill you, Harry," she replied in level tones. "I thought you were someone else. Why aren't you?" Then her eyes brightened, and a little laugh escaped her lips. "I'm annoyed—pay no attention to me."

"But what's the trouble?" he insisted. "Can't I help?"

"I'm starving," said Miss Oliver. "I haven't had a mouthful since I got up. I had a breakfast engagement at the hotel—and my friend, if you must know, has not showed up."

He laughed. "It's a situation easily remedied."

"I know," she said; "you'll take me to breakfast. Thanks! I

don't mean to be ungrateful, really. I may even let you do it. But I'm not sure that I ought to leave the lobby. Although I was just going to," she added grimly. "Look here, do you mind if I tell you about it?"

"I'd love to hear about it."

"Now that I have company, I'll give him another fifteen minutes," said Miss Oliver. "Isn't it a beast of a day? I've been feeling like Sadie Thompson—without a missionary! There are two chairs over there. Shall we sit?"

She told him the harrowing tale of the missing specialist and of her growing pangs of hunger. Mr. Prentiss was deeply sympathetic.

"You're a comfortable person to talk to, Harry," she admitted. "I can bare my soul to you. It's a funny soul—odd, you know; not humorous! It is disappointed and a little bit alarmed. You see, I don't know the man from Adam, really. I remember him from my youth—all right, my childhood then! At that time I felt a sort of romantic attachment for him. He must be nearly forty now!"

Miss Oliver mentioned the figure as if it were a tragic symbol of senility.

"What did he do? Call you up?"

"Yes—called me up. It was all right, of course. He was Dad's friend, too. He hadn't heard that Dad was dead." She added: "It couldn't be a hoax, I suppose?"

"Probably not," said Prentiss. "No, he's been detained, all right. Probably something fairly important, since he's a doctor. However, you're not bound to wait forever. Why not leave word at the desk—then let me take you to breakfast?"

"It's been in my mind," she told him. "But suppose something has happened to him?"

"You haven't been upstairs?"

"To his room, you mean? No, I haven't."

"I mean—if he had been taken ill, during the night—and couldn't answer the telephone——"

"I see!" She nodded. "Then I ought to go up. Well, it's giving him the benefit of the doubt. You'll go with me, of course."

"Of course."

"All right," she said; "let's go."

They crossed the lobby, pushed their way along the glittering corridor, and entered an elevator. The steel gates clanged twice, and they debouched upon the ninth-floor level. Before the door of room 940 Prentiss stopped with curious abruptness.

"Hello," he said, "there's a card on his doorknob. '*Please Do Not Disturb!*' By Jove, the beggar *isn't* up yet!"

Miss Oliver paled and laid a hand on his arm. "Harry," she said, "he's ill! He must be! You were right!"

He frowned—hesitated—then brought his knuckles up to knock. For a moment his hand seemed to hang suspended in the air; then it descended. Instinctively they turned their heads sidewise, listening. After an instant their eyes met.

Somewhere beyond the barrier a little clock was ticking briskly. It was the only sound from the bedchamber—and after a long moment it was suddenly intolerable.

"Try the door!" cried Miss Oliver. She stepped forward and laid her hand on the knob. "*Locked!*"

Prentiss was uncomfortable. "It's absurd," he said. "He can't be sleeping that soundly." He knocked again with greater violence. "Not a peep out of him!" he grumbled. "You don't happen to know whether or not he's a drinking man?"

Miss Oliver ignored the question; she was definitely alarmed.

"Harry," she cried; "we've got to get inside! Something *has*—happened! Don't you see? He's ill—or something!" She raised her voice and called through the panels: "Dr. Trample! It's *me*—Blaine Oliver!"

Prentiss yielded reluctantly; he hated trouble. "I suppose so," he agreed; and in the next instant was visited of an inspiration. "There's a house telephone in that little niche we passed. I'll call the manager."

In less than a minute he was jiggling the hook with nervous fingers. "Hello," he called; "hello—hello! Operator—give me the manager, as quickly as you can. Don't argue! There's a man sick up here. Room 940. Send up the house physician too."

He banged down the receiver and hurried back to Miss Oliver.

"That'll do it," he said. "We'll have the whole establishment up here in no time." Having taken this decisive step, he was suddenly all fuss and action. He peered savagely up and down the corridor. "Damn funny there isn't a maid around someplace!"

In a short time they heard the elevator doors crash open and crash shut again. Around the turn that concealed them from view came two men. They were not running; they were merely walking rapidly, until they caught sight of Prentiss and Miss Oliver. Then their footsteps slowed appreciably, and they came forward with a certain asperity.

"Did you telephone?" asked the manager, who was foremost. "About a sick man? Where is he?"

"He's inside," said Blaine Oliver. "We can't get in. The door is locked."

The manager's eye had spotted the card upon the knob. It worried him. "After all——" he began, and stopped. "I suppose you've knocked! Is he a friend of yours?"

"Of course he is!"

The manager's sense of propriety was still troubling him. "We're not supposed to disturb a guest who chooses to sleep late," he protested uneasily. "Have you tried the telephone?"

Prentiss was exasperated. "My God!" he exploded. "It's obvious that the man's ill. He needs attention. Of course we've telephoned! And knocked! Miss Oliver had an appointment with him for nine o'clock. What is needed to get in here—a search warrant?"

The manager stepped forward. He tapped tentatively on the panels with his nails; then cleared his throat and tapped a little harder. After a moment he gently shook the door handle, cocking his head like a fat robin.

His eyes sought those of his companion. The other nodded.

"You didn't say the door was locked," growled the second man. "We'll have to get a pass-key."

Very suddenly the manager came to life. He turned. "Wait here, Joe—I'll be back in a couple of minutes."

He hurried off on his mission, and there was little difference between his twinkling walk and a gallop. They watched him until he had turned the corner.

Prentiss and Miss Oliver turned their glances upon the man who was left.

"We looked around for a maid and couldn't find one," explained Prentiss courteously enough. "Are you the doctor?"

But the man did not look like a doctor; he looked to Prentiss like a retired pugilist. By an interesting coincidence, this was precisely what he was.

"House detective," growled the man laconically. After a moment he added: "The doctor's on his way up. If they can find him, he is. Who *is* your friend, lady?"

"Dr. Trample," said Blaine Oliver. "I had an appointment with him, and he didn't keep it." She explained briefly what had happened. "I'm afraid we are wasting valuable time," she finished a bit acidly.

The burly detective shrugged. "Can't be helped," he said. "We'll get in as quick as we can." He looked significantly at Prentiss. "Not much use, from the looks of it!"

Miss Oliver exclaimed in protest. "You mean—you think——?"

"Mr. Moffat thinks so, anyway." The big detective avoided the issue. His voice was not unkindly; he even ventured a smile that was intended to be sympathetic. "We've seen things like this happen before," he added.

"Like this?"

"Locked doors—and the card hanging on the handle. No answer when you knock! But I don't want to scare you!"

Miss Oliver drew in her breath. After a moment she leaned against the corridor wall, and Prentiss hastened to put an arm around her shoulders. "All right?" he asked.

"Yes," she said; "all right. Don't help me!"

Prentiss again was suddenly savage. "Damnation!" he cried. "I wish you *had* had your breakfast!"

He was not endeavoring to be funny; but she smiled faintly.

"I don't want to scare you," repeated the detective. "I was just preparing you, in *case.* Maybe it ain't as bad as we think. Was he a drinking man, this Dr. Temple?"

"I don't know," she answered; and did not bother to correct his notion of the doctor's name.

He blinked at her in slow surprise; then turned with alacrity as the manager, Moffat, rounded the turn in the corridor, followed by a stumbling maid. Their approach had been heralded by the ring of keys carried by the young woman, which jingled merrily with every bounce of her hips.

"Lucky!" puffed the little manager, coming up rapidly. "Found the maid on the other side of the corridor. We'll have the door open now in just a mo'." He indicated. "Open it up," he ordered briskly; "and then stand aside." He glanced at Miss Oliver. "Will you wait outside?"

She shook her head. "I'm going in," she answered. "I am the only one who knows him."

The maid was fumbling with her key; at length she turned the lock and flung open the door. They pushed past her in a group—the manager first, the detective at his heels.

Across the bed lay the body of a man, fully clothed. The bed itself had not been slept in, but the covers had been considerably disturbed; as if the man who lay outside them had tossed and turned intolerably.

Moffat, the manager, pushed forward slowly and stood beside the bed. The burly detective went around and viewed the body from the other side. He stooped and laid a hand above the heart of the man who lay supine. After a moment he shook his head.

In the doorway, just over the threshold, Blaine Oliver had paused, with Prentiss's arm around her. Her face was pale, her eyes wide and staring. With his free hand Prentiss touched the arm nearest him.

"All right?" he asked, for the second time.

"Yes," she gasped. Suddenly she whispered fiercely: "Harry, why did he do it?"

He answered her easily. "Probably ill or something, poor devil! Pay no attention to what that fellow suggested. It may have been perfectly natural."

The manager heard the remark. "It's true," he said, turning. "There's no blood—and no weapon. He's just—*er*—*twisted*—as if he was in pain." He glanced appraisingly at the girl in the doorway. "Do you want to—do you feel strong enough to—look at him?"

She advanced slowly, with Prentiss's arm still encircling her, until they stood beside the detective on the far side of the bed. From that position they could look down into the livid face of the dead man.

And suddenly Blaine Oliver cried out in bewilderment and terror.

"It isn't—it isn't—*he!*" she screamed. "It's—someone else! Harry—that isn't—Horace Trample!"

She collapsed against his shoulder.

Outside the door a quick voice sounded, in conversation with the maid. Then a bearded young man pushed into the chamber and strode rapidly to the bedside. He glittered as he walked.

"What's this, Mr. Moffat?" he asked briskly. "I just came in, and they told me there was a sick man in 940. He isn't——?"

"He's dead," said the manager dryly. "Better pay attention to the young lady, Dr. Marcus. I think she has fainted."

2.

To JOSEPH WHITE, chief of the detective staff of the Granada, fell the honor of identifying the man who was dead. He performed his task with great dispatch. He performed it, indeed, with considerable ease; a smarter detective might have made the thing appear more difficult.

The dead man was Jordan C. Chambers of New York. Beyond that, no one pretended to know anything about him. He was a guest of the hotel, having registered only the day before. He had been assigned to a room three doors beyond that assigned to Dr. Horace Trample—that is to say, to room 946—and had been immediately lost in the great maze that is the Hotel Granada.

White, in point of fact, had seen the man register but had not troubled to learn his name. The face, therefore, when he looked into it on Dr. Trample's bed, was simply a face he knew—presumably the face of Dr. H. C. Trample, who also had registered at the hotel the day before. Checking, against the register, his memory of the time the man had entered the hotel, it was possible—with two or three eliminations—to arrive at the man's name.

The next step was elementary, and it was made in haste by White, Moffat, and a number of other attaches. They descended in a cloud upon room 946 and entered without ceremony.

For a moment there was the appearance of another tragedy; then, as they shook and hustled the huge but drowsy figure in the bed, it stirred and stretched and, ultimately, sat up.

"What the devil is the matter?" asked a sleepy voice. "Is the place on fire? Who the devil are you?"

The dark eyes, at once fierce and humorous, opened more widely. They looked with astonishment into the clustered faces of the raiding party; then swung to a little traveling clock upon the dresser. The clock hands stood exactly at eleven.

"Good God!" shrieked the man in the bed. "Is that the *time?*"

He flung off the covers and bounded out upon the floor—a great animal of a man, in pajamas, with flailing arms like those of a gorilla.

Moffat was spokesman for the party. "Are you Dr. Horace Trample?" he demanded.

The gorilla was flinging himself into his garments at incredible speed, ignoring them completely. At the question, he paused long enough to ask another of his own.

"May I ask you what the devil the idea is—your breaking in this way? Not that I'm not glad you did; but what the devil is it all about?"

"We are looking for Dr. Horace Trample," said the manager.

"*I* am Horace Trample—yes! What is it that you want? Be quick about it, please. I had an engagement for nine o'clock, and it's now eleven. *Good God!* I can't imagine how I came to oversleep this way!"

Moffat was courteous but firm. "If your engagement was with Miss Blaine Oliver," he observed, "it can wait a little longer, Doctor. Miss Oliver is waiting for you in my office."

"The deuce she is! What office do you mean? Who are you?" With his tousled hair and savage brows, with one leg in his trousers and the other out, he was a picturesque and fantastic figure.

"I am the manager of this hotel. I am here to ask you by

what right you exchanged rooms last night with Mr. Jordan Chambers."

The doctor's face cleared. He slipped his other leg into his trousers and ran his fingers through his hair. "I had forgotten about that," he said. "It's easily explained. What's all the row about? It isn't a criminal offense."

Moffat, at the end of his resources, looked at his detective.

"Mr. Chambers was found dead, in your room, this morning," said White bluntly. "What can you tell us about that? Or do you want us to wait," he sneered, "until you've kept your blamed appointment?"

"Dead!" The doctor's voice rose sharply. "In my roo—— But it isn't my room. We exchanged." He frowned and added apologetically, "I'm sorry, of course; but I really didn't know the man. How did it happen?"

The manager shrugged a bit cynically. "We had hoped you might give us some clue," he retorted. "After all, your exchange of rooms was—shall we say, unusual? Such matters are ordinarily handled at the desk."

"I know—I know! It was my fault. He wanted to have the hotel fix it up. I was too sleepy; I wanted to get to bed." The doctor's eyes swung from the manager to the detective and back again to the manager. "Do you mean you don't know how he died?"

"There seems to be some doubt."

"He was all right last night, as far as I could see. Have you had a physician look at him? Look here—you don't mean that he committed suicide?"

White's heavy growl reëntered the conversation. "He's dead. We don't know what killed him. It could have been suicide, and it could have been natural. What interests us, right now, is how you happened to change rooms with him."

Dr. Horace Trample's arm made a wide gesture. "He asked me to—that's really all there was to it. I had met him at the bar.

Somehow he had discovered I was in room 940. It was a room he had asked for and couldn't get—so he said, anyway; your clerk will be able to verify that, perhaps. The room had sentimental associations for him, it appears. He had it on the first night of his honeymoon, some years ago."

"You believed that, of course!"

"Now, don't get nasty," said the doctor, "or I won't answer your questions. I don't have to, you know. Yes, I believed him. Why shouldn't I? Is there any better reason for preferring one hotel room to another? We were a bit sentimental about it, I suppose—over a couple of highballs."

"You say he wanted to go to the desk about it?" The question was Moffat's.

"Sure he did: it was his first suggestion. But I was sleepy and tired. I had had a long day. I wanted to get to bed. The more formal exchange would just have been a nuisance, and nothing was to be gained by it, that I could see. So it appeared to me last night, at any rate. I just picked up my traps and moved into 946, and he moved into 940. I went to bed soon afterward—and slept like a log: as you have observed! It was your excellent liquor, I suppose. I'm not used to it, that good. My God! What does Miss Oliver think has happened to me?"

"She doesn't know yet. She was relieved to find that it wasn't your body in 940."

"She *saw* the body?" The doctor was appalled.

"It was at her request that we entered the room," said Moffat.

"Oh, this is terrible," muttered the doctor. "Inexcusable! What *must* she think of me! I must go to her at once." He began to dress again in furious haste.

"She's with a Mr. Prentiss," continued Moffat.

Fumbling with his tie, in front of a mirror, the doctor cast a glance at them all over his shoulder. "Prentiss?" he echoed. "I don't know him." After a moment he asked: "What are you doing with Chambers' body? Did you want me to have a look at it?"

"Dr. Marcus, our staff physician, has seen it; and the police have been notified." The manager's tones were icy. "I suppose a coroner's physician will have to look at it, too."

"Undoubtedly. If there is any mystery about it, there may even be an autopsy and an inquest," said the doctor. "But I'm willing to be of service, if I can. Having caused you this inconvenience—after a fashion!"

"The police will want a word with you," contributed White in his rough voice.

"Doubtless," agreed the doctor. He slipped into his jacket. "Well, I'll be somewhere around. I hope they don't get the idea that I know anything about Chambers' death. But it was probably heart failure, after plenty of liquor."

"There was plenty, then?" Moffat's question was lightly tentative. "More than just 'a couple of highballs'?"

Dr. Horace Trample grinned at him out of the mirror. "Well, perhaps a few more," he admitted. "I was tired, and your liquor was admirable. Witness its effect upon me!"

"Thank you," said the manager dryly. "We feel certain our liquor had nothing to do with this case."

White entered the arena again. His blue jaw shot forward, and his eyes narrowed. "Did you know this Chambers before you came to this hotel?" He fired his question with blunt significance.

"I never saw him nor heard of him before in my life. Why?"

"You both arrived from New York yesterday; you both registered at this hotel; and——"

"And last night we exchanged rooms," finished the doctor. "But it's a silly flight of logic you are building, my dear man. If we had known each other, we could have arranged together, in advance, what rooms we were to occupy—always supposing they were to be had. There would have been no necessity for this eleventh-hour exchange. Do you agree?"

Mr. White retired behind his formidable eyebrows and sulked there—in ambush.

"Nevertheless," continued the specialist, "since you seem to be suspicious of me, for some reason, it may be that the police will be similarly curious. I assure you I can furnish excellent references."

"You mean Miss Oliver?" Moffat was politely sarcastic. "As I understand it, she has not seen you for a number of years; and your recent conduct will hardly recommend you to her."

"Perhaps not," agreed the physician. "I have other friends in Chicago, however." A little light of suppressed anger shone in his eyes, under the heavy brows. "Let me again remind you to be very civil in your remarks to me. I recognize your right to ask questions, but I shall not stand for any insolence."

"Quite right!" Moffat was suavely managerial again. "But the circumstances, as you admit, are curious. Chambers' story is not a particularly plausible one. I think you will find the police even more skeptical than we."

"I thought it very plausible indeed," replied the doctor. "You may be right about the police. But what the devil can they think? That I aided him to commit suicide? If I did, it was unintentional. I gave up a room that he told me had sentimental associations for him. There can't be any *great* mystery about the matter. If Chambers' door was locked on the inside, he locked it himself. That's plain enough, isn't it? So his death was either suicide or from natural causes."

"Nobody said the door was locked on the inside," growled White, the hotel detective.

The doctor's brows met in a frown. "That may be so," he agreed; "but you have conveyed that impression to me. It was, wasn't it?"

"Yes, it was," said Moffat.

"Then there's your case!" Dr. Trample was triumphant. He glanced at his fingernails and shot a final swift look at his portrait in the mirror. "I have no intention of running away," he added. "I shall be around when the police want me. In the meantime, if you will take me to your office, I shall be greatly obliged."

Miss Oliver's apology was destined to be further delayed, however. Sounds of a new activity entered the hotel room from the corridor. The door, which had been almost closed, was flung rudely open, and three men entered. Two of them were bulky individuals in soft hats and loose, light overcoats; the third was the assistant manager.

"These gentlemen are from the Detective Bureau, Mr. Moffat," explained the assistant. "I have told them briefly what has happened; and they have seen the body in 940. The doctor from the coroner's office is in there now." He cast a curious glance at Dr. Horace Trample, nodded casually to the two detectives, and vanished from the room.

Moffat looked around him. The chamber was becoming congested. He nodded his head, and his own assistants, except for White, the detective, reluctantly departed in the wake of the assistant manager.

"Roach and Barry," said the headquarters spokesman, *staccato*. "Your assistant said something about a doctor named Temple, who was missing. Know anything about him?"

"Trample," said the doctor, speaking for himself. "My name, gentlemen. The lost has just been found."

Moffat hastened to explain. "Dr. Trample and Mr. Chambers—the dead man—exchanged rooms last night. The doctor has just been telling us about it."

The police detective turned the information over in his mind. "What'd they exchange rooms for?" he asked, after a moment.

He turned his cold blue eyes upon the doctor and repeated his question in another form: "What'd you change rooms for?"

He listened without emotion to the doctor's explanation.

"That is the story of my entire connection with the late Mr. Chambers," observed the specialist, in conclusion.

Roach merely grunted. "And you were still sleeping when Mr. Moffat found you," he said, after a pause. There was just a suspicion of derision in his voice. He looked at Moffat. "How did you get into the room?"

"Pass-key," answered the manager. "Dr. Trample had not left his key in the lock."

"You weren't drugged, were you?" Roach looked again at the doctor. "Being a doctor, I suppose you'd know."

"I don't believe so," replied the specialist. "I can't quite imagine it. Being a doctor, as you say, I probably would know."

The police detective made up his mind. "Well, Doctor, I'll have to ask you to tell your story over again, at headquarters."

"I rather thought that might develop." Trample smiled and shrugged. "All right, I'll go along with you, when you are ready. Present my apologies to Miss Oliver, Mr. Moffat, if you will be so kind. Tell her I am abysmally ashamed."

"Oliver?" echoed the detective. "That's the girl that sounded the alarm. I'd like to have a talk with her myself. Where is she?"

"In my office—waiting for Dr. Trample."

The eyes of the two police detectives met, and the silent Barry rose. "I'll go down and keep her company," he observed; and tramped out of the room.

The shifty eyes of his companion swung again to Dr. Horace Trample. "Would you like to have a look at this Chambers, Doctor?"

"If I can be of service, certainly. Do I understand correctly that there may be some mystery about his death? What does your physician think?"

Roach chewed reflectively on an unlighted cigar. "Looks like poison," he said at last, with great deliberation. He cocked an eye at the doctor and asked a question of his own: "That in your line?"

"Very much," said the physician. "As a matter of fact, poisons are my specialty. I am a toxicologist." He added: "Then it *was* suicide!"

Roach shrugged his heavy shoulders. His mouth took on a peculiar twist. "Maybe it *was*," he said. "We don't know anything about it yet."

"Look here," cried the doctor suddenly; "I was with him in that room, last night—for a little while. We had a final drink together. And this morning I slept until eleven o'clock. You asked me a minute ago if I thought I had been drugged. Confound it, I wonder if I *was!*"

It sounded a bit like a crawl, to Detective Sergeant Roach. White, the hotel detective, pricked up his ears. "You didn't say anything to *us* about being in the room with him," he scowled.

"Shut your trap, White!" ordered the official investigator. "We're handling this case."

But the physician looked around him with perfect coolness. "Didn't I?" he retorted negligently. "I said we had exchanged rooms, didn't I? I said he had moved his things into my room, and I had moved mine into his. We had a final drink together, in his room—the one that *had* been mine; and when I left I heard him turn the key in the lock."

"What time was that?" asked Roach sharply.

"It was after eleven sometime. It was eleven when we came upstairs."

Moffat ventured suddenly where White now hesitated to intrude. "There was a card on Chambers' door when we came up, Doctor," he said. "One of those 'Do Not Disturb' cards that hang on the knob, to keep the maid out in the morning. Did you see Chambers put it out?"

The doctor turned the question over in his mind. After a moment he shook his head. "I have no memory of it," he answered. "But he must have hung it out, I suppose; then or shortly afterward. He was going straight to bed."

"Nothing on his mind in particular?" The question came from Roach.

"To indicate that he might commit suicide? No—nothing whatever. Nothing that emerged in our conversation, anyway. It was all a bit sentimental, as I say. I listened to the story of his honeymoon at least twice, I suppose. While it was all a bit silly, I felt sympathetic."

"Wife dead?"

"I don't recall that he specifically said so; but I assumed that to be the case. Maybe they were only separated; I really don't know."

Roach caressed his jaw with his fingers; he needed a shave. "Well," he said, at last, "if you'd like to see the body, Doctor, I've no objections. Since you're an expert on poisons, maybe you can give us a hint."

The party left the room and entered another, three doors along the corridor, where a middle-aged political doctor, somewhat shabby, was bending over the corpse of Jordan Chambers. Marcus, the house physician, was sprawled in a chair, smoking a cigarette. Both doctors were laughing, as the party entered, as if a boisterous story had just been uttered; but they sobered with commendable promptness and looked with interest at the formidable dimensions of Dr. Horace Trample. It must always have been Trample's fortune, good or bad, to stand out among his fellows, in any company.

He went directly to the bed, and the coroner's physician

moved aside for him. His face was unmoved as he looked at the twisted body of the dead man. "Yes," he said, after a pause, and as if there had been some doubt in his mind; "it's Chambers, all right."

Stooping, he sniffed at the dead man's lips; then pushing up the stiffened eyelids with his thumbs, peered earnestly into the corpse's eyes. He examined as much of the wrists and forearms as was immediately possible. Finally he glanced at the man from the coroner's office. "What would you say it was, Doctor?"

The other shrugged. "If you are a physician, your guess is as good as mine, at this stage," he replied. He was promptly and frankly hostile to the newcomer.

"It is *better* than yours, at any stage," retorted the specialist coolly. "I suggest morphine—in some quantity. The eyes would seem to indicate it; and it is the easiest drug for the ordinary citizen to obtain." He smiled faintly. "An overdose, perhaps? But it's curious. He didn't look to me like an addict."

Again he examined the wrists and forearms. "I can't find any needle scars—and there appears to be no hypodermic in the room."

Detective Sergeant Roach reached suddenly beneath a miniature desk and plucked forth a metal waste-basket. He upset it on the floor with a single motion of his hands and burrowed amid the papers.

"Good shot, Doctor," he said, after a few moments. "Here's the container—a tube of quarter-grains, eh? It's empty now."

"Mmm," commented the specialist.

But Roach was tired of further beating about the bush. He had a temporary victim, and the triumph was sufficient for the moment. His voice was rough and faintly sneering.

"And you're a toxicologist yourself," he added. "A poison specialist!" His broad shoulders lifted and fell. "Well, Doctor, if *you've* seen enough, *I* have. Let's be on our way."

"Very well," answered the doctor. He produced a silver cigarette case, and struck a match. "It's a villainous habit to smoke before breakfast—but a man must do something at a moment like this! The gesture is traditional, I believe."

Then for an instant everybody paused and listened. In the corridor, beyond the closed door, a whistle was heard approaching, low-pitched but clear, and in the circumstances singularly incongruous. Somebody was whistling the staccato melody of the *Habanera*, from *Carmen*, and doing it remarkably well.

Moffat jerked suddenly. "Riley Blackwood!" he exclaimed, as if the name were a profane expletive. "And the Big Boss," he added, "is probably with him." He shrugged, and for the first time since he had been called from his more usual duties a smile played for a moment about the manager's lips. It would have been difficult for a stranger to say whether it was a smile of pleasure or dismay.

"Just a minute, gentlemen," he continued, holding up a hand. "You are about to witness an exhibition of detective work that will curl your hair and eyebrows."

Light fingers were tapping now on the door panels; then the doorknob turned. A reconnoitering head was thrust around the corner, and the door opened more widely.

"Ah, Moffat!" cried the proprietor-in-chief of the Hotel Granada. "Thought perhaps we'd find you here. Come in, Riley!"

But Mr. Blackwood was already entering the room. The ghost of the *Habanera* was still upon his lips, from which, however, no sound now emanated. A tall, loose-jointed young man, with horn-rimmed spectacles, he bore a faint resemblance to the published portraits of Mr. Aldous Huxley—although without the mustache. His garments were of loose gray cloth, the jacket cut in Norfolk fashion. His eyes, behind their little panes of glass, seemed to survey the room with mingled insolence and amusement.

Mr. Riley Blackwood—in person.

Moffat nodded shortly. He introduced the newcomers to those already in the room. It was a large room, but it was beginning to take on an appearance of glut.

Then a glassy silence fell upon the company, in the midst of which Riley Blackwood, in his turn, strode to the bedside and looked down upon the corpse of Jordan Chambers.

3.

WIDDOWSON, principal owner of the Hotel Granada, was jealous of the high repute of his establishment. In support of his conviction that he was himself an important figure in its personnel, he maintained an extravagant suite upon the premises. This comprised an office and several anterooms, beyond which lay a sumptuous living room, two bedchambers, and a private bar. He moved in the city's best society, sailed a racing motor launch, in season, and sat a horse with easy mastery—albeit a trifle heavily. He was unmarried and a collector of expensive curios, including women.

One of his enthusiasms was young Mr. Riley Blackwood, that admirable wastrel, who divided his undoubted talents between dramatic criticism and the alluring problems of fantastic crime. He watched him now as the long, angular figure bent across the body of Jordan Chambers, on the bed. Six other pairs of eyes were similarly occupied. Their owners were disposed haphazardly about the chamber, which to Moffat seemed suddenly to have become a convention hall or an auditorium.

Young Mr. Blackwood—he was perhaps thirty—straightened. He looked negligently around the room. His glance, at length, rested upon the dramatic proportions of Dr. Horace

Trample, the only man in the place whose height was the equal of his own. After a moment it swung reflectively to Moffat.

"Door locked, Mr. Moffat?"

"Yes—by the man himself, undoubtedly. The key was not in the lock, however. There was a card on the door handle, outside. That card, on the dresser there."

Mr. Blackwood looked at it without emotion. "Better have it dusted for fingerprints," he observed with a casual glance at Roach.

The official detective stared, then frowned. "I intended to," he replied shortly, although in point of fact the idea had not until then crossed his mind.

"Two glasses and a whisky bottle," continued Riley Blackwood easily. "Is it known who the gentleman's visitor was?"

"He has confessed," said Dr. Trample, with a smile. "It was I. Would you care to hear my story? I have already told it several times, but I am still in good voice. One version might be checked against the other—for discrepancies."

Mr. Blackwood's sudden grin was not unfriendly. "So you exchanged rooms, Doctor! The possibility had crossed my mind. I have heard the early history of the—*er*—episode, from Miss Oliver. And from your assistant," he added, turning upon Moffat; "he told us what he could. Is the doctor under arrest, Mr. Roach?"

"Certainly not," said Roach. He seemed to bite at the words as they emerged from between his teeth.

"Merely a bird in the hand, as it were, while your search for the murderer in the bush goes forward!"

The police detective moved uneasily. "Nobody has said anything about murder in this case," he growled. "On the face of it, it's suicide."

"That is true—but you are not revealing all that is in your mind, Sergeant." Mr. Blackwood was reproachful. "Of course, you know it *could* be murder, quite as well as I do. A locked door—the 'sealed-room' problem—is not proof of suicide where the weapon used is poison."

"Oh, the case against me is very black," insisted the doctor, with smiling irony. "I am in point of fact a poison specialist—a toxicologist."

Riley Blackwood offered his cigarette case. "It may flatter you to hear that I have read a number of your pamphlets," he observed.

Only three of the men who stood about accepted his cigarettes; they were Widdowson, Marcus the house physician, and Dr. Horace Trample. Mr. Blackwood burned his fingers and swore thoughtfully. "Four on a match," he said. "I really think, Doctor, that you would be well advised to tell me your story."

"With pleasure," said the doctor; and he did so.

Riley Blackwood listened with a sphinx-like not-there-ness that must have been exasperating. His eyes, during the recital, continued to rove about the room in casual examination of its contents.

"Very plausible," he said, at last. "Very plausible indeed. And what is your own opinion, Doctor, of the death of Mr. Chambers? I suppose you have one?"

"Suicide or accident," replied the physician promptly. "An overdose of morphine—let us say—taken either by accident or by design, Mr. Blackwood."

Mr. Blackwood nodded. "He was undoubtedly in great distress. It is your profession that makes the case particularly awkward for you, of course. You could have furnished him with the means of destruction—hence Mr. Roach's interest in you. Accessory before the fact, perhaps, is the idea that is hazily forming in his mind; not deliberate murder. You deny, of course, that you gave him the stuff that killed him!"

"Oh, of course!"

"Of course," said Blackwood. "When you exchanged rooms, Doctor, you moved *everything* of yours into the other room?"

"As far as I know, yes. In fact, I am certain of it."

"Then those binoculars which I see on the side table were Chambers'? Not yours, by any chance?"

The eyes of seven curious men were turned upon the indicated glasses. Dr. Trample seemed puzzled.

"They are not mine, certainly," he replied. "Therefore, presumably, they were Chambers'. I didn't notice them last night."

"And they were not mentioned, I gather. Probably they had not been unpacked. But why under the canopy should Chambers have required a pair of binoculars? At eleven o'clock at night! Why, for that matter, was he traveling with them at all? The racing season's about over, I think, in these parts."

"H'm! But there are other 'parts,' Riley, after all." Widdowson's suggestion was tentative. "For all we know, he may have been going South."

"True enough—but the glasses are not in their case. The case is there—on the floor—where he dropped it. It is a fair assumption that the glasses were in use."

"Cleaning them, perhaps?"

Mr. Blackwood shrugged. "Well, well! It may not be important. But you might dust them for fingerprints, also, Mr. Roach, if the idea appeals to you. You will find, I think, that only Chambers used them."

The burly Roach was faintly—and reluctantly—respectful. "There'll be a squad over here before long," he said. "And a cameraman. I'll see to all that."

Riley Blackwood continued his casual cross-examination. "When you left this room, last night, Doctor, in what condition did you leave the late Mr. Chambers? He had been garrulous, as you have suggested; but—*ah*—was he drunk?"

"N-no, I think not. No more than I was. We had had perhaps

half a dozen drinks in all. They were fairly stiff. Neither of us was reeling, if that is what you mean. I suspect our tongues were a trifle thick."

"You did not at any time suspect that Chambers might be an addict?"

"Certainly not! I don't believe that now. If he had been, he would probably have used a needle. There's none around."

"None in *sight*, would perhaps be the police view of it," smiled Riley Blackwood. "He didn't mention drugs to you, however, in any way, shape, or manner?"

"He did not."

"Do you carry anything of the sort around with you?"

"Not often. I have none at present."

"And you had none last night?"

"I had not. When I require anything of the sort, I can always get it. I had no reason to think that I would need it. I have a syringe, of course."

"You came here merely to attend yesterday's medical convention?"

"That is all. The convention, however, lasts for a week. I planned to stay through."

"Are you acquainted with a Mr. Harry Prentiss—Miss Oliver's friend?"

Dr. Trample smiled and shook his head. "I had never heard of the young man until a little while ago."

"His appearance, this morning, struck me as being a trifle fortuitous, that was all." Riley Blackwood smiled in his turn.

"Very," agreed the doctor. "I'm damned glad of it, speaking for myself, Mr. Blackwood. I hope he got the poor girl something to eat."

Mr. Blackwood returned to his lazy attack. "This Chambers, Doctor—did he appear to you as somewhat of a melancholy fellow?"

"No—rather the contrary, I should say. But the liquor may have accounted for that. He was *eager*—eager to tell me his story; then grateful— grateful to me for giving up my room to him. I don't think I noticed any melancholy."

"Did you tell him that you were a physician?"

"I believe I did—after he had asked me."

"A specialist?"

"I think so, yes."

"Did he mention his own line?"

"I don't recall that he did. I don't believe I asked him."

"Is that the bottle out of which you poured liquor last night?"

"It is the bottle out of which *he* poured liquor," corrected the doctor. "That or one just like it, anyway."

"It's quite empty," commented Riley Blackwood significantly.

"Yes, so it is—By Jove!" exploded the doctor. "I see what you are getting at! He must have done a lot of drinking after I left him! The drinking we did together, for the most part, was at the bar. We had only one drink, here in this room, before I left."

"Odd, isn't it?" said Riley Blackwood. "The ginger ale bottle is also empty. Are those the shoes you were wearing last night, Doctor?"

"Eh? Yes—of course."

"May I see the soles of them?"

Dr. Trample sat down, laughing; for some time he had been leaning idly against a chair back. He thrust forth first one foot and then the other, while Blackwood inspected his soles. Widdowson rubbed his hands together delightedly. His friend's remarkable activities, he felt, in some fashion reflected credit on himself.

Riley Blackwood grinned cheerily. "Right-o, Doctor! You may put your feet down. By the way, which chair did you occupy last night?"

The doctor considered. "This one," he said, at length. "And Chambers sat *there*, facing me."

"The chairs are much as they were?"

"Almost precisely, I should say. The liquor table, too."

"That's fortunate. And strange, considering the herd of trained elephants that has been let loose in here. Well, it's a small indication perhaps; but this second glass appears to be just a little out of reach of either chair. It is as if someone sitting in this third chair—now occupied by Dr. Marcus—had set it down. You haven't touched it, have you, Doctor?"

The dapper house physician looked offended. "I haven't touched anything but the body since I came into the room," he said. "Nor has anybody else, except yourself and Sergeant Roach."

"And I have been very careful," smiled Riley Blackwood. "Now, with reference to soles: I am glad to note that none of you gentlemen who have trampled up this room has mud upon his shoes. Nor has the late Mr. Chambers!" He cast a glance at the twisted body on the bed. "Yet under Doctor Marcus' chair there is a small patch of mud—quite dry—that obviously has dropped from someone's sole. It is about the size of a twenty-five cent piece. Imbedded in its center, unless my eyes deceive me, is a black speck that I suspect to be a cinder."

Detective Sergeant Roach crossed the room in two swift strides and knelt beside the chair in question. His voice, however, when he spoke, was deprecating.

"Well, you're right about that, anyway. But what's it prove?"

"Nothing whatever," said Riley Blackwood. "It is perhaps suggestive."

Moffat spoke with a certain asperity; he had a feeling that he had been too long silent. "If you mean it may have been there for weeks, Mr. Blackwood," he observed, "I don't agree with you. This room was thoroughly cleaned after the last tenant left it."

"Still," said Mr. Blackwood, "it could have been overlooked. It's not impossible. What I was really suggesting, however, is that it may have been dropped there no longer ago than last night. It may have been dropped there by Chambers, himself, for all that his soles are now quite clean. And it may have been dropped there by somebody who has not yet entered the circle of our knowledge."

Roach turned a baleful eye upon the specialist, and Trample responded to the unspoken accusation.

"No," said the doctor, "I didn't lie, Sergeant. These are the shoes I wore last night, and all day yesterday. I came and went in taxicabs, and had no opportunity to step in mud or cinders."

"But you've got another pair of shoes?"

"I am the fortunate possessor of *three* other pairs of shoes," replied the doctor pleasantly. "All of them are open to your inspection."

Riley Blackwood shrugged and yawned. "Please don't be silly," he implored. "There is no point in saddling the patch of mud on the doctor. Nothing is gained, if that is the explanation. He has admitted being in this room last night. I am suggesting the possibility of a stranger."

He turned to the seedy coroner's physician, who had been a silent listener for many minutes. "How long has Chambers been dead, Doctor?"

"From eleven to twelve hours, perhaps."

"That is, since twelve or one o'clock last night. Do you agree to that, Dr. Trample?"

"Yes, I think so. It is difficult to be exact. The time may have been a little shorter."

"What is the lethal dose of morphine, Doctor?"

The specialist shrugged. "It depends upon the individual. Half a grain might kill a delicate woman. Two grains might kill

any healthy adult, unused to opiates. Under the influence of cus-
tom, however, large quantities may be taken."

"I see. And what would be the symptoms of a lethal dose?"

"Well, they would begin to manifest themselves in about half
an hour, I should say, the time depending of course upon the
dose. Giddiness at first, then drowsiness, and finally stupor. In-
sensibility ensues fairly quickly. The patient appears to be sleeping soundly. As the poisoning progresses the breathing becomes
slow and stertorous, the pulse weak and feeble, the countenance
livid. The eyes are closed, and the pupils are frequently contract-
ed—sometimes almost to a pinpoint; they are insensible to the
stimulus of light. In some cases the skin is cold; in others it is
bathed in perspiration."

White, the house detective, his June-bug eyes upon the body
of Jordan Chambers, was avidly checking the doctor's information against the appearance of the corpse.

"I see," said Riley Blackwood again. "No possibility of rous-
ing such a patient as you suggest, Doctor, once the drug has
begun to get in its work?"

"A loud noise might perhaps rouse him for an instant; but the
relapse would be almost immediate."

"And death, at last, comes peacefully!" Mr. Blackwood was
piously sententious.

Dr. Trample smiled. "Not always; it is occasionally preceded
by convulsions."

"H'm! It is a little strange that Chambers made no effort to
summon help. There must have been a few minutes before the
pains seized him—in which he might have grabbed a telephone.
Were you in the hotel last night, Dr. Marcus?"

The house physician blinked. "Yes, I was—after one o'clock,
at any rate. I live here, you know."

Young Mr. Blackwood drummed his fingers on his knee.

"And yet," he mused, "he would probably have called on Dr. Trample first."

"I think he had no idea he was dying," said the specialist. "Anyway, until it was too late to try to save himself. He had been drinking, remember; and his inclination would be to ascribe any stomach difficulties to what he had consumed. That would be the case if death was the result of accident. Of course, if this is a case of suicide——!" He shrugged.

"He would know precisely what was happening to him and would be unlikely to call for help, you mean. Exactly!" said Riley Blackwood. "Was the room next door to Chambers' occupied last night, Mr. Moffat?"

The manager was pensive. "Was it, White? Upon my soul, I don't know. But it can easily be discovered. I suppose it *was,* since—if we are to believe Dr. Trample—Chambers wanted room 940 and had to take 946. I mean, if room 942 had been unoccupied, he might have been willing to compromise and take that. I'll go into the whole matter with the clerk who talked to him."

"Please do! And it would be interesting to discover whether the occupant of room 942 heard anything after midnight. Or, for that matter, the occupant of room 938. That sort of thing is rather in Mr. Roach's line, I think."

"Yeh," said Mr. Roach dryly. "You can leave all that to me. In fact, you can leave the whole investigation to me, after you get tired of asking questions. After all, I've got to earn my salary." He grinned a bit maliciously at Riley Blackwood, but with less unfriendliness than he had previously manifested. "That's not such a bad line you got, young fella!"

"All thanks for your approval," murmured Riley Blackwood. "Praise from Sir Hubert—and all that sort of thing! I now retire to luncheon and reflection. Don't overlook any bets, my good Roach. This room must be lousy with fingerprints—not all of them Dr. Trample's and Mr. Chambers'. There was a bellboy here, last night; he left these glasses—and before the advent of Chambers there was a maid. It will be a case of too many fingerprints before we are through with it. But I doubt that you will learn much from the fingerprints. Probably the murderer wore gloves. I commend you to the binoculars! Yes, and the little patch of mud. With those clues, Sergeant, you should make a name for yourself. May you rise high in your profession!"

He uncoiled his long length from the chair in which he had been sprawling and stalked majestically out of the chamber, followed by the delighted Widdowson. In an instant he had returned. A faint grin hovered about the corners of his lips. Six pairs of eyes looked at him with amazement, and Widdowson teetered expectantly in the doorway.

"By the way," said young Mr. Blackwood casually, "are any of you familiar with the card and glass trick? It's very simple and highly instructive. I dislike to use one of these tumblers which may be required in evidence. Perhaps there is another. Ah, this will do!"

He strolled into the bathroom as he spoke, ran the water for a moment into the basin, and emerged with an ordinary tumbler borrowed from the bathroom fixtures. He set it carefully upon the small liquor table.

"That is a handsome diamond you are wearing, Doctor. May I see it for a moment?" He extended his hand for the brilliant finger ring worn by Marcus, the hotel physician, who drew it off in astonishment. "Thank you!" And Blackwood dropped the glittering bauble into his own waistcoat pocket.

His right hand explored the side pocket of his jacket and brought forth a deck of cards. "I am a little out of practice," he apologized; "but I believe I can still place these cards, one at a time, wherever you would like them placed. Bear in mind, please, that the quickness of the hand deceives the eye. That is proverbial. Now, what about this ace of spades? Have any of you any choice?"

Trample burst into a roar of laughter, quickly subdued, and the coroner's physician grinned. There was a frown of annoyance on the brow of Detective Sergeant Roach. Dr. Harold Marcus, puzzled, was secretly disturbed about the disappearance of his ring. Moffat cleared his throat angrily and seemed about to speak; but the presence of his employer sealed his lips. It was Widdowson who broke the uncomfortable silence with a remark.

"Really, Riley!" he protested, good-humoredly enough. "At this time—*ah*—is this really necessary?"

"Suppose we say the window cornice, then." Mr. Blackwood was undisturbed. "It is sufficiently difficult," he added, "and, as I say, I am somewhat out of practice. However——"

He drew back his arm and with a gentle toss sent the ace of spades fluttering upward toward the corner of the window top. It alighted as easily as a bird on the designated spot.

"Bull's-eye!" said Riley Blackwood in triumph. "With a drink of whisky—even a glass of water—I could do it fifty-two times, hand running. However, ten should be enough to prove my point."

Again his arm drew back; and again, and again. Ten cards he flung easily toward the ceiling, and each alighted gently on the designated ledge above the window.

"Very pretty," commented Mr. Blackwood in self-congratulatory tones. "The quickness of the hand deceives the eye. It's just a trick, of course. Any one of you could do it with a little practice. Thank you for your attention, and once again good-bye."

He dropped the balance of the pack of cards carelessly onto the low table and turned to the door.

"Pardon," said Dr. Marcus acidly; "but if your idea was to make off with my ring, you've failed. May I have it back?"

"You have it back," said Riley Blackwood. "At least, it is in the glass of water, on the table in front of you. May I take it that seven pairs of eyes failed to see me drop it there? That is a tribute to my skill that I appreciate. It would have been just as easy with a tube of morphine. Sorry to have been so dramatic. Life, as somebody has remarked, is like a pack of cards. I have forgotten the precise argument; but the aphorism, I think, is sound. Good luck to you, Dr. Trample. If Roach & Company fail you, look me up."

He vanished around the corner of the door, leaving behind him an almost visible sense of his mocking, shadowy smile.

4.

In PRIVATE, Mr. Riley Blackwood was somewhat less of a poseur than his numerous acquaintances imagined. He was, indeed, a serious-minded youth, who dropped his cloak of motley when he entered his apartment and closed the door behind him. For one thing, it pleased him to think that the public didn't really understand him; and for another, there was always the possibility that his aunt would be upon the premises: she occupied the adjoining suite. For that formidable old bluestocking Blackwood entertained a high respect—just faintly touched with apprehension. Sometimes they discussed together such clamorous and timely problems as the mystery of Dickens's *Edwin Drood* and the influence of Ibsen on the English drama.

Her own influence was chastening and salutary. "My nephew," Julie Blackwood told her intimates, "has a good mind, if only he would learn to use it." Thus the colorful public reputation of Riley Blackwood, the brilliant young critic of the *Morning Chronicle*, tripped and fell on his own doorsill. It was as well for Blackwood, for it kept his egotism within bounds and helped to humanize him.

His flair for mystery—and its solution—was his principal enthusiasm, and it was genuine. More so, perhaps, in literature than in life; he recklessly identified himself with the great fathomers of fiction. But his passion for justice, while less a reasoned conviction than a literary tradition, was sincere enough. He was an impatient observer of the human comedy, and frequently a bitter commentator.

A trifle ashamed of his theatricality, now that it was over, young Mr. Blackwood took leave of his admiring friend and hastened toward his rooms, in the Pomander Mansions, where his aunt, a terrier, and a Chinese servant would be awaiting him. Tea with Miss Blackwood—twice a week—was a rite as well as a ritual, and nothing lightly to be dismissed.

It would be as well, he reflected, to say nothing immediately about the body in the hotel bedroom. His aunt would only ask questions; and he had a column of stage gossip to turn out, at the office, before dinner. Tea would be served in the living room, and the scene from the windows—as usual—would remind Miss Blackwood of the bay of Naples, a safer and less protracted subject, and one in which he knew his cues.

He lightly kissed his aunt upon the cheek and apologized for being late. "I've had a fairly busy morning," he explained; "and Tony Widdowson sends you his devotion. How are you, Aunt Julie?"

The ancient maiden lady sniffed. "You and your Tony Widdowson and your blarney!" she retorted. "I'm well enough," she added, and lifted the silver teapot in her thin white fingers. "Pass me your cup, Johnnie," ordered Miss Julie Blackwood; and John Riley Blackwood passed up his cup like a little gentleman.

It had been that way as far back as he could remember; and Riley Blackwood hoped that it would always be that way. But it inclined him to a certain recklessness in other quarters.

Miss Blaine Oliver, in the meantime, released by the hotel and the police, drove slowly southward along the Outer Drive, toward the home of a friend with whom she might discuss the startling developments of her own morning. Her home, in Evanston, was quite the other way; but she had need of conversation.

She was entirely self-possessed and just a bit complacent. She had lunched tardily with Harry Prentiss—stuffing herself like a python to make up for the breakfast she had missed—and had then dismissed him with her thanks. Her mind, at the moment, was on the difficulties of Horace Trample.

Was it not conceivable—*just* conceivable, perhaps—that he knew more than he had told about the death of the mysterious stranger? His hurried explanation and apology, in the few minutes allowed him by the tough policeman who had him in charge, were not entirely satisfying. But he was a likable scapegrace, she admitted to herself; and his remorse about the failure of their breakfast had been quite sincere.

He had had his impudence right with him, too—to urge a further tryst upon her, after the outcome of the first one! She rather liked that. The dinner engagement was tentative, of course: the police might not let him off in time. But on the whole she hoped he *would* telephone. Now that the shock and horror of the adventure had passed, she realized that curiosity—her besetting sin—had taken possession of her.

It was not that she believed him guilty of murder: she didn't. On the face of it, the man in the hotel had committed suicide, poor devil! In her secret heart of hearts, Blaine Oliver was convinced that Horace Trample had aided him to do it.

She drove leisurely past the long fence that shut in the second annual session of the Century of Progress exposition, still functioning as the days grew shorter, and was surprised at the number of umbrellas pouring through the gates. A muggy, sticky day for sightseeing, she reflected; and a sticky, muggy day for Horace Trample, perspiring at the Detective Bureau, while the police hurled questions at him.

What an idiot she had been to faint at sight of the body! That was what came of going without one's breakfast, she supposed.

"If he doesn't call," she told her friend, when the exciting story had been related, "I don't think I shall be able to stand it."

Miss Clelia Mason looked back at her with speculative eyes. "What does he look like?" she pertinently asked.

Blaine Oliver told her. "He's bigger than he used to be," she finished; "but otherwise he hasn't changed a bit."

Miss Mason was not greatly impressed. "He sounds enchanting," she lied. "He'll call, of course!"

Dr. Horace Trample, meanwhile, was keeping his temper with some difficulty. He was too important a citizen, however, to be bullied like a taxi driver, and in time the ordeal was over. He gave his solemn word that he would not attempt to leave the city without permission, and returned to the Granada to await developments.

He was grateful to Roach for one thing: that before departing for the Bureau he had been permitted to make his peace with Blaine Oliver. In the knowledge of her forgiveness he took some comfort. She had been swell! It had taken nerve, he reflected, to suggest another engagement; but somehow he had to prove that he was not the frightful ass his earlier conduct must have indicated.

He raised the telephone receiver from its hook and then replaced it. A light knock had fallen upon his door.

It was Widdowson. The Granada's proprietor was jovial and smiling; a little tentative.

"Well, Doctor, they told me downstairs that you were back. Hope the ordeal wasn't too awful! Our master minds are frequently pretty nasty, I believe." His smile widened. "You seem unscarred, at any rate."

"Oh yes! They didn't beat me up!" The doctor also smiled. "Tired me out a bit, that's all. Well, I suppose I had it coming to me."

"You've got an apology coming to you," said Widdowson frankly. "Speaking for the Granada, we're damned sorry."

"Even White?" The doctor's eyebrows lifted humorously. "And Moffat?"

Widdowson grinned. "They appear to be satisfied that you were just an innocent bystander. The clerk who received Chambers has testified that Chambers *did*, as a matter of fact, ask for room 940. And seemed distressed when he couldn't get it."

"I see. But how did he find out who had it? Or did your clerk tell him that too?"

"He says not. If I thought he did, I'd fire him." Widdowson frowned. "No, it would be simple enough, you know. He watched the box numbered 940, I suppose, until you came along and called for your key."

"When I came in after the afternoon session, that would be." Trample nodded. "Then he waited until he found me at the bar, and told his little tale."

Widdowson agreed. "It was suicide, of course. In the room where he'd been happiest, eh? Insane, perhaps, but understandable. Not nice for the hotel; but there's nothing we can do about it now." He shrugged easily. "Look here, Doctor; I didn't come to bother you about Chambers. I came to speak my little piece. Blackwood's dining with me tonight. Will you join us?"

"To tell the truth," replied the doctor, faintly embarrassed, "I've another engagement with Miss Oliver. Naturally, I'd like to keep this one! I was about to call her up."

"Possibly Miss Oliver would join us also."

The doctor thought it over. "All right," he said. "Why not?"

"That's fine," said Widdowson. "Shall we say seven o'clock, then? In my rooms? They're on the third floor. Fine! I'll tell Riley, and we'll get a couple of actresses."

"Good Lord!" cried the doctor. "What for?"

"For Riley and me," said Widdowson. "Oh, it will all be perfectly respectable. Don't worry about that!"

He bustled out of the room, and Dr. Horace Trample, a trifle dubious, again focused his attention on the telephone.

Miss Oliver thought the arrangement an excellent one, and they dined at seven, as arranged. The actresses, however, did not materialize. It developed that Blackwood had objected.

"Widdowson thinks that no dinner is complete without an actress," he explained. "I apologize for the low level of his mind. It's what comes of owning hotels. I have been looking forward to a chat with you, Miss Oliver."

"With *me?*"

"Crime fascinates me even more than actresses. You had a box seat for this curious performance. You were on hand when the curtain rose. I should be interested to hear your impressions."

"I fainted," said Blaine Oliver.

"I know: it was a very significant action. But I imagine you have some opinion about the case?"

"Significant?" Miss Oliver was puzzled. She was also disturbed. Could it be that this clever young man was trying, through her, to get at Horace Trample?

"I think Mr. Chambers committed suicide," she answered, at length. "But you used the word *crime!* Do you mean you *don't* think so?"

"I haven't any final opinion yet," said Riley Blackwood. "The police, I suspect, think that our friend the doctor either murdered Chambers or helped him to commit suicide. But there are other alternatives."

There was a faintly satirical quality in his wry smile, she felt certain; and in the shrug that accompanied it. Perhaps the whole dinner party was a trap! She looked uneasily at Horace Trample, but he was smiling negligently, apparently without suspicion.

"What are the other alternatives?" she asked.

"That *somebody else* murdered Chambers or helped him to commit suicide," said Riley Blackwood. "There is, also, of course, the simplest solution of them all—that Chambers committed suicide without help from anybody. It is most unlikely that his death was accidental."

She nodded. "I suppose so! I mean, I suppose it *wasn't* accidental." She blushed and glanced apologetically at Trample. "To tell the truth, I *did* think it was possible that Dr. Trample had helped him! Helped him to get the drugs, I mean."

"I didn't," said the doctor. "Honor bright!"

"You didn't murder him, either," she cried loyally. An idea occurred to her; she believed it to be an inspiration. She spun toward Blackwood in some excitement. "Could Dr. Trample have been drugged himself? After all——"

"After all, he was a long time getting up," smiled Blackwood. "We've considered the possibility, Miss Oliver. Well, that depends!" He paused, his owlish gaze upon the model of a ship, under glass, which occupied a shelf in Widdowson's living room. "That depends on whether Chambers was murdered or committed suicide," he finished suddenly.

"He committed suicide," said Widdowson, setting down his cup of strong coffee.

Riley Blackwood grinned. "That's the hotel point of view, I realize. Still, a man *might* manage to get himself murdered, Tony, even in the Hotel Granada. Miss Oliver's question goes rather to the heart of things. Was the doctor doped or wasn't he? If he was, it seems likely enough that Chambers committed suicide. If he was not, it's possible to build a very plausible argument for murder."

"I don't follow you," said the doctor.

"If Chambers committed suicide, he may have thought it worth while to insure you a comfortable slumber. For all he knew, you might take it into your head to return to the room—perhaps for something you had forgotten; perhaps because you suspected his intention. I mean, he wouldn't care to be interrupted."

"And if I was *not* drugged, it follows that Chambers was murdered?"

"Not inevitably; but the indications, in that case, are obviously stronger. A murderer would have no valid reason to drug you, unless he thought you had knowledge of his plans; and the chances are against his knowing anything about you. In any case, how could he have done it? You could have been drugged only while you were having that last drink with Chambers. There was no potential murderer in the room with you, at that time, if I have not been misinformed."

Trample laughed. "Very plausible and ingenious," he said. "And perhaps just a little specious?"

Mr. Blackwood made a splendid gesture. "This process," he remarked, "goes on night and day and requires no oil. Widdowson doesn't like me because I am trying to stir up a murder mystery."

"Well," said the doctor, "I *don't* believe I was drugged. To that extent I must support your argument."

"Murder it is, then," spoke Riley Blackwood.

"Not in this hotel," said Widdowson firmly. "It's a dirty enough break to have a suicide."

Trample was still annoyed with himself. "I can't think how in the devil I came to oversleep that way," he complained. "Just tired, I suppose. There was the train journey from New York; I don't sleep well on a train. And the two sessions of the convention—God knows, they were tiring enough, too!"

The dinner proceeded, and Miss Oliver continued to be puzzled. She felt a vague distrust of Riley Blackwood, who seemed to argue first one way and then the other. He was very clever, she was sure; but she was certain she was going to dislike him.

That faintly superior, faintly satirical way he had of speaking was really a little bit infuriating. Like his reviews in the *Morning Chronicle*. He had a boyish grin that was sometimes rather nice.

One of his remarks kept coming back to her. At length she reverted to it.

"Just what was the significance of my fainting, Mr. Blackwood?"

"Ah!" said Mr. Blackwood, briskly buttering a biscuit. "That *is* the question, isn't it?"

"I wondered about that remark myself," said Horace Trample. "You don't mean that you think Miss Oliver——?"

"Dissembled? I don't *think* it—no! It is merely one of the things about which I have wondered. Why *did* you faint, Miss Oliver?"

"I don't know," she answered. "It was an idiotic thing to do— particularly as the body wasn't that of Dr. Trample. I had been thinking, you see, that it *would* be; and then when it wasn't—— Oh, I don't know!"

Riley Blackwood chuckled a particularly odious chuckle. "It hasn't occurred to you that you might yourself be suspect?"

"Good heavens!" said Blaine Oliver. "*I?*"

"Oh, come off it, Riley," protested Widdowson. "You know you're only showing off."

Mr. Blackwood seemed pained. "You think I am accusing Miss Oliver?" he murmured. "Quite the contrary! I simply suggest that in a detached consideration of the problem of the late Mr. Chambers' death, Miss Oliver's connection with Dr. Trample is one of the early question marks. She had an appointment with him that he was unable to keep. It was she who first expressed fear that something had happened to him and led the search party to his room. She has just told us that she expected the body to be that of Dr. Trample; and she fainted when she discovered it was not. Whatever *I* may think of the episode, from first to last, you may bet your final dollar that the police have thought of these several circumstances in the order of their enumeration. They are wondering whether Miss Oliver was preparing an ingenious sort of alibi."

"That's nonsense," snapped the doctor.

"Possibly it is." Blackwood was unperturbed. "But the argument is sound. It would be a very clever thing to do. Who would be likely to suspect a young woman who herself pointed the way to the body of her murdered victim?" He grinned his schoolboy grin. "Everybody, of course, except the young woman asking herself the question. Nevertheless, it would be a clever trick."

The young woman thus accused decided to conduct her own defense. After all, she reflected, this amusing idiot *might* be serious.

"I'm really not that clever," she said; "but let it go. Assume that you are right. What about Mr. Chambers, poor dear?"

"He complicates the case," admitted Riley Blackwood. Then he brightened. "Of course, he might have been the instrument of your vengeance! You sent him to murder Dr. Trample, let us say; but Trample turned the tables on him. That covers the facts and accounts for your very natural faint when you discovered that your hellish plans had gone awry."

The doctor had recovered his good-humor. "Now *I'm* the murderer again!" he said. "I hope the police imagination is less ingenious than yours, Blackwood. And you promised to clear me, remember, if Roach & Company failed. By the way, what was the significance of those field glasses? You appeared to be making quite a point of them."

Riley Blackwood's facetiousness was no longer in evidence. "Yes," he said quite seriously, "I did rather call attention to them, didn't I? They are probably the key to the mystery. I hope to know more about them by tomorrow. Tonight, in fact."

"Which reminds me," broke in Widdowson hurriedly, "we've

got another party on tonight. Hope you don't object, Riley! Cope Haviland called me up a little while ago and made me promise that if the rain stopped we'd join him on a cruise. Small party, I believe, but very select, wot ho! He's entertaining that English traveler fellow—what's his name? Ford something! Holderness—Ford Holderness! They're dining at Haviland's, and we're to join them about nine-thirty. I told him we had a party of our own, and he said to bring 'em along." He looked apologetically at Blaine Oliver and the doctor. "You'll go, won't you?"

"A cruise?" Miss Oliver echoed the word that interested her most.

"On Haviland's yacht. We won't go far! Up around the Fair Grounds, to look at the lights, and back again to Belmont Harbor. Maybe we won't go at all. Depends on the weather. If we don't, we'll hang around at Haviland's and drink some highballs."

Blackwood pushed his chair back and strolled over to the window. "It's stopped raining," he said morosely.

"Well, that means the yacht, then. Come on, Riley! Don't be a detective all the time."

"All right," grumbled Blackwood ungraciously. "But I want to be back by midnight, Tony. By golly, I've got to be! Well, anyway, by one o'clock. You'll have to arrange it for me."

Horace Trample echoed the word that had interested *him*. "Holderness?" he said. "That's the fellow who wrote the book on Yucatan, isn't it?"

"Or Siberia. Or Tibet!" Widdowson shrugged. "Hanged if I know exactly. He's been every place." He glanced at his watch. "Plenty of time; but we'd better get along with the rest of this dinner."

He telephoned the Haviland apartment, when they had finished, and reported back to Blackwood. "Haviland says they're starting in a few minutes. He wants us to join him at the harbor.

We'll pick up a taxi at the door and drive over to the garage for my car: that'll be the easiest way."

"All right," said Blackwood. "I'll join you in the lobby."

He collected his outer garments, including a heavy stick of snakewood, and left the room with some abruptness. But he did not go directly to the lobby; instead he caught an elevator going upward and disembarked at the ninth floor. From his pocket he brought up the key to room 940 and, after a hasty glance to be certain he was not observed, let himself in.

The room was in darkness; but his exploring fingers found the light switch. He closed the door behind him and stood for a moment in casual inspection. The body of Chambers, as he had anticipated, had been removed; but otherwise the place was much as he had left it earlier in the day. No maid had been admitted to clean up. Certain of Chambers' belongings also had been removed, including, he noted, the binoculars—whatever might offer a possibility of fingerprints. It was obvious that Roach had taken his tip.

For some minutes he moved softly about the room, touching nothing, his lips puckered in a soundless whistle. The *Habanera* was running in his mind. Then he moved leisurely to the door, snapped off the lights, opened and closed the door as if in departure, and in the darkness strode swiftly back to the windows giving on the street.

Very gently he moved the hangings and peered out. Immediately across the street bulked the great mass of the Hotel Jamaica, the Granada's nearest rival. Here and there in its exposed façade a window showed a square of light, but for the most part the rooms were still in darkness. He waited patiently for several minutes. From his pocket, after a time, he produced a small but powerful pair of opera glasses and focused them upon the building opposite, swinging them with solid movements of his shoulders as he scanned all visible aspects of the other hotel.

At length he returned the glasses to his pocket, with a little shrug, and left the room. He descended swiftly to the lobby and joined the others of his party on the pavement outside the hotel door.

"Hope I haven't delayed matters," he apologized. "There was a little job I really had to do. Don't forget, Tony, that I want to get back here by twelve or one o'clock."

In Widdowson's big Cadillac, speeding northward along the border of the lake, Miss Oliver's curiosity—a troublesome intelligence—got the better of her breeding. What was it, she wondered, that the drama critic of the *Morning Chronicle*, that extraordinary creature, planned to do at midnight or one o'clock? The opportunity for inquiry seemed excellent. She put the question.

"Why do we have to get back by one o'clock, Mr. Blackwood? I mean, does it have anything to do with this case?"

"I, not *we*," said Mr. Blackwood. "It does indeed! A Mr. Chambers was found dead in his room at the Hotel Granada, this morning, it seems—greatly to the annoyance of Anthony Widdowson, Esquire. His door was locked, on the inside, apparently by Mr. Chambers himself. Death, we have reason to believe, resulted from an overdose of morphine. All indications point to suicide; yet Riley Blackwood, the brilliant young criminal investigator, ventures to think otherwise. He plans to spend the night in the room occupied by the late Mr. Chambers."

A swift picture of that room as she had last seen it flashed for an instant before Blaine Oliver's eyes.

"Good heavens!" she said. "With that terrible thing on the bed?"

"Oh no!" Mr. Blackwood patted her gently on the arm. "The body, I fancy, already has been removed."

"But *why?*" she persisted. "What can you expect to find?"

Dr. Horace Trample also was interested; he was leaning forward to catch the amateur's reply.

"I may even invite the doctor to sit up with me," continued Blackwood pleasantly. "There is a little experiment I want to make."

Trample nodded. "Glad to, if I can be of service," he assented. "You said the door was locked, Blackwood; and of course it was. But how about the windows? I've been wondering about them."

"Nine floors up from the street, for one thing," growled Widdowson, from his seat beside the chauffeur. "And I can't quite see anybody crawling from one room to another across the face of the building."

"It could be done," said Riley Blackwood. "By a very agile fellow. One of the windows was locked, Doctor; the other unlocked and slightly open. But the windows have no bearing on the actual murder. The murderer entered by the door, at Chambers' invitation, and was later ushered out by Chambers. Mr. Chambers, you see, didn't know he had been poisoned."

Widdowson was glum. "Have it your own way," he murmured. "Here's Belmont Harbor, anyway!" He glanced from the window. "Run her up to Addison Street, Fred, and take the Drive right in. We could get out here and walk across the bridge; but the park looks pretty sloppy."

Lights danced on the waters of the little yacht harbor, and from the farther shore, where the motor launches were moored, came the tinkling strains of music. They swung into a strip of parkway, turned eastward toward the lake, then doubled back to the north along the peninsula that formed the eastern shore of the harbor.

The night was clear and fine, after the rain, but damply cold.

Blaine Oliver shivered and was glad she had not gone home to dress. The clothing she had on would be none too warm, out there on the water, she reflected, and evening garments would have been ridiculous.

Haviland and his guests already had arrived. On board the *Flying Fish*, a radio was blaring. The jackdaws and the peacocks already had begun to dance.

5.

"CHICAGO'S REPUTATION for violence has always interested me; but I am beginning to wonder if it is deserved. I have been among you now for two days, and—upon my soul—I haven't seen a single murder!"

Ford Holderness laughed his pleasant, patronizing laugh, quite unaware that every contemporary European visitor before him had uttered the same witticism. "Give you my word!" he added brightly.

Blaine Oliver showed her pretty teeth in a smile. "Not even a very *little* one, Mr. Holderness?" she questioned. "We must really see what we can do for you, I think. I understand it's possible, in almost any of our neighborhoods, to get a throat cut for a dollar and a quarter."

"Jolly!" said Mr. Holderness. "From ear to ear, Miss Oliver?"

"We advertise 'em," said Riley Blackwood dryly. He was sprawled in a deck chair, smoking a cigarette. "'Bigger and better murders,' is our motto, you know. As a result, you hear about them. Just as many in Detroit and San Francisco; in New York, *more*."

He yawned and tossed his cigarette stub overboard. The water was making him drowsy; he sat up with a certain decision. "I've lived in Chicago nearly all my life and never seen one," he added.

"I mean, in the act of happening. So have lots of policemen. It's a secret profession—murder, I mean."

"Poor Mr. Holderness," smiled Blaine Oliver. "After exploring all the wilder parts of the old world, he naturally turns to Chicago—and finds us discussing cricket and Noel Coward."

The Englishman laughed. "No, no," he protested. "I didn't really expect to find Indians west of the Alleghanies. But, after all, your gangsters, eh? What about them, now?"

"We *are* a race of savages yet," said Widdowson dryly. "Look at Blackwood!"

"When they caught *me*," said Miss Oliver, "I was living in a tree." She added thoughtfully: "An oak, I think it was."

They were seated on the after-deck, keeping their feet away from the shuffling feet of the dancers, now struggling to the more modified uproar of a phonograph. It was possible to speak without shouting. A steward, shivering somewhat in his white jacket, was weaving in and out with trays of tall glasses in which blocks of ice swam noiselessly.

Cope Haviland came to the rescue of his distinguished guest. "Queer things happen in Chicago, just the same," he maintained. "Shots in the night, for instance—whole volleys of them—after one is in bed; and not a word of explanation in the morning papers. I always wonder what is being suppressed."

"Heard some last night, by Jove!" exclaimed the visiting Briton. "I'm at Mrs. Melton's, you know; my window's right on the boulevard. Sounded like a revolution! I bounded out of bed, expecting to find a barricade before the house." He spread his hands in humorous bewilderment. "Nothing! Thought I had been dreaming."

Widdowson laughed. "Roving squad car shooting at suspicious speeders," he said. "Suspicious speeders maybe shooting back. They'd be out of sight before you could reach the window, Mr. Holderness. They never catch anybody, you know; it's just a game between the minor gangsters and the police." He had an inspiration. "You ought to get some of your friends in the department to take him around some night, Riley."

"I'd love it," cried Ford Holderness eagerly. "Do you mean it can be done?"

Blackwood thought it could be arranged. "I'll speak to Drury and Howe about it," he said.

"Speaking of murder, Widdowson," said Cope Haviland, "the papers reported a man found dead in the Granada. Nothing sensational in *that*, I hope?"

The Granada's owner made a hideous grimace. "So do I," he answered heartily. "Riley's trying to persuade us it's a mystery; but the police have more sense, I think. Suicide's bad enough."

"What happened?" Ford Holderness screwed his monocle into his eye and turned the astonishing orb on the hotel man. Miss Oliver watched the proceeding with fascinated gaze.

"Overdose of morphine, presumably. So the doctor, here, says; and he ought to know."

"Dr. Trample?" The single eyeglass swung in the direction of the specialist, who had taken no part in the conversation. "That's very interesting," said Ford Holderness. "Was he an addict, Doctor?"

"I think not," answered the doctor, a trifle shortly. He disliked being drawn into an inquiry that he felt was embarrassing to Widdowson; but there appeared to be no help for it. And it was Widdowson who had called attention to him, after all.

He smiled. "No, I don't believe he was an addict, Mr. Holderness. On the face of things, I'm bound to say that I agree with Mr. Widdowson."

"That he committed suicide, you mean?"

"I think so, yes. It is rather to my own interest to think so," he added dryly. "For a time there seemed to be some notion that I had murdered him."

"Get out!" said Haviland.

In his surprise, Ford Holderness relaxed the muscles of his eye, and his monocle dropped swiftly toward the deck. He caught it with a dexterous movement of his hand and thoughtfully replaced it. "Of course, you *didn't* murder him?" he questioned. "By Jove, I almost hope you *did!* I'll put it in my book."

Trample laughed. He beckoned to the steward, passing once more upon his interminable round, and accepted one of the tall glasses. "Of course, you realize," he said, sipping at his highball, "that even if I had, I would deny it."

"But not here, tonight, among your friends!" smiled Holderness. "Gentlemen—and Miss Oliver!—I submit that we are a jury of more than ordinary intelligence, in whose hands the doctor may rest his fate with perfect confidence. Wild horses shall not drag his confession from us! If he murdered this unfortunate man, whose name and misdeeds we have yet to learn, it was because the unfortunate man deserved to be murdered. Am I not right, Miss Oliver?"

Blaine Oliver glanced at Riley Blackwood with a malicious twinkle. "I'm in it, too," she said. "Don't look to *me* for information."

For a moment it appeared that Holderness again would lose his monocle. He plucked it forth and put it back more tightly in its aperture. "You surprise me," he murmured. "But I begin to see the game. You are putting up a job on me. Chicago's reputation is to be made secure. All over the yacht are murderers and gangsters." He chuckled his appreciation.

The *Flying Fish* was approaching the Fair Grounds. Steaming slowly, it bore down upon the scene of carnival. Red, blue, and yellow lights wavered across the water, and the sky was a canvas of flaming modernistic color. The confused murmur of thousands of voices was borne to them on the light breeze, punctuated at intervals by the crash and din of bands playing in the several casinos.

The dancers halted their shuffling feet and pushed toward the rail; the idlers who had been sitting aft went forward. There was a general rearrangement of groups, in the midst of which a tall young man, holding a cravenette around his evening garments, uttered a sudden exclamation.

"Blaine!" he said, in tones of pleased surprise. "What the dickens! I didn't dream of finding *you* on board."

It was Harry Prentiss, whom she had last seen at luncheon.

She gave him her hand. "What a fortuitous person you are, Harry," she smiled. "When you spoke, I had a nightmarish sensation that it was all beginning over again. Have you met Mr. Holderness?"

But Holderness had been swept away by another group of voyagers: he was nowhere to be seen. Neither was Widdowson or Haviland. So she introduced Blackwood and the doctor.

Prentiss stared at Horace Trample with great interest. "Glad to see you alive and well, sir," he observed. "For a little while, this morning, you had me frightened!" There was now only amusement in his dark eyes, however.

Trample was only slightly embarrassed. "I think," he said, "you are the last remaining person to whom I owe an apology. And I'm grateful to you for standing by Miss Oliver. I hope you know what happened. To tell the truth, I'm a little tired of talking about it."

Prentiss grinned. "Sketchily," he answered. "Rumors of it floated downstairs to the office, while we waited. And there's a small bit in this evening's papers. You aren't mentioned. The fellow's name was Chambers, wasn't it? You didn't know him?"

"Beyond what he told me of himself last night, when he persuaded me to change rooms, I know nothing about him."

"Mysterious case," said Prentiss lightly. "Most mysterious!"

His bright manner, however, almost wholly discounted the meaning of his words. He turned to Blaine Oliver. "I didn't know you knew this particular group, Blaine."

"I don't," she retorted. "It came about through Mr. Widdowson. I don't know him either, really; so figure it out. And be very careful—Mr. Blackwood has turned detective!"

"Good Lord!" exclaimed Prentiss. He smiled at the long, languid figure in the deck chair. "What are you detecting tonight, Mr. Blackwood—if it isn't a secret? Have you found any clues?"

Blackwood decided to be affable. "Miss Oliver is having a great deal of fun at my expense," he replied. "I was faintly interested in the case of Chambers because he died in Widdowson's hotel; that's all. A little murder now and then is relished by the best of men: that's a poem, you'll observe. Since you are here, do you mind if I ask you a question?"

"Not at all. Please do ask one!"

"What were you doing in the Granada when you met Miss Oliver, this morning?"

Prentiss laughed. "That's pointed enough," he commented. "I was doing precisely nothing. That is to say, I was passing through the lobby. It was raining, as you know; I took a short cut—or intended to—from one street to another, through the hotel. On the way, I ran into Blaine. She was in some distress." He struck an exaggerated posture: "It was my happiness to aid her!"

Riley Blackwood nodded. "That's all," he said good-humoredly.

"Oh, ask another," pleaded Prentiss. "Make me account for my movements last night, that's a good fellow!"

Blackwood's annoyance did not show on the surface. "Sorry," he smiled. "Only one question to a customer."

Harry Prentiss drew up a chair and sat down. "That's that, then," he said. "Throw me out, if I intrude! The Fair looks rather attractive from the water, doesn't it? I'd rather look at it from the deck, here, than *go* to it. A million guinea pigs last week, I believe. I shouldn't mind being a stockholder! By the way, have any of you met this odd bounder Cross?"

"Cross?" Blaine Oliver echoed the name idly.

"Gene Cross, I think he's called. Now, if you had told me *he* was a detective, I'd have believed you! Short, stocky fellow, with a pair of shoulders. I wondered who he was. Looks a bit out of his element; and I thought his tails were bothering him."

"What's he done?"

"Nothing but drink, that I know of—and paw the younger girls. Lovely pastimes, both of them; but I thought some of his language was a trifle loose and careless." Mr. Prentiss laughed. "My Puritan blood coming out, perhaps," he murmured.

"Well, he didn't come with us," said Miss Oliver. "I haven't seen him."

Harry Prentiss rose to leave them. "Got to go," he said. "Dot Harvey will be looking for me. Happy to have made your acquaintance, Mr. Blackwood—or is it Inspector Blackwood? Good luck, Doctor!" To Blaine Oliver he said: "I'm driving north with Dorothy, when we get back; but I suppose you are already provided with transportation?"

She glanced tentatively at the doctor. "Thanks, yes. Dr. Trample will see that I get home all right."

Prentiss nodded and moved away in the direction taken by the party he had deserted. An orchestra on shore was playing "One Minute to One," and Blackwood glanced at the illuminated hands of his watch: but actually it was not yet eleven.

He yawned. "Is Mr. Prentiss an old friend of yours, Miss Oliver?" he lazily inquired.

"M-yes. So-so, that is! His people and mine have known each other for a long time, anyway. And in the North Shore suburbs people are fairly chummy." She added: "He's really a very nice boy."

The *Flying Fish,* meanwhile, had reached the farthest southern extremity of the Fair Grounds and was turning for the return cruise. Horace Trample stood up and stretched his huge body.

"I'll have a look at the thing from the rail," he said. "Last chance, perhaps, to see it from the water." His look of inquiry suggested that possibly the others would care to accompany him; but neither of them did, and he moved away in the semi-darkness, shouldering his large way gingerly through the groups that littered the deck. Blaine Oliver and Riley Blackwood were left alone together.

For some time neither of them spoke.

"Having a good time, Miss Oliver?" he asked at last.

"I think so," she replied. "Fairish! Aren't you?"

He shrugged and slipped farther down into the comfortable deck chair. "Parties of all kinds bore me rather," he admitted. "This isn't bad—I like the water. Widdowson has a launch, the *Charming Sally.* I'd like to take you out in her sometime."

"One would never dream that you were eager to be up and doing." There was a note of mockery in her voice. "The architect who designed that long chair had you almost perfectly in mind."

"You should have seen me this morning! It *was* just this morning, wasn't it? But I do rather like comfort."

"You mean, when you can't be the center of attraction, you won't play," she retorted. "You're just spoiled, I think."

He smiled at her without rancor. "I *am* a bit of a show-off," he confessed, "but there's more to me than just that." His glance became quizzical. "Sorry you don't like me!"

"Did you want me to?"

"N-no, not particularly. I mean, it's unimportant. But one likes to create a good impression. I'm an egotist, of course; I mention the fact to forestall your own comment. In some ways I'm rather nice, really. I can do tricks with cards, and in other ways I am very entertaining. You should give me a trial."

"You may leave one of your cards," said Miss Oliver, perpetrating a joke. "When I am in need of entertainment or a detective, I shall give you a ring, Mr. Blackwood. By the way, are you detecting at present, or is this a pause in the day's occupation?"

"Just loafing," he assured her. "I had no notion, for instance, that Prentiss would be on board."

"But you are sticking rather closely to Dr. Trample's trail, aren't you?"

"Perhaps; but without prejudice to Trample. He isn't trying to run away."

"I don't think Mr. Chambers was murdered at all," said Miss Oliver with decision.

"I should like to be able to agree with you," said Riley Blackwood.

She regarded him for a time from under half-closed eyelids. "Why do you do this sort of thing at all?" she asked at last. "In a sense, it isn't any of your business."

"It's everybody's business, isn't it?" he retorted, but without conviction. "Murder is a fairly serious matter. However, that isn't the answer. I've that kind of a mind, that's all. A mystery fascinates me; I'm unhappy till I've solved it. The morality of it all concerns me less, I'm afraid, than the excitement of the problem. I used to be a reporter."

"I think it's morbid," said Miss Oliver severely. "What is it you are planning for tonight?"

Blackwood grinned. "Well," he began, "as one of the suspects in this case, I'm not certain that you ought——"

He stopped short. A heavy splash had sounded in the water somewhere up ahead; it was followed by a piercing scream. Then a confused babble of voices arose, in the thick of which a powerful single voice was raised in a sudden shout of "Man overboard!" A bell rang sharply, and the *Flying Fish* seemed to pause on her course and shudder. The yacht's engines slowed and stopped;

along her sides the hiss of water ceased and was succeeded by an alarming and momentous silence.

Riley Blackwood sprang to his feet with an agility that belied his previous attitude. He hurried forward without further attention to Miss Blaine Oliver and vanished around a corner of the cabin. As quickly as she could, she followed him.

The yacht rolled easily in the long swell of the lake. Half a mile off the port bow stretched the fantastic, colored skyline of the Century of Progress exposition. And clustered at the starboard rail were half the company of guests, with the other half pushing at them from behind. Their voices were excited but subdued.

Blaine Oliver clutched at the nearest sleeve. "Who is it?" she inquired breathlessly.

"Don't know yet," said the man addressed, a bit impatiently.

With some difficulty she forced a passage to the rail and peered downward at the water. It was dark and cold, and she half expected to see a drowned face float past on the crest of one of the black waves. But on that side of the yacht there was only cold, dark water. She looked farther seaward and saw nothing but a confusion of sky and water, in which—far away—a little light appeared and vanished, like fox-fire on a marsh.

Some sailors were wrestling with a small boat, endeavoring to launch it. Someone was shouting orders at the wheel-man. "Bring her head around and use the searchlight," called a powerful voice that she recognized as Haviland's. Again a bell rang sharply, twice; the engines throbbed slowly: the propeller began to thrash.

At that instant, in the pressure of the bow, she heard with relief the voice of Horace Trample: "He's well astern by this time, I'm afraid. No use looking for him where he went in!"

That was Haviland's idea, also, it was obvious. The *Flying Fish* once more was turning on her course. Her nose was pointed southward again. The exposition's noise and color were on her starboard bow. A small searchlight was pointing a path on the water. The yacht cruised slowly.

She heard the voice of Horace Trample again, raised in excitement: "There he is," it cried. "I see him, Blackwood! No, he's gone again." The words were followed by another splash in the water, and for an instant Blaine's heart sank. Then she was scrambling through the crush of watchers in the bow, with some wild motion of rescue in her mind. She was an excellent swimmer, and she had heard the doctor remark that he could not swim a stroke.

But it was Trample himself against whom she brought up at length. He glanced at her without emotion. "Hello," he said calmly enough. "We've just spotted the fellow, I think. Blackwood's gone in after him. The light picked him out for a moment, and then he vanished."

"Who is it?" she asked again; but this time the question was less frantic than when she had asked it first.

"Nobody appears to know," replied the doctor. "Funny! Nobody seems to be missing."

Their eyes scanned the water. Somewhere out and beyond they could hear the flailing strokes of Riley Blackwood. He was not visible in the path of light. He was swimming rapidly, and he seemed to be swimming outward. The sounds of his passage became indistinct and then appeared to cease entirely. The doctor's eyes were anxious.

"Don't worry about Riley," spoke up Widdowson, in the darkness; "he swims like a fish. Wish we were in my motor launch!"

It was some minutes, however, before a muffled hail came to them across the water. The yacht's nose swung seaward, following the sound. A light fog was beginning to roll in from the lake, and Blaine Oliver shivered.

"Better go down into the cabin, hadn't you?" suggested the doctor.

The hail was repeated from the darkness; it seemed to ricochet along the waves. "Keep her head the way she is, Haviland," called the voice of Riley Blackwood. "Come ahead slowly. Don't run me down!"

"Have you got him?" roared Haviland.

"Got him," answered the voice across the water, like an echo of the question.

Blaine Oliver strained her eyes into the darkness. Quite suddenly she saw the swimmer. He was closer in than she had imagined. He was swimming slowly, using only one arm, as he approached, and he was towing something horrible behind him. She turned away her eyes. In a few moments there were scrambling sounds along the ladder, and the doctor spoke again. "All right, Blackwood," he said. "Look out for the ship's side!"

For an instant she saw again the twisted body of the man called Chambers, sprawled across the bed. Now another body was coming up the side. The day had been a slightly harrowing one! For a moment she was a little sick. A shudder shook her, and she pushed free of the groups that lined the rail. She returned to the after-deck and sat down in the chair she had deserted. After a moment she lighted a cigarette and peered closely at her watch. In spite of everything it was only eleven-thirty.

She smiled faintly. There was still time, if he hurried, for Blackwood to conduct his "experiment" at the Granada!

It was close upon twelve-thirty, however, before anyone came near her—except a steward, from whom she gratefully accepted a jolt of whisky so powerful that it staggered her. Then Ford Holderness appeared, still jauntily immaculate, a dowager on either arm. He deposited his burdens with an air of polite relief.

"Well," he opened brightly, "that was almost a tragic end to our adventure." He adjusted his single eyeglass and pretended to peer through it at the girl who occupied the deck chair. "Ah, it's you, Miss Oliver!"

"Yes," she said. "I'm still hanging around, you see. It *wasn't* a tragedy, then? I didn't stop to hear."

"The doctor's brought him around, I believe; that was the last report that came up from the cabin."

"Who was it?" asked Blaine Oliver for the third time. The question was quite casual, this time; she no longer greatly cared.

"Fellow named Cross, they tell me," said the Englishman. "Queer sort of blighter, I believe. I only met him for a minute."

That was the name of the man about whom Harry Prentiss had spoken, she remembered. His other name was Gene. "How did it happen?" she inquired, without much interest.

"Drunk, most likely," responded the dowager who sat beside her. "Lost his balance, I suppose. Last time I saw him he was perched on the rail like a blackbird."

"Sporting of your friend Blackwood to go in after him," commented Ford Holderness. "And a lucky thing," he added, "that your friend the doctor was on board."

"All in all, a jolly little incident for your book," said Blaine Oliver jauntily. She was beginning to feel more like herself, now that the curiously artificial evening appeared to be drawing to a close. Glancing up, she noted that the yacht was almost opposite the harbor. In a few minutes they would be inside.

She smiled mischievously; there was a question that she had intended to ask, if opportunity offered.

"I am fascinated by your monocle, Mr. Holderness," she said. "What *would* you do if it were to be broken?"

The eye that gripped the monocle relaxed; the glass wafer fell crashing to the deck. Ford Holderness kicked the broken pieces into the water. From his waistcoat pocket he brought up a second patch of crystal and stuck it firmly in his eye. No smile accompanied the transaction.

"I carry spares, Miss Oliver," he bowed. "Your question is such a popular one, when I am out of England, that I never venture out without a pocketful."

After that rebuke she liked him better.

In Widdowson's car, a little later, she agreed that it would be pleasanter to accept a room at the Granada than to drive to Evanston. Blackwood, impatient, had threatened to take a taxicab and leave them. He was wearing a suit of Haviland's yachting clothes, which fitted him in only one or two particulars.

His impatience communicated itself to all of them. It was as if they realized that tidings were awaiting.

In the lobby, White was doing sentry duty. He came up swiftly.

"Here's a pretty mess, Mr. Widdowson," he growled. "The police have found that Chambers isn't Chambers, after all. He's Jeffrey Cottingham, the New York banker!"

6.

IT SIMPLIFIED MATTERS, after a fashion—the police discovery of private papers in Chambers' effects, establishing his correct identity. As Chambers, the dead man might have remained a mystery for weeks; but as Jeffrey Cottingham he became a person of importance. His history was known. So, too, in some part, were his associates.

At the same time the second identification complicated matters. It made a national sensation out of what had been a local problem of only minor interest. Mr. Blackwood felt himself trembling on the verge of large disclosures. He said nothing about his adventures at the office, however. The prospect of writing a daily story about the progress of the mystery did not attract him. Probably it would not have been permitted.

Blackwood's confrères were familiar enough with his peculiar habit of mind; they even called him "Hawkshaw" to his face. But they made no serious call upon his abilities. He was too much the facile theorist—the dilettante—for his superiors; there was always the danger that he would plunge the paper into a libel suit. Occasionally, when a particularly troublesome crime had stirred the city, he was permitted to write a Chestertonian essay on the subject.

But his reputation was tremendous. A nod from him was

something in the nature of an accolade. His long, lank figure swinging along the boulevard was one of the minor spectacles of the windy city.

He had read the early afternoon editions with attention. The story of the private life of the late Jeffrey Cottingham, as revealed in dispatches from New York, bore faintly on the story told by the spurious Chambers to Horace Trample. Cottingham had been married in Chicago, some years previously, to Effie Leedom, an actress; Blackwood recalled her vaguely as a large and puzzled blond. Presumably, then, the fellow *had* spent his first night of married happiness in a Chicago hotel. They had been separated—divorced—for almost a year, it appeared.

There was a possibility, at least, that Cottingham, in his Chambers rôle, had been telling nothing but the truth.

However, Blackwood didn't really think so. A hazy memory had entered his mind the night before, when White had made his sensational announcement. It still troubled him. Somehow he associated the name Cottingham with quite another actress.

"Now, who the devil was it?" He put the question up to Widdowson, an almanac of stage celebrities.

It is not part of a drama critic's job to remember the details of *any* actress's marriages, and Riley Blackwood did not stuff his lively mind with such ephemeral information. Such matters are in the files of newspapers, if one has need of them. In the present instance, the files afforded no clue to the state of Cottingham's heart and mind, however, after the brief account of his divorce.

Widdowson could not remember any whisper of the matter. "Probably just gossip, anyway," he ventured. "God knows we hear enough of it!" An idea occurred to him. "Could it have been in Winchell's column?"

"It might, at that," said Blackwood. He shrugged. Unhappily, there was as yet no index to Winchell.

He had drawn a blank, the night before, during his long vigil at the window of the dead man's room; and the circumstance annoyed him. The idea had struck home like an inspiration; its failure was disheartening. The doctor, obviously weary, had been excused from the nocturnal vigilance.

Over a tardy breakfast, Riley Blackwood—a little haggard—was thinking the problem out afresh. He had finished the night, and a large part of the morning, in his own room at the hotel—a courtesy of Widdowson's that was frequently a godsend. It was a small chamber near the proprietor's own, containing among other matters a small cabinet of liquor.

Blackwood excused himself abruptly, leaving the hotel man staring. Another inspiration had occurred.

There was one feature of his theory, at least, that he might possibly test, he reflected as he took the elevator upward. And once more he shut himself into the ninth-floor bedroom in which the puzzle had originated.

What he needed was a flag of some sort. However, his pocket handkerchief would do. He opened one of the windows several inches and pushed the handkerchief out upon the sill, weighting it with a copy of the Bible—furnished by the hotel—which he borrowed from a dresser drawer. Then he thoughtfully retired.

Six minutes later he was alighting from another elevator on the eighth-floor level of the Hotel Jamaica, just across the street. A little ell, near the shaft, gave onto a window that looked upon the street. There was no one in the corridor to wonder at his actions.

He raised the window swiftly and thrust forth his head. Yep, there it was! His handkerchief. It was bravely fluttering in the light breeze, to mark the room that he had left behind. And he had been right, he felt certain, in his mathematics. The eighth floor of the Jamaica was almost level with the ninth floor of the Granada. No doubt the ceilings were higher in the Jamaica, an older hotel. Standing at a window of the Granada—say the window of room 940—it would not be difficult to see into a room across the way, particularly if that room were lighted. More particularly if one had a decent pair of field glasses. The line of vision would be slightly downward, and that was all to the good.

His own operations, the night before, had been fruitless, to be sure; but he was confident his thinking had been sound.

And the room in the Hotel Jamaica that figured as precisely opposite the marked room of the Granada was——

Blackwood leaned out of his window like a locomotive fireman leaning from his cab. He counted the Granada's windows carefully, from the alley to the aperture that he had flagged; then—at greater peril—checked them against the parallel windows of the Jamaica.

Then he closed the window that he had opened and strolled tentatively along the corridor. On the door of room 827 he gently knocked.

There was no reply and, after he had knocked again, he tried the knob. But room 827 was unqualifiedly locked. There was still no maid in sight, or he would have tested the creature's integrity in the face of half a dollar.

It was annoying. This was the room, however; he felt certain of it. It had to be this one or the one immediately adjoining. Cottingham himself had obviously figured the matter rather accurately; he had even changed his room at the Granada to correct his view. An ingenious fellow! But no more ingenious than Riley Blackwood, if it came to that.

Inside the room that he was picketing a clock began to strike the hour. There was a stuttering sound in the mechanism, as if the thing were tired, and after six halting bell-like blows it gave up the attempt. If the occupant of room 827 kept appointments by the contraption, reflected Mr. Blackwood, it was likely that she was often late.

Conceivably it had run down. If she had forgotten to wind it the night before, what would be the significance of that omission? He turned the question in his mind, but reached no conclusion.

His own timepiece showed the hour to be eleven. His task now was to discover who occupied the room, if possible before that occupant returned. It was so easy that it surprised him. The switchboard girl, when he had called the room from the lobby, was almost chatty.

"I don't think Miss Mock has come in yet," she observed. "You called a little while ago, didn't you?"

Blackwood lied gracefully. He was sorry to be such a nuisance.

"I'll ring her for you, anyway," purred the switchboard.

The attempt was as vain as Blackwood had expected; but he was satisfied with his progress.

Kitty Mock, then, was the occupant of room 827. It was the name he had been seeking. The syllables "clicked" with the vague memory that had been teasing him. Somewhere, at some time, he had heard her name associated with Cottingham's. And the circumstance that Cottingham had died mysteriously in a room directly opposite that occupied by the actress was too remarkable to be regarded as mere coincidence.

She was playing a decent part in *Uncle Claude* at the Hyperion. A character part of some importance. Blackwood, in point of fact, had singled her out for eulogy, on the occasion of the piece's opening, some weeks before.

It occurred to him for the first time that the day was Wednesday. There would be a matinee at the Hyperion. Presumably the young woman would be on hand, as usual.

Or would she? There were circumstances, after all, in which it was possible to imagine her as preferring to be absent.

Well, *Uncle Claude* was a fairly tiresome work of art; but he supposed he could stand it again, if necessary. However, it was not yet even twelve o'clock.

Sitting loosely on the small of his back, in a comfortable chair in the Jamaica lounge, Blackwood again turned matters over in his agile mind. Cottingham was supposed to have arrived from New York on Monday, and certainly he had been murdered sometime Monday night. His body had been discovered in Trample's room on Tuesday morning, largely as a result of Miss Oliver's insistence. The show in which Miss Kitty Mock held forth had been in evidence for several weeks. It was, of course, possible that Cottingham had been in the city for a longer time than anybody knew; that he had merely removed his belongings from one hotel to another on the Monday that he had registered at the Granada as from New York.

Either way, it seemed a plausible hypothesis that he had come to see the actress.

On Monday night, quite late, for reasons of his own, he had elected to spy upon her—through a pair of field glasses—and his murder had promptly followed. The inference was obvious. It was in point of fact almost *too* obvious. Too easy! For how did the actress know that Cottingham was spying?

There was the telephone, to be sure, that useful instrument. Had he called her on the telephone, to upbraid her? Had she, then, infuriated, sped across the street with murder in her heart and morphine in her purse? It seemed a little silly, looked at in that way.

Blackwood sighed. If Cottingham had been a drama critic, now, the whole episode would have been understandable—even forgivable, perhaps. Mr. Blackwood smiled happily, thinking of his confrères—silent, white, and beautiful, with lilies in their hands.

But no—the alternative was better. An emissary had been

employed, and that emissary had been a man. A man had been his choice for murderer in the beginning; it was the entrance of Kitty Mock into his thinking that had balled things up. There had been no traces of a woman in Cottingham's death chamber; none whatever. All right, then, there had been an emissary—a man—and the man had murdered Cottingham. Before the murder, pleasantries had passed between them, good whisky had been offered and accepted; and the actual murder had been the subtle and cowardly crime of poison. Kitty Mock was merely an accessory before the fact—although guilty, no doubt, as Judas Iscariot himself.

"Cheers!" murmured Mr. Blackwood. "Now we're getting along."

The hell of it was, however, that as soon as one began casting about for a male murderer, one was dismayed to realize how miraculously Horace Trample filled the bill. Cottingham and the doctor were known to have been together, and drinking, after a highly curious exchange of rooms. And Trample was a poison specialist, a man who without difficulty or suspicion could obtain a tube of morphine; who might indeed carry such an item on his person.

Somehow Blackwood could not imagine Trample as poisoning a fellow creature; and yet—one never knew!

Assuming that Trample had told the truth about the exchange of rooms, he had never seen Chambers, or Cottingham, before; he simply did not know the banker. If it could be shown that Trample knew Miss Kitty Mock, his statement about Cottingham would be seen to be highly improbable, however. On the other hand, if it could be shown that Trample did *not* know Kitty Mock, the doctor's innocence might safely be assumed.

It was a point, reflected Blackwood, that ought to be put to a test as soon as possible. Meanwhile, the Hyperion was close at hand.

In the office of the theater he found the company manager and the theater manager preparing to go in different directions for luncheon. They seemed to have been annoyed by something.

"What can you tell me about Kitty Mock?" asked Blackwood brightly.

Steep, the company manager, regarded him morosely; he spoke bitterly. "Well, what would you like us to tell you?" he inquired. "That she's a bitch? I've no objections. Write your own ticket! But how did *you* happen to hear about it?"

"About what?" asked Blackwood, startled. Was the story already out? he wondered. Had the police anticipated him, after all? Then he remembered the locked door at the Jamaica, and a sudden, paralyzing thought went speeding through his head. "Has anything happened to her?"

There was a note of cynical regret in Steep's voice. "Not to *her*," he said. "Not likely! No, it's her husband that's dead. In consequence, Miss Mock is sorry that she must leave the company."

"Ah!" said Blackwood sapiently. He was, however, quite flabbergasted. "So she's left you," he added.

"Flat," said Steep. "No warning whatsoever—just a telephone message, half an hour ago. We're shoving Ora Thornton into the part for the matinee. That's all I know."

Blackwood was digesting the information he had received. "So Cottingham was her husband," he mused, trying to fit the circumstance into his mental picture.

"She didn't mention his name," said Steep. He was suddenly interested. "You mean this banker person who committed suicide at the Granada? Well, well!"

Mr. Blackwood was not proud of himself. Anger filled him and congested his arteries. "Well, what *did* she say?" he snapped. "What *did* she say, Steep? Why is she a 'bitch'?"

"Ditching the company like that," said Steep. "It's only our good luck that Thornton happens to know the part."

"I see! 'The show must go on,' and all that sort of rot, eh? *Marbles*!" said Blackwood profanely. "Cannon balls and cartridges, Mr. Steep! Nothing would be lost to the world if this lousy piece of avuncular stupidity were to cease entirely, from now on."

He was deeply annoyed with himself for his revelation about Cottingham. Steep, he supposed, would somehow turn the situation to his own advantage in the way of publicity, and the fat would be in the fire.

Well, let him. To hell with Steep!

"You don't happen to know where she was when she telephoned, I suppose?" he said.

"She didn't say. At her hotel, probably."

The two managers were looking at him curiously. A new grouping of the figures in the case was trying to form itself in Blackwood's mind. Since Cottingham had registered under a false name, it was probable that he had not wished the delectable Kitty to realize his presence in the city, after all. If Cottingham had been in truth her husband, Riley Blackwood's first easy assumption of an illicit tryst, complicated by the appearance of a second lover, was already knocked into a cocked hat. For one of the two lovers he must now substitute the dramatic but slightly tiresome figure of a wronged husband. It was a threadbare situation; but, for that matter, so was the other. Only in art—once in a blue moon—did one escape the obvious.

Well, it was a situation that opened up new vistas.

Was it conceivable that Cottingham and Kitty had not met at all? Blackwood hardly thought so, in view of all the circumstances. Yet she had waited until Wednesday to quit the company—as if the tidings had come suddenly. A subterfuge, perhaps?

The revelation of the dead man's identity had been withheld from the morning papers; it was in the early afternoon editions, on sale by ten o'clock. She had telephoned to Steep somewhere around eleven, according to the manager. It was quite possible, therefore, that she had read the death news in the papers. But, in any case, why "ditch the company" entirely, as Steep expressed the outrage, when she might with perfect propriety have asked a few days off?

It was all a little muddled, thought Mr. Blackwood testily; but one thing, at least, was certain—as soon as possible he must see Miss Kitty Mock and ask some questions. Failing that, he must somehow gain entrance to her room.

"Who's been dating Kitty these last few weeks, Steep?" he asked pensively. "Anybody in particular?"

"Search me," said Steep, and the theater manager also shrugged. "I saw her with Burton, of the *Telegram*, one night last week," added the latter helpfully.

Blackwood grinned a sudden satanic grin. "That *would* be jolly!" he observed; and did not further elucidate the delightful thought that had crossed his mind. Not that he really would have liked to send Burton to the electric chair, but the idea was a droll one.

"I'm afraid Burton won't do, Halpin," he continued. "Find out for me, will you? Somebody back stage must know."

"What's the big idea, Riley?" asked Halpin, the theater manager.

It occurred to Blackwood that he might as well go the whole hog: it might stop their filthy mouths for the time being.

"Cottingham didn't commit suicide," he told them. "At least, I don't believe he did. I think he was—*ah*—helped out of the world. Keep that under your hats, however. It may be only an idea of mine."

He smiled at their expressions of surprise.

Steep was stuttering. "You mean that—Kitty—that Kitty ——?"

"Not necessarily. I'm not sure of anything, just yet. You can help by digging up that information. And it's just between ourselves, eh? Until we decide to bust it? Right! We'll talk about it later."

Less dissatisfied with himself than he had been, Mr. Blackwood took his gloves, his hat, his stick, and his departure. But he reopened the door and put his head back into the room. "If Kitty calls again, try to find out where she is, will you? She *wasn't* at the Jamaica when she telephoned you. I want to see her."

It was possible, he reflected, that Kitty was meditating a departure from the city. Her abrupt severance of relations with the theater seemed to indicate it. If Cottingham had been as wealthy as the papers hinted, there would be no further necessity for Kitty to continue as a trouper. She could collect the body of the late lamented and vanish from the scene. Blackwood had small hope of help from the police. A coroner's jury would probably call the murder suicide, and that would be the end of it. Unless they tried to fix the crime on Trample.

With burglarious intention, he returned to the Jamaica and somewhat to his confusion found the actress in her room. He had gone straight up without telephoning. They greeted each other on the threshold.

"Why, Mr. Blackwood!" said Kitty Mock.

He could not be certain whether she was frightened or just astonished. Certainly she did not look precisely grief-stricken by her loss.

"Then you do remember me," he said. "May I come in?"

"Why, of course I remember you! And *do* come in," said Kitty Mock.

It was astonishment, he decided; not fright. She was puzzled by the sudden visitation. Wondering what could have brought the mountain to Mahomet—if he might so flatter himself! In the circumstances, it occurred to him, his still troublesome suspicion of Horace Trample, whom he liked, was probably unwarranted. If the doctor and the actress were acquainted, Kitty

Mock would not have been bewildered by a visit from Mr. Riley Blackwood; she would have heard of his activities from Trample, the day before, when—it was reasonable to suppose—they would have been in touch with one another. She would have guessed what such a visit portended.

The idea pleased him. Artistically considered, Trample's complicity must have been regarded as atrocious: he was too outstandingly the obvious suspect. It should be a fundamental rule—although it wasn't—that in life, as in fiction, the individual at whom suspicion pointed with most damning finger should be innocent. Mr. Blackwood liked his mysteries complex; his denouements surprising. The play writers were aware of this.

He sank into a chair. Miss Mock did not appear to be considering flight. There were no evidences of haste.

"And so you've left the company," he said.

Miss Mock exposed her knees. "You've heard that, then! I didn't think I was important enough to rate attention." Her smile was friendly and attractive. "Yes, it's true. My husband died— rather suddenly. It shocked me. I didn't feel that I could go on." She added: "It was a break for Thornton. I knew she knew the lines."

She was older than he had thought. In her middle thirties, he judged, although still a handsome animal.

Blackwood made a sympathetic noise in his throat. "Have I met him?" he asked. "To tell the truth, I didn't know you were married—Kitty. Nothing recent, I hope!"

The flippant irony of the remark was disguised by the seriousness of his voice; but he felt that she resented it. She shook her head.

"Not many people knew about it," she answered indirectly; and added, "About a year."

"I'm sorry," said Riley Blackwood. "An accident, I suppose! You said he died rather suddenly?"

"He committed suicide," said Kitty Mock. Her answer was abrupt, but there was a dignity in it that he was forced to admire. She was an admirable actress.

"Forgive me," he begged. "I can understand that it *must* have been a shock. You will be going back to New York shortly, I suppose."

"New York?" She raised her eyebrows.

"It was my impression that your home was in New York."

"My home," said Kitty Mock, "is in Carthage, Texas. But you are right. I *shall* be going to New York shortly. It was my husband's home."

They were fencing cautiously now. It was obvious, he thought, that she was suspicious of his questioning.

"I'm sorry," he said again. "There's nothing you would care to have me say about him, in the paper, I suppose? In the circumstances, perhaps the less said the better."

She greatly surprised him. "There has already been enough said in the papers to satisfy *me*, Mr. Blackwood. There really isn't any secret about the matter, you know. There won't be long, at any rate. As I say, not many people knew about it—but my husband was Jeffrey Cottingham, the banker."

"Great Scott!" said Riley Blackwood. He was a bit of an actor himself, he reflected immodestly.

"Yes," she said, nodding; and her little smile was everything it should be. "So you see, it isn't publicity I shall be needing."

He agreed; with sympathetic heartiness he agreed. "Why," said Blackwood, "it was only yesterday you heard of it, then!"

She avoided the trap without faltering. "Only today," she corrected him. "I read about it in the papers—less than two hours ago."

"Then you haven't seen him!"

"I've seen him," said Kitty Mock a little grimly. "I couldn't believe it—so I went at once to the place where the papers said he had been taken. It was horrible! An undertaker's shop, in Randolph Street. I kept hoping, you see! But it was Jeffrey. I almost fainted. Then I went to a drug store and telephoned the theater."

It was a careful and plausible story, Blackwood admitted to himself. She had been away identifying the body while he was trying to reach her here at the Jamaica.

"Do you mean that you identified him—officially—for the police?"

She shook her head. "There was no necessity. A Mr. Melton—a banker of this city, and a friend of Jeffrey's—had just left. He had seen it in the papers, too, and gone right over. The undertaker told me."

The name rang familiarly in Blackwood's ear. Where the dickens had he heard it spoken only recently?

"What did you tell the undertaker?" he asked her curiously.

"I said I thought I knew the—the man who was dead—and he let me look at the body. When I recognized it, he told me about Mr. Melton. He told me there wasn't any mystery about it, though; the police already knew who Jeffrey was. I think Mr. Melton was going to them, anyway."

"You didn't tell him that Cottingham—that Mr. Cottingham was your husband?"

"No."

"Why not?"

"I don't know," said Kitty Mock. She hesitated. "I just don't know!"

"You'll have to tell the police sometime, you know," he pointed out. "You'll have to claim the body, won't you?"

"I suppose so. Yes, of course I will. And you mustn't misunderstand me—I was fond of Jeffrey. I really was! You see," she burst out, "it's going to be messy, Mr. Blackwood—I'm *afraid* it is. Why was Jeffrey in Chicago, masquerading as Jordan Chambers? I suppose you've read the papers."

"You haven't any idea?"

"No."

"And you think there may be something—*er*—'messy' behind it all?"

"I don't know what to think," said Kitty Mock. She smiled a wan little smile. "There's a situation for you—an actress afraid of publicity!"

An idea crossed his mind. "Is there a *real* Jordan Chambers?"

"Not that I ever heard of."

"I thought you might have been suggesting it. Probably not, though. The initials are Cottingham's own. That usually happens when a man takes another name. It helps to keep him from forgetting the name he has selected."

A silence fell between them. Blackwood was puzzled; he admitted it. But he was far from being convinced that the actress had had no hand in her husband's death. She seemed to be sincere enough, and at the same time she seemed to be concealing something. It was incredible, he thought, that she really feared any revelation other than the one he believed to be inevitable— that her husband was a murder victim and not a suicide. And it was always to be remembered, he told himself again, that this woman was a skilled and seasoned actress. He had himself had occasion to praise her ability. Her stage work was consistently excellent.

She shrugged, and broke the silence that had succeeded his last remark. "However, you didn't come here to listen to all this! I'm sorry. Why *did* you come, Mr. Blackwood?"

"To tell the truth," said Blackwood, "I came to ask you about a man named Trample—Dr. Horace Trample. You know him, I believe. A toxicologist!"

Her eyes were thoughtful; her glance level. "Dr. Horace Trample? I don't think I've ever heard the name before. It's a name that one would be likely to remember, isn't it? No, I'm almost certain I don't know him. A toxi——?"

"—cologist," said Blackwood. "That is, a specialist in poisons."

"I was thinking you meant a man who stuffed birds!" she told him with a smile. "No, I'm sorry. What made you think I knew him?"

The drama critic of the *Morning Chronicle* also smiled. "Perhaps it doesn't matter now," he said. "But about your husband—Kitty. That's important. I rather think you had better tell the police about him before long. It's good advice. It'll look better—later on—*whatever* may develop."

Miss Mock agreed. "I believe you are right," she said.

He was standing now; and suddenly—on an impulse, for he had until then forgotten all about it—he crossed the room and pushed aside the window curtains. Yep, it was still there! His handkerchief, fluttering in the breeze, nine floors above the traffic of the thoroughfare.

"That's rather odd," he commented; and she came and stood beside him at the window. "Isn't it?" he questioned. "Somebody's handkerchief—it almost looks as if it were a signal of some kind!"

She steadied herself against the window frame. "It *is* odd," agreed Miss Kitty Mock, "isn't it? *Very* odd!" And after a moment, with a trace of confusion, she said: "You know, I've never thanked you for your marvelous review. Particularly what you said about *me*. It was wonderful!"

She was a very attractive woman; there was no possible doubt about that. He slipped an arm around her, and for a few moments they both breathed hard.

In other circumstances, now, thought Mr. Blackwood, glancing tentatively toward a little alcove—a veritable love nest——

Well, well! Always the gentleman, eh, Riley, old fellow?

He dropped his arm, and they moved apart, each one a little ashamed. Mr. Blackwood resolutely took himself in hand. He fumbled for his cigarettes. Turning, a moment later, to offer her the case, he saw that she was standing rigid, her eyes fixed upon something on a table, in the corner. In the next instant, she had stepped forward and obscured it. Her back was toward him; but he sensed that with a quick movement she had dropped her handkerchief over some object that had been conspicuously in view.

He had not noticed anything out of the ordinary; but then, he had had, as yet, no opportunity to explore the corners of her apartment.

It occurred to him that her action was significant.

With her eyes squarely upon his, he moved to the table and lifted the handkerchief, to look down upon the thing she had concealed.

It was a hypodermic syringe, neatly laid out upon a piece of absorbent cotton and filled with a brownish-looking fluid.

"Sorry, darling," said Blackwood, "if I've been a brute!"

7.

WELL, THERE IT WAS! The direct connection! Morphine in the stomach of Jeffrey Cottingham, and a needleful of it on a table in his wife's apartment.

Blackwood was a little shocked by his discovery, certain as he had been that Kitty held some vital clue to the murder. The way in which this new development implicated the doctor was almost alarming. Morphine, unless illegally obtained from dope peddlers, was to be had only on presentation of a prescription. If Kitty Mock, in private life, employed the needle of happiness and horror, who furnished the materials?

But he could not ask for better melodrama, he admitted. All the props were being drawn forth and dusted off for the occasion. One thing, he fancied, the drama ultimately would lack—a moral conclusion. The wronged husband—if that had been Cottingham's rôle—being jolly well dead, could hardly triumph in the end.

Blackwood sought the Jamaica's manager in his rosewood office and spun a tale of great ingenuity. Steep, he was confident, would back him up in anything he cared to invent. And anyway, the manager did not know him.

"I am an assistant to the producer of the *Uncle Claude* comedy, now playing at the Hyperion," he explained in confidence. "It is possible that I am only one day ahead of the narcotic squad on this investigation—I don't know. On the other hand, it is possible that my investigation may keep them from coming to you at all. Frankly, Mr. Holabird, has it ever occurred to you that dope peddlers might be operating in this hotel?"

Mr. Holabird was horrified. "Good God, no!" he replied. "What do you mean?"

"Remember that what I am telling you is confidential," said Blackwood. "The fact is, Kitty Mock is getting morphine from somebody. We're worried about her at the theater, and we're trying to locate the source of her supply."

Once more the manager of the Hotel Jamaica called piously upon his Maker. "Kitty Mock!" he exclaimed.

"Yes, I'm sorry to say she's somewhat of an addict. The maid who makes up her apartment could bear me out, I think, if it were necessary." Blackwood's voice was filled with regret. "I'm not prepared to say that the stuff is always delivered to her here; but that's the way it looks. We've checked the theater end of it carefully."

"I can't believe it," said Holabird.

He found no serious difficulty in believing it, however. God alone knew *what* went on in a great hotel, under the noses of its authorities, was what he was thinking, unless Blackwood was mistaken.

"It should be easy enough to prove," said Blackwood, "one way or another. We happen to know that she received a supply of it on Monday night. And we know there was someone with her, here, after eleven o'clock; say between eleven and twelve. There may have been no connection between the two circumstances, but it's likely that there was. Now, who is there that can tell us about Kitty's midnight visitors?"

"Visitors?"

"My information is that there were two of them."

"I see," said the manager. He thought the situation over with some care. It was a nasty spot in which he found himself, he realized; and he must appear to wish to be of help.

It was fairly notorious among the members of the staff that Kitty had had several midnight visitors, at one time and another; but one did not inquire too earnestly into such matters. After all, the private life of an actress began after the show was over. She was entitled to her friends, like other people. It was simply that her hours were different.

"There's the night clerk, of course," he suggested dubiously. "But it's obvious that anybody on that kind of an errand would not report where he was going. He'd just slip in and hustle for the elevators."

Blackwood seemed struck by the objection. "That's true," he agreed. "Then you suggest the elevator man?"

Mr. Holabird thought it unlikely that the elevator man could know anything about it, unless he had actually seen the actress and the secret salesman in conference together. "I'll speak to him myself, however, when he comes on duty," he promised.

"It's only Monday night we're interested in, you know," said Blackwood. "How about the occupants of the adjoining rooms?"

The manager of the Jamaica was uncertain at the moment who occupied the rooms adjoining room 827; but he would ascertain and, if the proper opportunity presented itself, would——

He spread his hands. "You realize the difficulty?"

"I know!" Blackwood realized the other's difficulties very well. He felt a sneaking sympathy for Holabird. Making furtive inquiries of one guest about the possible shenanigans of another, was not good politics. "But we must get at it somehow," he insisted. "Look here! What about your boys? They're coming and going at all hours, I imagine. And they're not exactly fools."

It occurred to Holabird that he would rather allow his boys

to be cross-examined than his guests, if there were no other way out of this unhappy business.

He brightened. "Yes, that's possible. I'll speak to them and let you know what they say. Where can I get in touch with you, later on?"

But Blackwood had no intention of allowing himself to be put off. And he was familiar with the workings of hotels, through his association with Tony Widdowson.

"Oh, let's get it over with at once," he urged. He glanced at his watch. "It's after twelve. You run your lads in several shifts, don't you? Some of your evening boys are certain to be back on duty." A warning note crept into his voice. "Better you and I, after all, than the narcotic squad!"

With luck, he reflected, he might catch a boy who had been on till midnight on the day in question. He realized that Holabird also thought this possible, and that he feared the consequences.

The hotel manager lifted his receiver, without enthusiasm, and gave the necessary orders; and shortly there stood before them, easily enough, an alert young person in buttons, with freckles beneath his eyes.

"You were on duty Monday night?" asked Holabird a trifle crossly.

"Yes, sir, from six to twelve. I'm on today from twelve to six."

"This gentleman wants to ask you some questions about Monday night. You are to answer them as accurately as you can. Remember, however, that everything that passes between us is in confidence. Do you understand?"

"Yes, sir." The boy's eyes opened a trifle more widely, and Blackwood understood that his curiosity had been aroused. Holabird appeared to wash his hands of him; he glanced at Blackwood.

"What's your name, son?" asked Riley Blackwood pleasantly.

"Jamieson, sir—Charles Jamieson."

"On Monday night, fairly late—after the show, in fact—Miss Mock, the actress, had a visitor; possibly several visitors. Did you happen to see any of them?"

"Yes, sir."

Holabird was greatly alarmed. "No names just yet, Jamieson," he warned sharply; then he apologized to Blackwood. "After all, the man you have in mind would not be one of Miss Mock's more usual visitors, I take it!"

Blackwood concealed his annoyance. "Possibly not," he agreed; "and yet—can we be sure? After all, the exchange may have been given the appearance of a social visit." He wheeled upon the boy. "Do you *know* the names of Miss Mock's visitors on Monday night, Jamieson?"

"No, sir."

Holabird's relief was evident in his face. "Sorry," he said. "You may be right, of course. That hadn't occurred to me."

Blackwood shrugged. He was disappointed by young Mr. Jamieson's answer to his important question, but he hoped the interview might now go forward without interruption.

"That's all right, Jamieson," he said. "Never mind the names, just now. So there were two of them, were there?"

Jamieson, a bit embarrassed, turned his eyes upon his employer, who graciously nodded. "Answer Mr. Blackwood's questions, Jamieson," he ordered.

"There were three of them, sir," said Jamieson.

Blackwood was surprised. "Well, well!" he commented. "Were they all together?"

"I don't know, sir." The bellboy hesitated. "I think so; but I can't say for sure."

"What do you mean by that?" asked Blackwood. "Perhaps you had better tell me all about it in your own way, Jamieson."

"Yes, sir. I mean that two of them came out together, and the other one stayed behind; so maybe they weren't all together in the first place."

"I see. But you saw them all, didn't you? All three of them?"

"No, sir. I only saw the two who came out together. But I knew there was another man in the room, because I heard his voice."

"I see," said Blackwood again. "Well, what time was all this, Jamieson; and how did you happen to see them leave the room? Just go ahead and spill it in any way you like."

Young Mr. Jamieson considered the questions for a moment, with wrinkled brow. "Well, sir, it was somewhere close to midnight; I know that because I was figuring on going off duty in a little while. A call came through from 827 for two bottles of ginger ale and some set-ups. I took them up. But when I got there two of the men were just leaving, see? I met them in the hall."

"Good!" cried Riley Blackwood. "Then you had a look at their faces. Can you describe them for me?"

Jamieson's eyes flickered for an instant toward those of Holabird, where they found no help—only a certain anxiety. "They looked excited," he answered.

"Excited, eh? That's fine!" Blackwood was enthusiastic. "Now, what I want, Jamieson, since we do not know their names, is a description of the men, from which I might possibly recognize them if I saw them. Hair, eyes, weight, height—clothing—you know the sort of thing I mean. Do you ever read detective stories?"

"Yes, sir."

"Well, that's what I want. A description of the suspects."

He rather hoped that, without actually saying so, he had conveyed the impression that he was himself a detective. Then he listened with increasing interest to the descriptions vouchsafed by young Mr. Jamieson. The second man described—the shorter of the two—troubled him; but of the first there could be no doubt whatever. It was an accurate portrait of the late New York banker, Jeffrey Cottingham.

Who the dickens, then, could have been his companion? He was certainly not Horace Trample.

He pressed the question. "Short, you said, and sandy? You saw him before he put his hat on? And a bit *thick,* eh? A fairly tough-looking baby?"

"Yes, sir. Looked as if he could put up a pretty good scrap, if he had to. Looked to me like he was a sort of bodyguard to the other fellow." An expression of interest crossed the boy's face. "Say!" he cried. "The other fellow called him 'Gene'—I just remembered!"

Good Lord! thought Riley Blackwood. *Gene Cross!*

But was it possible? The ugly-looking thug that he had himself rescued from the lake only the night before? What possible connection could Gene Cross have had with Jeffrey Cottingham? But the description was almost letter perfect. The coincidence of names was astonishing.

Here was food for thought. And the boy's impression of the man as a "sort of bodyguard" for Cottingham was almost an inspiration.

"It rather looks to me, Mr. Holabird, as if this second man is the man we're looking for," he commented. "What do you think?"

It looked very much like it to Mr. Holabird. The manager asked a question of his own: "You never saw this man before, did you, Jamieson? The one you heard called 'Gene'?"

"No, sir."

Holabird was both relieved and interested. He seemed to be on safe ground. "And what about the third man, Jamieson?" he hesitated. "The man you didn't see. You didn't recognize his voice, I suppose?"

"Couldn't, sir. All I heard him say was, 'Never mind'!"

" 'Never mind,' " repeated Blackwood. He cocked his head and tried it with a different inflection: " 'Never mind'?" But the vocal experiment told him nothing. "You didn't see him leave the hotel later?" he questioned.

"No, sir—not that I know of, anyway. I might have, without knowing it was him."

"*He*," corrected Blackwood. "Well, Jamieson, I'm certainly much obliged to you. By the way, what happened after the two men left?"

"Nothing that I know of. Miss Mock took the tray from me at the door. I didn't go in. When she closed the door, I went away."

"Did Miss Mock also look excited?"

"Sort of—yes, sir. But I just figured they'd all been having something to drink, and two of them knew when they'd had enough."

"I see. That sounds very plausible. But I think that second fellow is our man, Mr. Holabird. I think he came to deliver the goods. The fellow with him was just a blind. I don't know about the third man. He may have been in the room when the other two arrived—one of her regular visitors. I wish we knew who he was. He might be able to give us a clue to the others."

Blackwood looked pensively at the manager of the Hotel Jamaica, who shook his head.

"I'm sorry too," the manager lied. "Oh, don't bother to give Jamieson anything."

Blackwood was digging into a billfold. "He's earned a dollar, anyway," he retorted. "Wish I could make it two. Nothing else you can think of, on Monday night, Jamieson?"

"No, sir. I think that's all there is." The bellboy grinned. "Thank you, sir."

It occurred to Mr. Blackwood, seated on his shoulder blades, a little later, in the gorgeous lounge of the Hotel Jamaica's principal rival, that he had not done too badly. He could visualize the scene now with some clarity. The third man—the "mystery man," as the newspapers would no doubt be calling him in a day or two—had been already in the room when Cottingham and Cross arrived. The order for two set-ups seemed to prove it; these were for Cottingham and his companion. He had always believed that Kitty and Cottingham had had a meeting on Monday night. But where in hell did Cross come in?

Blackwood had half a mind to dig up Widdowson and lay this new discovery before him. But he decided to postpone the revelation until dinner time. There was still a fair part of the afternoon left to him for further research.

He tossed his cigarette stub into a tub of palms and strolled into the telephone alcove. The phone book revealed that one Gene Cross had an office in La Salle Street; but there was no clue to the tough baby's professional activities. It was Blackwood's idea that he was a lawyer, and possibly a shady one.

The distance was not great; but he took a taxi, just the same.

It was a dingy old building: one of the remaining landmarks of an earlier and vastly dirtier Chicago. Over near the river. The rentals, Mr. Blackwood ventured to think, were relatively cheap. He found Gene Cross's name in capitals on the index board and took a wheezy elevator to the top floor.

Then for a startled moment his eyes considered the legend underneath the name upon the door.

There was a card beside it. "Back in Five Minutes" read the fly-blown placard in the corner of the ground-glass pane; but there was no indication how long before his arrival the thing had been put in place. A swift impression crossed his mind that the placard was as much a fixture as the building. These strange old buildings in La Salle Street! Second-rate lawyers had their offices here, and unsuccessful beauty specialists, and Western representatives of dubious Eastern corset manufacturers. The rabbit holes looked gloomy and uninviting. A perpetual twilight brooded in the halls.

And private detectives!

His eyes returned to the painted advertisement of Cross's business. He was a "Special Investigator."

Blackwood turned the door handle and pushed inward. But the door was really locked. Whatever the length of time he had been away, Gene Cross was not now in his office.

A little song that he had heard somewhere, probably in vaudeville, years before, was running in Blackwood's head; he softly hummed the melody. The words of the song, if he had given voice to them, would have run as follows:

> Oh, I broke a lock in Lockport,
>> And they gave me time, you bet.
> It's hard to sing at Sing Sing
>> Or be jolly at Joliet!

The locks in these old buildings were notoriously inexpensive. The one he now confronted would not have troubled a child. There was a key in his pocket that would open it as if it were a can of sardines.

The only alarming feature of the set-up was the "Five Minutes" card, and this he reexamined carefully. He was prepared to swear that it had been there since the great fire of 1871. And, after all, he had saved the fellow's life. Cross would hardly feel like punching his jaw for a little thing like housebreaking. As a matter of fact, he could say he had found the door unlocked.

Happily, he was out of sight of the elevator; but he waited until he heard the thing descending, after a fruitless visit to the top. It made noise enough, he reflected, to give him plenty of warning.

His conscience—a well-trained and well-subordinated intelligence—did not trouble him for a moment.

Blackwood took his key out of his pocket and let himself in as neatly as if he had been opening his own back door.

There were two offices within, beyond a small barrier with a swinging gate. One was apparently for visitors, so he chose the other to begin with. Cross was not a tidy man, he noted with regret; his desk was littered with legal-looking papers and presumably unanswered correspondence. On the walls were a calendar, donated by a great insurance company, and a framed photograph of Gene Cross in the uniform of his country's service, standing beside a military plane.

Blackwood pivoted slowly in the center of the small chamber; then he turned his attention to the papers on the desk. Their lack of order was reassuring, at any rate. It seemed unlikely that Cross would know that anything had been moved.

He did not know precisely what he was looking for. Something—anything—that would verify the presumed connection between Cottingham and Cross.

Once he looked up and heard the elevator returning to the top. But it went down again before he had closed the outer door behind him; and he returned to his wearisome picking up and laying down of papers. Dislike for Cross kept mounting within him as he worked. It occurred to him that the investigator's principal activities were along the lines of espionage, and he was inclined to wonder if they did not include a little blackmail on the side.

In the end, he said, "Damn!" softly, under his breath, and sat down in Cross's chair. It seemed obvious that if the fellow had been in correspondence with Jeffrey Cottingham he must be carrying the documents upon his person.

However, he changed his mind immediately. Cottingham's letters would be in the safe, of course! He had forgotten the safe. It stood in a corner near the window. Blackwood eyed it speculatively. After a moment he rose to his feet and tried the handle. Then he sighed and lighted a cigarette. His accomplishments were many, as he had pointed out to Blaine Oliver; but they did not include safecracking. Somehow, it seemed an oversight.

"What a hell of a place for a detective," he mused, eyeing his surroundings with distaste. But the view of the river from the window was rather striking—in a Joseph Pennell sort of way. Confound Cross! He almost hoped he *would* come in and catch him.

He became bolder and telephoned to Widdowson.

"Listen, Tony!" he said. "You'll never guess where I am."

Widdowson was disinclined toward guessing.

"I'm in Gene Cross's office," said Blackwood. "What do you suppose the gentleman's business is?"

But Widdowson had not the faintest idea.

"He's a private detective," reported Blackwood, with a certain triumph. "You know, the sort of Dashiell Hammett dick who trails your wife and the other fellow to a hotel. What does that suggest to you?"

It suggested nothing immediately to Widdowson, who was interested to know, however, what Blackwood was doing in the investigator's office.

"I'm waiting for the blighter to come in," said Blackwood. "I've discovered that he was with Cottingham on Monday night. *What?* No, at the Jamaica! There was a scene of some sort; I don't know what it was about, just yet—but both of us can guess. For all I know, he may have been at the Granada too. That's what I want you to find out. Tell White about it, will you? See what he can turn up. I'll be along for dinner."

He hung up the receiver and returned to his inspection of the melancholy office. He stood upright, pinching out his cigarette, and tossed the stub into a reeking cuspidor. As he did so, a desk pad caught his eye; it had been beneath his nose for some time.

Its top sheet announced the current date, in large letters, but was otherwise blank.

Reversing time, he turned quickly to the preceding day—Tuesday—and read a penciled note. "Bourbon," it read simply, and then some figures. They looked like "$3.75." The modest record, no doubt, of one of Mr. Cross's purchases. The short and simple annals of the poor.

"Backward, turn backward, O Time, in thy flight!"

He turned another page and read, beneath the printed legend—Monday—the one word "Chambers."

At the Granada, en route to Widdowson's quarters, the speeding Blackwood crossed the path of Dr. Harold Marcus and was greeted cordially.

"You don't happen to want my ring again, I suppose," said the house physician amiably; and instantly added: "Well, it begins to look as if your friend the toxicologist is in for trouble!"

"The deuce he is!" Blackwood already had begun to excuse himself and push on. Now he turned back. "What's happened?" he demanded.

The house physician shrugged. "Nothing yet, I believe. But Roach was here a little while ago, looking for Mr. Widdowson. I saw him talking to Moffat, in the lobby, and Moffat told me what he said. No fingerprints of any kind in 940, except Trample's and the dead man's—and I believe those of the boy who brought the bottles. Roach had been trying to reach the doctor and couldn't find him."

"He's at that infernal medical convention, I suppose," said Blackwood irritably. "Trample isn't trying to run away."

The hotel doctor grinned. "Maybe not," he answered; "but, believe me, I'd run if they had a case against me like the one they've got on Trample!"

"You'd be a chump," said Blackwood, with intense dislike.

He burst into Widdowson's living room, muttering, and suddenly realized that Roach and Barry had not yet left the hotel. They were seated, very much at their ease, in comfortable chairs, while drinking some of Widdowson's good Scotch.

The proprietor of the Granada was relieved. "I'm glad you've come, Riley," he said. "Roach is worried about the doctor. He's been trying to get in touch with him all afternoon."

"He's at his medical convention, I suppose," retorted Blackwood. "He'll be along for dinner now at almost any minute."

The spokesman for the two detectives cleared his throat. "Maybe he will, Mr. Blackwood," he observed pacifically. "But he *wasn't* at his convention, this afternoon: we tried to reach him there." He sipped his highball with great enjoyment. "You haven't seen him, I suppose?"

"I haven't seen him since last night," said Riley Blackwood. "I intended to look him up myself, tonight."

"I hope you find him," said the police officer. "He promised us he wouldn't leave the city without telling us." He sipped again. "I suppose you've heard the latest news?"

"I supposed that I was listening to it now," said Blackwood.

"I mean about the dead man. His wife's come forward to claim the body. Just a little while ago. Perhaps it isn't in the papers yet—but you have ways of finding out things for yourself!"

Blackwood laughed softly. "Oh yes! It's Kitty Mock you're talking about. It was I who urged her to lose no time about it. I suppose she told you that."

"She did," said Roach, without rancor. But he was distinctly curious. "How'd you happen to know she was his wife?" he asked.

Blackwood laughed again. "Sheer inspiration, Roach," he answered. "Some people call it genius. I went to her, I asked her, and she told me." It was not a precisely accurate statement of the case, he reflected, but it was near enough.

He asked a question of his own: "What's your latest theory

about the doctor? How does the revelation of Miss Mock have any bearing upon Trample? She never heard of him before."

The big policeman shrugged. "Maybe she didn't," he agreed; "but it all looks kind of funny. She didn't know her husband was in the city, yet he was right across the street from her on the night he died. She didn't know this Dr. Trample, yet he's a poison specialist, and Cottingham was killed with poison. And the only fingerprints in that room upstairs were Cottingham's and this Dr. Trample's."

It was an able enough summary, Blackwood inwardly admitted. He had himself had difficulty in getting past the incriminating facts. Indeed, he had as yet no adequate alternative for them.

Cross? But there was no telling yet where Gene Cross came into the tangled picture. He hoped that Widdowson had said nothing about his telephone call from the investigator's office.

One thing was certain—he would keep the tale of Kitty's hypodermic to himself. Trample might be the murderer of Jeffrey Cottingham and he might not; but there was already sufficient trouble brewing for him.

"Whose fingerprints were on that card, Roach?" he asked abruptly. "The one that was hanging on the door knob."

"Nobody's," admitted the detective. "Not even Cottingham's. But I suppose he hung it out himself. You called the turn on that."

"I'm smart," said Blackwood. "I'll call the turn on Trample, too. He didn't do it. I don't know yet who did—but it wasn't Trample."

He sincerely hoped that he was right. If the doctor had disappeared, as this fathead of a police detective seemed to think, it *might* be Trample, after all.

8.

WHERE THE DICKENS was the doctor?

His belongings were definitely in his room; he had left no tidings at the desk for any who might care to see him. Miss Oliver, reached at her home in Evanston, by telephone, replied that she had seen nothing of him since early morning. They had breakfasted together, then had parted without a definite engagement. She was quite sure that he had intended to attend the morning session of his medical convention. Yet, if Roach's information were correct, he had not been near that distinguished mobilization in the Hall of Science.

He might, of course, be simply wandering through the Fair. There was his own testimony that he found the convention a trifle of a bore.

Widdowson was worried. He was inclined to be annoyed with the police; in some degree, even with Riley Blackwood. Three hours and more had passed since the hotel man's unwelcome guests had taken their departure, and there had been still no sign of Horace Trample.

"There's no sense in blaming the police," quoth Mr. Blackwood, in mellow mood after a satisfying dinner. "Their present theory of the case was practically inevitable. What else can they believe? Let them worry about Trample for an evening; it gives them something to occupy their minds." He drew reflectively upon his cigarette. "But for Trample actually to be guilty is to violate all the canons of detective drama." He gestured splendidly. "You may respond that life and literature are unlike, and that——"

"I don't respond at all," said Widdowson testily. "I know nothing whatever about it."

"No matter," said Blackwood; "your responses are an open book to me—a primer, Tony. I reply that, in spite of all appearances to the contrary—including the admitted exceptions to the rule—life frequently *does* plagiarize the drama. And for reasons that are demonstrable! In the beginning, we agree, it was literature that first plagiarized from life. After a time——"

The proprietor of the Granada moved sharply in his chair. His nerves were becoming frayed. "For God's sake, Riley," he implored, "cut out the lecturing! The question is, what are we going to do about the doctor? You started this investigation—and unless it's stopped this hotel is going to lose a lot of money."

"I think not," said Riley Blackwood. "Your premise is a false one to begin with. The bigger the scandal the more money you will make. And I didn't really start the investigation, my dear man: if anything, I delayed it. Sooner or later it was bound to be assumed that Trample was the culprit—*re*assumed, I should say, since that was the police idea at the beginning. Probably it never entirely left their heads. Why should it? The doctor is the logical candidate. Ultimately, unless a stronger suspect appears on the horizon, he will be taken into custody."

Widdowson seemed despondent. "*Is* there a stronger suspect on the horizon?" he asked.

"Oh yes! I have already suggested Cross to you—still unknown to the police—and there is the man who murdered Cottingham, if the murderer doesn't happen to have been Cross. Possibly he is the third man of the conclave at the Jamaica,

Monday night—the 'man of mystery.' Possibly he is someone to whom, at present, we have no clue at all."

Blackwood leaned forward in his chair. "Seriously, Tony, I'm not fool enough not to realize that Trample may have done this job. The fact that I might prefer it otherwise has no bearing on the matter. But there's a feature of *that* theory that bothers me. If Trample murdered Cottingham—in other words, if Trample is the third member of an unsavory marital muddle—what part in the enterprise was played by Miss Oliver of Evanston?"

"Blaine Oliver!" Widdowson was surprised. "I supposed that she was out of it completely."

"It's a pleasing assumption; but if Trample lied, so also may Miss Oliver have lied. You heard me tease her on the subject of complicity; yet it's a possibility one has to bear in mind. I don't mean that she may have committed the actual crime: there isn't a chance of it. But suppose she knew that Trample intended to. Suppose, then, that Trample had this breakfast engagement with her, the following morning—at which he was to report. It would explain her agitation, wouldn't it? There's Prentiss, too—a friend of the Oliver woman. He showed up with surprising fortuity. Was that just an accident? He was on the yacht, too."

Widdowson frowned. "Prentiss couldn't have known that either the doctor or Miss Oliver would be on board," he pointed out. "They didn't know it themselves until I asked them and they agreed to go."

"I know," said Blackwood. "It's a bit murky. Cross too was on the yacht, however."

The hotel proprietor seemed puzzled. "I don't quite see what you're getting at, Riley," he protested.

"Neither do I," grinned Riley Blackwood. "I'm not attempting to draw conclusions. I'm indicating some of the puzzling features of the case and wondering about them—that's all."

Widdowson was silent for a moment. "It's beyond *me*, Riley," he burst forth at length. "I'm worried about the doctor—but I'm inclined to bet on Blaine Oliver. She seemed all right, to me."

"To me, too," agreed Blackwood. "And if Trample is the murderer, because he was interested in Cottingham's wife and Cottingham didn't like it—her rôle is very mystifying indeed. You see," he shrugged, "it's a lot simpler to believe that Trample had nothing to do with it, and that Miss Oliver too is innocent."

"I've no objections," said Widdowson grimly. "*You* brought all this up, you know."

"I know," said Riley Blackwood. "Underneath my confident exterior it's worrying me. Damn Trample, anyway, for running off like that! What about White? Did you ask him about Cross?"

Widdowson shook his head. "Sorry—those infernal coppers came in just as I was getting around to it."

"See if you can find out," urged Blackwood. "I'm interested in Cross. He's a key piece in this puzzle. He has a very irregular outline, and God knows where he fits. There's one man who may be able to tell us something about him, and that's Haviland. Cross was certainly on the yacht—I plucked him from the raging main, myself! But what the devil was he *doing* on the yacht?"

He glanced at his wrist watch. "If Haviland isn't at a theater or some place, I might catch him at his home right now."

From the littered dinner table at which he sat, Blackwood abruptly reached an arm to the small telephone stand near by. "What's Haviland's number, Tony?" he inquired. "Hello, operator! Get me Majestic 4844—Mr. Haviland . . . Haviland, yes! Riley Blackwood speaking. Put him on Mr. Widdowson's private phone."

There was a pause, while Widdowson waited morosely for what might follow. Then the bell rang sharply.

"All right, Blackwood speaking. Hello, Haviland—Riley Blackwood! I called to see if you were at home. I want some information about Gene Cross—the thug whose life I saved last night. I thought perhaps you——"

He interrupted himself to listen.

"The hell you say! Well, the doctor's missing, too; I hope it doesn't become epidemic. Trample, I mean; the medico you met last night. Maybe they're off together, somewhere."

He listened again . . . "All right, I'll be along in twenty minutes."

He banged down the receiver and turned to Widdowson. "Cross vanished from the yacht last night shortly after we left the party. He must have *dripped* his way across the city, unless Haviland had another suit of clothes! Well, I'm off to Haviland's. It seems he would a tale unfold."

In the taxicab that bore him northward Blackwood again heartily cursed the missing doctor. Was it possible that Cross knew of the disappearance and was after him? Cross was a detective; he had been employed, apparently, by Cottingham. At any rate, the two had been together at Kitty Mock's apartment, where they had seemed "excited." What other alternative was there? Cross obviously knew that Cottingham was masquerading—the name "Chambers" was scrawled upon his desk pad. Who but Cottingham could have told him? They had met upon the Monday night after the meeting between "Chambers" and the doctor; after the specialist had given up his room and gone to bed in Cottingham's.

A swift picture of their several activities ran in Blackwood's mind. Cottingham had not been going straight to bed, as he informed the doctor. He was even then looking forward to his rendezvous with Cross. But would Cross know that the exchange of rooms had been effected? Probably not at that time. Their meeting then was outside the actual room—possibly even in the lobby; it would be fairly crowded between eleven and twelve. Cottingham had already, probably, used his binoculars to advantage; there would have been no necessity for taking Cross upstairs.

Very well, then, they crossed the street to the Jamaica; it was close to midnight when young Jamieson went up with ginger ale, and the excitement, by that time, was over, whatever it may have been.

The time element was almost brilliantly involved, it occurred to Blackwood; but the program he had imagined seemed to check. It had been eleven, or a little after, when Cottingham and Trample left the bar; and there had been only one drink after they had made their curious exchange. Fast work, all of it; but it could have been done.

And *after* the "excitement" at the Jamaica? Surely it was reasonable to suppose that Cottingham and Cross had returned to the Granada! That they had discussed their problem, after midnight, in Cottingham's new quarters. Had there been a quarrel?

A tough detective, with the experience Cross must have had, would not be fool enough to leave his fingerprints around. It was likely enough, also, that Cross—with his knowledge of the underworld—would be able to obtain a tube of morphine.

All this supposed the doctor to be innocent. If Cross had murdered Cottingham, there was now no reason to suppose that his own disappearance and Trample's were connected—was there?

On the other hand, if Trample were the murderer, Cross—as an agent of the murdered banker—might very well be on the trail. Might have been on the trail from the beginning! For if Trample's circumstantial story were a fake, the whole problem must be attacked anew, as far as Blackwood was concerned. He realized how nervously he shied at anything new involving Trample, even while he played with the idea of the doctor's guilt. It was the very overwhelmingness of the superficial case against

the specialist that turned him from it. That and the simple circumstance that Trample—in a tone of voice that Blackwood
liked—had quietly denied all knowledge of the murder.

That hypodermic needle he had found in Kitty's room!

Feeling his mind in the act of departing from its foundations,
Mr. Blackwood ceased his tortured cerebration. It was time: he
was already in sight of Haviland's apartment on the Drive.

"Frankly," said the yachtsman, when they were seated in his
library with glasses in their hands, "I don't know what to think
of this damned Cross. He's a bit of an embarrassment. I suppose
you know he's a detective!"

"I discovered that this afternoon," said Blackwood, "when I
went looking for him at his office. A very lousy one, I should
imagine."

Haviland seemed puzzled. "His office?" he echoed. "You
mean he has an office in the city?"

"He calls it that, I fancy. It's a dirty hole in La Salle Street,
over near the river. Where'd you think he hailed from?"

"You mean that—he's a *private* detective?"

"What did you think he was?"

"Well, I'll be damned!" said Haviland. "Why, the lying rascal
told me he was from New York—a member of the regular detective force!"

Blackwood was interested. "He came to see you?"

"Just yesterday afternoon. Showed me his credentials, said he
understood I was giving a big party in the evening, and asked
permission to attend it. I asked him what the big idea was, and
he said he was keeping an eye out for somebody he expected to
turn up. Naturally, I was interested; but he wouldn't mention
names. When I pressed him, he said the man was an international crook, and I'd have to take his word for it. Promised not
to make any trouble at the party—just wanted to keep an eye on

the fellow—and so on! I didn't know what the deuce to do about it. His credentials seemed in perfect order. I never thought of doubting him."

"Faked the credentials," said Blackwood. "He probably has 'em for every city in the union. Who did you think he had in mind, Haviland?"

"Well, I think I know my own friends," the yachtsman answered; "but I had to admit that there would be a number of strangers, probably, on hand. There always are. People bring other people, in spite of hell and high water—and there are usually one or two gate crashers. But as a rule they're not any of them international crooks!"

Blackwood laughed at the expression on the other's face. "Well?" he said.

Haviland grimaced. "I see the same idea is in your mind that was in mine. *Holderness!* What else could I think? As far as I knew, he was the only 'international' figure who was certain to be among the guests; and I had an idea it was Holderness he was talking about, because he was so determined not to mention him. A lovely predicament! My principal guest—supposed to be a distinguished English writer and explorer!"

The yachtsman shrugged. "What was there for me to do? I didn't know the fellow, after all—Holderness, I mean. You take a man like that on trust. He was a guest at Melton's; but he had gone to Melton because he thought Melton would be interested in financing some sort of an exploration. Nobody, I suppose, really *knew* him, beyond what he had to say about *himself.* Anyway, I didn't want him to make a fool of *me.* I told Cross to rent a pair of tails and come along."

Blackwood was staring. "Melton!" he said. "By Jove, I knew I had heard the name before!"

"He's a well-known banker," Haviland explained.

"I know," said Blackwood. "I was wondering, a little while

ago, where I had heard his name. It was Holderness who mentioned it. He said he was staying with the Meltons, on the Drive—or something of the sort—last night."

In the name of everything wonderful, Blackwood was thinking, what could Holderness or Melton have to do with his own problem? It was certainly Melton who had identified the body of Jeffrey Cottingham. Was that circumstance in some fashion significant? If it were true that Holderness was an "international crook"——

But at the moment it was all too muddled. He gave it up.

"You haven't heard whether anything happened to Holderness after the party, I suppose?" he asked.

"I don't know," said Haviland. "I understood from him, last night, that he was leaving on the *Century* for New York, today. I imagine he's gone. If so, I suppose Cross is after him. You're quite sure, Blackwood, that he *isn't* a New York detective?"

"I'm not very sure of anything, any more," said Riley Blackwood. "But if Cross is a New York detective, I'm the Crown Prince of the Belgians. You say he vanished from the yacht, last night. When would that be, Haviland?"

Haviland considered. "Shortly after you and Widdowson left, I think. His clothes were still fairly wet, so I suppose he took a taxi when he reached the Drive. He wouldn't have far to walk."

"Had Holderness already left?"

"Yes, he and the Meltons left right after you did."

"The Meltons were there too, were they? But, of course, they would be. I'm sorry I didn't meet them. Well, I'm certainly obliged to you, Haviland! You're probably wondering what the devil all this has to do with me. Somehow—I'm not quite certain—this Cross reptile is mixed up in Tony's jolly little mystery. It appears that he was in the employ of Cottingham, the man who turned up dead in one of Tony's beds."

"I've been reading about that, a bit. What about this Dr.

Trample? Didn't you say he had disappeared? But he was joking, of course, when he said he had been suspected."

"He was *not*," said Blackwood. "He's still the principal suspect, from the constabulary point of view." He entertained the yachtsman with a swift and humorous account of the exchange of rooms. "You see how beautifully he fills the bill!"

Haviland shook his head. "I don't believe it," he said. "He doesn't fit the rôle, Blackwood. I never met a more likable fellow."

"My sentiments to a T," said Blackwood; "but there it is! And his disappearance—if that's what it is—doesn't help his case a particle. However, I don't believe he's disappeared. I more than half expect to find him at the hotel when I return."

He stood up. But Haviland checked him with a gesture.

"Hold on," he protested. "You've only heard half the story."

"The deuce!" said Blackwood. "About Cross, you mean?"

"Yes—and this is the queerest part of it, it seems to me. I was with him after he came around, last night; right after you and the doctor had gone on deck. He insisted that somebody had *pushed* him overboard."

Blackwood subsided in his chair. "The hell he did!"

"I told him he was crazy, and he just grinned at me."

"Holderness?" asked Blackwood.

"God knows! He wouldn't mention any names, as usual. Naturally, I guessed that he meant Holderness. Which raises an interesting point. Was Holderness in a position to *do* it?"

Blackwood cast his mind back to the night before. "He was with our party for a time; but *was* he at the moment Cross went overboard? Damned if I remember. No, by George, he wasn't! I was alone with Miss Oliver when that happened. Holderness had gone away. So had everybody else, come to think of it; even the doctor—*he* went last. We heard a splash, and then a scream——"

He paused, cocking his head sidewise like an owl. "Now who the devil was it that screamed, I wonder! A woman, of course. Somebody who knew what had happened, right *after* it had happened. She might even have seen something."

"It's possible," agreed the yachtsman. "I remember hearing somebody scream, myself. Well, it's a clue! I'm going to find out. After all, I know *most* of the people who were on the damned boat!"

Blackwood slowly nodded his head. "Yes," he said, "it's a clue. Let me hear what you discover, Haviland. But I'll be hanged," he added, "if I can understand what any of it has to do with Cottingham."

He glanced quickly at a clock, standing on a bookcase, and rose again. "I'm off, Haviland," he said. "I promised Tony I'd see him before I tucked in. Keep me posted on anything you hear. You've given me something to think about, that's certain."

It was true. He had plenty now to think about. For one thing, if Holderness, the Englishman, were Cross's quarry, and it seemed quite possible, another shuffling of the cards was indicated. How long, he wondered, had Holderness been in Chicago?

"He was here on Monday night, at any rate," mused Riley Blackwood, speeding back to town. For he now remembered the English traveler's remarks about the shots that had awakened him while he was sleeping at the Meltons'. That had been Monday night.

Melton was acquainted with Jeffrey Cottingham: he had identified the New York banker's body. Melton was also the host of Ford Holderness, who, according to Haviland, had come to him for financial backing in some piece of exploration. Did any of it make sense?

And Cottingham also was a banker. But if Cottingham and Melton were associated in a venture involving Holderness—a reasonable enough supposition—why did it seem expedient for somebody to murder Cottingham, and where did Kitty Mock fit into the picture?

There was one satisfying feature of the new development, at any rate. It did not further involve the unfortunate Horace Trample. If Cross was on the trail of Holderness, he was certainly not off somewhere looking for the doctor.

In which case, reflected Mr. Blackwood happily, it was about time for Trample to return and give a satisfactory account of himself. No doubt he was even now at the hotel.

Widdowson and White were waiting up for him. The hotel proprietor shook his head in answer to the question.

"Hasn't come in yet," he reported. "Roach has been telephoning every five minutes for the last half hour. He's been pestering Miss Oliver, too, I think."

"What about Cross?" asked Blackwood testily.

"He was here on Monday night, all right. White says he saw him."

The house detective nodded. "That's right. I could have told you that yesterday, Mr. Blackwood, if I'd known you were interested in the mug. I saw him twice, in fact: once a little before midnight, and then again when it must have been close to one o'clock."

"Well, well!" said Mr. Blackwood. "*Here?*"

They were standing in the lobby.

"The first time he was sitting over there by the cigar stand, smoking a cigar. The second time, he was just going out the door. Looked to me as if he might have been coming from the elevators, but I can't be sure."

9.

Mr. Blackwood rose late—his most pernicious habit, according to his aunt—and breakfasted in a favorite window nook, from which it was possible to watch the speedboats race along the surface of the lake and horsemen gallop in the parkway. The room was at once living room and library, and it was a remarkable anachronism. There was not a stick of really modern furniture in it. Its principal pieces had been his grandfather's, in point of fact; but Blackwood liked his setting very well. It gave him a sense of detachment from the present, which he found restful if not always stimulating. The world was sometimes too much with him—at any rate, the flesh and the devil.

The number of the books was legion. Behind him, as he sipped and nibbled, Blackwood felt their presence and was complacently content. He liked to idle there among them, in certain moods, and feel himself a part of that great company of crime savants who stalked and blustered in so many of their pages.

A wire-haired terrier, named Whisky by his proprietor, had come in with the breakfast tray. He was all white, except for his ears, which were black. He now sat motionless upon his haunches, with upturned eyes imploring food. Blackwood pulled his ears and made a number of absurd remarks which, in a play, he would have found revoltingly sentimental. He came across with a full strip of bacon and brought his mind back to the problem that was troubling him.

It made a difference—the mounting conviction that Trample had actually disappeared. Blackwood was annoyed. And just as he had been upon the point of clearing him, too! Something had happened to warn the doctor, he supposed, that the police were planning to crack down upon him. Rather than face the music he had gone away. It seemed unlike him.

Blackwood was stubbornly unwilling to believe the specialist guilty; but what were the alternatives? He gave the wire another strip of bacon. That the doctor had once more fallen from grace and taken too much liquor with a stranger? Absurd! That he was protecting somebody of whose complicity he had guilty knowledge? Possible, perhaps. Indeed, as one came to think of it, rather plausible. It was in line with Trample's character as he understood it.

In the circumstances, the mysterious "somebody" could only be Miss Oliver. Cross had been in the hotel lobby twice, at least, on the night of the murder. If the tough detective were not himself the guilty man—an attractive possibility—it was quite on the cards that he had seen something significant. He would be aware, of course, before the night was out, of Trample's meeting with Cottingham, for Cottingham would have told him. But what the deuce could he have seen?

"Blaine Oliver?" Blackwood spoke the name aloud, with a rising inflection and an eye upon the terrier. The wire did not reply.

No, no! Not on Monday night. He refused to consider it.

"Prentiss, perhaps?"

Assuming it to be a game involving bacon, the wire barked loudly and bounced the height of the table.

Blackwood nodded. After all, Prentiss was Blaine Oliver's friend. Was it possible that he was also the doctor's?

But Cross—hang it!—was almost certainly on the trail of Holderness, wasn't he? And where did Holderness touch either Prentiss or Miss Oliver?

"Ring-around-a-rosy!" spoke Mr. Blackwood bitterly, and fell to wondering who else would vanish before the day was out. Holderness, he had already learned, had really gone. Somebody at Mrs. Melton's—"on the Drive"—had told him so, at any rate, over the telephone. Assured of Melton's backing and the backing of the others, the voice had said, the Englishman had returned to New York. Shortly he would go to England. Ultimately he would go to the Gobi Desert—if he didn't go to jail in the meantime, reflected Blackwood.

Oh yes, Mr. Melton and Mr. Cottingham had been "well acquainted." Naturally they would be, "being in the same line of business, as it were!" Mr. Melton had simply seen the story in the papers, that was all; he had had no notion that Mr. Cottingham was in town. "Not at all! Good-bye!"

It had been Mrs. Melton, he supposed.

"Thursday morning," mused Blackwood pensively, "and what have I accomplished? Nothing! The admission fills me with shame."

But it didn't really. He thought that, on the whole, he had been particularly clever. Trample, he reflected, he could now safely leave to the police—poor devil! They had ways of tracing people. The coroner's inquest would now be safely over—he glanced at his watch. It would be continued, of course, in view of Trample's disappearance; and there would be activity among the flatfoots. Telegrams would go forth—Kitty would take her dead back to New York—and Miss Oliver and Harry Prentiss were at the moment, probably, en route for Evanston.

A peaceful spot! He would go to Evanston himself.

The deferential China boy brought him his hat and stick.

"Jim," said Mr. Blackwood, "once more I go forth upon a trail of wickedness and evil. And don't give that dog any more bacon! He's had enough."

He saluted the signed photograph of the late distinguished *caballero,* Holbrook Blinn, which hung beside the door—a pleasant habit that annoyed his aunt—and closed the door behind him.

But he did not go at once to Evanston. Instead, he drove to the Jamaica, some miles out of his way. Miss Mock had not yet taken off her hat. She seemed less pleased to see him than his vanity had whispered that she might be.

"Darling," he said, "was it an ordeal?"

"It was ghastly," said Miss Mock. "I thought you would be there."

"I'm here," said Mr. Blackwood. "I just stopped off to sympathize. When are you leaving for New York?"

"Tomorrow probably. The funeral will be Saturday, I think. He will probably be buried in the family vault."

"Creepy," said Mr. Blackwood. "I've always thought I should like to be buried in a tree-top. Swung in a hammock, perhaps, or something of the sort. The idea of a coffin and a tomb is terrifying. The emotion is known as claustrophobia, I believe. I've sometimes felt it in a theater. That Englishman was speaking about you, the other night—Ford Holderness, you know."

The eyes she turned upon him were puzzled. "Ford Holderness! An Englishman? You mean an actor?"

"A traveler and author, I believe." He laughed. "I mean, he liked your work in *Uncle Claude.* Thought you were 'ripping' in that last scene—as indeed you were. I met him on a yacht. I didn't tell you about my heroism, did I?"

"Heroism?"

"When Gene Cross fell overboard—with your name upon his lips!"

"My God!" said Kitty Mock. "What are you talking about?"

But he had winged her that time, he reflected. Her face had gone pale. Cross, then, was the name to conjure with. The man her husband had employed to watch her.

Suddenly he felt sorry for her. "Somebody's name, at any rate," he grinned. "Or is it some play that I'm remembering? Pay no attention to me, Kitty. But if ever you feel you want to have a talk with me, don't hesitate." He hesitated himself for a moment, then went on: "The doctor I mentioned to you yesterday is missing, Kitty. *Horace Trample!* You said you didn't know him. But the police are looking for him; they think he killed your husband. Perhaps he did—I don't know anything about it. If he didn't, and some other fellow *did,* an effort should be made to clear him. In my feeble way, I have been making such an effort, without notable success. If you should happen to feel like helping me——"

He paused and waited.

"Was that why the inquest was continued? To give them time——?"

"To saddle somebody with a charge of murder. Yes! And you may take it from me that you will not be left alone yourself. I mean, for some time to come there will probably be some flatfoot trailing you."

"You don't think that I——"

"Honestly, I don't; but you *could* know something about it, you know."

She hesitated. "I think Jeffrey committed suicide," she said at last. A little piteously she added: "I wish I knew why!"

Blackwood was disgusted. "And you never heard of a doctor named Trample?"

"I never did, really!"

"Or an English explorer named Holderness?"

"No."

"Or a tough detective named Cross?"

"You have no right to question me this way, Mr. Blackwood."

"I'm trying to help you," said Blackwood angrily. "*Did* you?"

"N-no."

"Who the devil *are* you protecting?"

"I'm not protecting anybody—except myself, against *you!*"

Blackwood's grin was somewhat wicked; but he resolutely fought down the ungentlemanly retort he was about to make.

"Never heard of a man named Prentiss or a girl named Oliver?"

"Their names were mentioned at the inquest. I believe they testified. They found the body, didn't they?"

"You're asking *me?*" said Blackwood.

"I don't think I care to continue the conversation, Mr. Blackwood," said Kitty Mock.

Mr. Blackwood shrugged and agreed. "It *doesn't* appear to be getting us anywhere," he admitted. "Well, remember, I'm your friend. Come to Daddy when you want to cry a little."

He stalked out of the room.

It occurred to him that, if he hurried, he might catch Blaine Oliver and Prentiss at a tardy luncheon—supposing they had not tarried in the Loop. Probably he should have telephoned first; but catching people off their guard—after a harrowing morning at a coroner's inquest—was not a bad idea. In the case of Kitty Mock, he reflected, it had been a rather good idea.

He entered the peaceful university town of Evanston, stopped at a drug store and consulted a telephone directory. Then, armed with the address of Blaine Oliver—which he had forgotten and was able to identify only through his memory of the telephone number—he continued his journey. One thing was certain, he vowed, frowning at the taximeter: Widdowson would receive an expense account, when this inquiry was all over, that would freeze his eyeballs.

Miss Oliver, it developed, had returned alone. She received him in a drawing room that was pleasantly old-fashioned; even a trifle quaint. These older families didn't go in for jumbled periods—they clung frankly to their Civil War atrocities and made people like them!

"Why, Mr. Blackwood!" said Miss Oliver. "This *is* a surprise!"

"'This *is* a baby!'" quoted Mr. Blackwood joyously. "If you haven't heard the story, I'm afraid I sound a trifle crude. Phillips Brooks, wasn't it—the old clergyman? You don't mind my dropping in this way?"

"Of course I don't. I'm flattered."

"Don't let me turn your head," said Blackwood; "but I came all the way from town to see you."

"Do sit down," she suggested. "Of course, I'm dying to know why." The probable solution of the mystery crossed her mind. "Are you still detecting?"

"I'm puzzled," said Blackwood. "I come to you for help. I rather hoped that Mr. Prentiss might be here. As it is, I am afraid I shall seem to be talking a bit behind his back. You were both at the inquest, of course, a little while ago?"

Miss Oliver was puzzled also. "Of course," she agreed; "but I left Harry—Mr. Prentiss—in the Loop. He was going back to his office."

"I should have known that, I suppose. Although in point of fact I don't know where his office is. He's a lawyer, isn't he?"

"He's an architect—*Freeman, Prentiss & Palmer.*"

"Do you know him well, Miss Oliver?"

"Reasonably well—yes. Quite well, I suppose."

"Do you happen to know whether he is acquainted with a man named Cross—a detective?"

She shook her head; then, as the significance of the name occurred to her, her eyes opened more widely.

"You mean that—that man who was on the yacht—who fell overboard? *That* Cross?"

"Yes."

"Good heavens, no! I don't know anything about it; but I should imagine that he *didn't* know him. Why under the sun do you ask?"

He smiled. "I'm just checking up on names, Miss Oliver." The assertion was sufficiently vague, he fancied. "Trying to find out who knows who—and why." A phrase out of a book or play came to his assistance. "It's purely a matter of routine, you know."

"But," she protested, still puzzled, "it is this case of Mr. Cottingham that you are investigating, isn't it? What has Mr. Cross to do with that?"

"Ah, of course," said Blackwood; "you wouldn't know about that. It develops that he *is* connected—somehow. I don't know in what way."

She washed her hands of the mystery. "Well, I'm sure I don't know. Perhaps Harry knows him—but I certainly can't answer for him. Why don't you ask Mr. Prentiss himself?"

"I will, when I see him. But let's forget Cross, for the time being. Let's think of Holderness."

Miss Oliver frowned. "Holderness! That Englishman, you mean?"

"Yes. Do you know whether Mr. Prentiss was acquainted with him, before the party on the yacht?"

"I haven't the faintest idea; but I should certainly think *not*."

"Had you ever met him before, yourself?"

"This gets wilder and wilder," smiled Blaine Oliver. "But I never had. Why? Is he in it, too?"

"I don't know," said Blackwood. "I'm trying to find out. There are indications that rather suggest it."

"It's amazing," she said. "But, in any case, why should I——?"

"Routine," said Blackwood, laughing. "You know, I told you that you were yourself a trifle suspect. You were on the scene so early!"

Her answering laugh was nervous. "I think I feel my mind slipping, Mr. Blackwood! Do you mind if I ask you a question. It's this: Are you playing some sort of a joke on me this afternoon, or are you seriously investigating Harry Prentiss and me in connection with this murder?"

"You agree that it is murder, then?"

She frowned. "I know you think it is."

"You had never met Cross before, yourself?"

"I have never met him at all. He was mentioned, the night on the yacht, I remember——"

"By Harry Prentiss," he reminded her.

Miss Oliver looked shocked. "Yes," she confessed, "I had forgotten that. It *was* Harry who mentioned him. But I didn't meet him; and all I saw of him was a dark shape in the water, when you were towing him back to the yacht."

"Do you know where Harry Prentiss was on Monday night, Miss Oliver?"

"No, I don't. Working, I think." The answer was abrupt—annoyed. She added: "You haven't answered *my* question."

"He wasn't with you?"

"No!"

He raised his hand. "One more question, please! Where were you, yourself, on Monday night?"

Her lip curled. "Now you *have* answered me! You are actually serious in all this!"

He grinned without embarrassment. "Do you decline to answer?"

"Of course not! But you are being so completely ridiculous.

For a few minutes I felt myself growing angry. Now I am only amused."

"And perhaps disappointed in my intelligence?" suggested Blackwood, chuckling.

"I know so little about that," said Blaine Oliver. "I've seen no evidence of it, one way or another."

"*Sock!*" He clapped a hand over his right eye. "But I can 'take' it! Shall we return to our muttons?"

She shrugged. "On Monday night—let me see. I had dinner with the Coltmans, here in Evanston, and stayed until about ten. They drove me home, and I was here the rest of the evening. My mother and father could testify to that, if you think it necessary. Dad's away, just now; but perhaps you would like me to call Mother, Mr. Blackwood?"

"Don't bother," grinned Mr. Blackwood. "I am convinced that your alibi is unshakable. But you have none for Mr. Prentiss. I'm sorry about that."

"So am I—since you seem so determined to involve innocent persons."

He offered his cigarette case, but she refused. The shadowy smile that had hovered about his lips since the beginning of the interview was gone. His voice, when he spoke, was serious.

"Speaking of innocent persons," said Blackwood, "Horace Trample is really missing—and the police are looking for him."

"Oh, no!" she cried, distressed.

"Oh, yes!" said Blackwood. "I am sorry if my questions have annoyed you. They were intended as much to *clear* you, as anything else. I have to understand all possible relationships; and what happened on Monday night, at the Granada, has become a very troublesome riddle. The lobby of that delightful hostelry seems to have been actually congested with possible murderers or accessories. In view of Trample's predicament, if there is anything you can add to what you have said——?"

She shook her head. "On my honor, there's nothing! But I *do* understand, Mr. Blackwood! I wish there were something I could do to help."

"There is," said Mr. Blackwood. "Find out for me what Prentiss's alibi is for Monday night—from eleven o'clock until, say, one."

She twisted her fingers together. Dismay was in her eyes.

"You can't really believe——!"

"I don't know anything about it," shrugged Blackwood. "He may be as innocent as eleven of the apostles were. Anyway, what is Prentiss to you?"

"He's an old friend," she said in a low voice. "All right, I'll try."

"That's splendid," Blackwood encouraged her. They rose upright at the same time, and he placed an arm around her shoulders and patted her with artless guile. "That's splendid," said Mr. Blackwood.

"Oh dear!" she sighed.

"Darling!" said Mr. Blackwood.

She flushed and drew away from his embrace. "Don't be an idiot," snapped Blaine Oliver.

"The manner of a fool," said Mr. Blackwood, "when it masks the mental processes of a wise man, is an advantage of great worth to a detective."

She smiled in spite of herself. "Please go away, now," she implored. "You have worried me a great deal."

Mr. Blackwood went away.

There was no doubt, he reflected, as he was driven back to the city, that he really *had* worried her. And her worry, as he sensed it, was for Prentiss even more than it was for the doctor. She was wondering if he could have had anything to do with Cottingham's murder.

The situation pleased him well enough. She was herself now quite out of the picture—not that he had ever seriously considered her as part of it, he told himself!—and beyond suspicion. Her obvious fear that Prentiss might conceivably be guilty absolved herself. It was a neat point. A guilty person does not fear another's guilt. His apprehension for another is presumptive evidence of his own innocence. Anyway, Blaine Oliver's alibi for Monday night was certain to be genuine. It was one of those simple, natural ones, too susceptible of verification to be anything else.

The offices of Freeman, Prentiss & Palmer, architects, were in a tall building on the Boulevard; they overlooked the lake and the Illinois Central railroad structure.

Blackwood seated himself and smiled blandly across a desk at Harry Prentiss. He admitted to himself that Prentiss did not appear either surprised or worried by the visitation.

"Smoke?" questioned the architect, pushing a box of cigarettes across the desk. "They're not the sort that make you appear nonchalant—but I like them."

"Do I look nervous?" asked Blackwood amiably. "Or is it to your own shaking hands and twitching lips that you are referring?"

They both laughed easily, and Prentiss extended his lighter across the interval between them. "You know," he said, between puffs, a moment later, "I've been expecting you."

"You haven't!"

"Cross my heart, my dear Holmes! You will admit that I gave you every opportunity, on the yacht, to ask me the question that now trembles on your lips."

Blackwood grinned. "You did suggest it, I believe."

"Quite—I implored you to ask me. There were only two questions you could have asked me, and you neglected the second. 'What was I doing in the lobby of the Granada on Tuesday morning, when I so fortuitously met Miss Oliver?' and 'What were my movements, if any, with respect to the Granada on Monday night?' You asked the first; I frankly answered it. I think I annoyed you by suggesting that you ask the second. You refused."

"You did, rather," admitted Blackwood. "Well, what would you have answered?"

"Exactly what I should answer now, if you were to ask the question."

"We are becoming quite roguish," said Riley Blackwood. "Well, then, Mr. Bones, where was you, prezackly, on de ebening and night of Monday de—what date was it, by the way?"

"It doesn't matter—it was Monday night: the night Cottingham was murdered, as I understand it. The answer is: I'd rather not say. If necessary, I *will*—not now, but when it becomes necessary. But I wasn't in the room of Jeffrey Cottingham at any time, and I didn't murder him."

"Had you ever heard of Jeffrey Cottingham at that time?"

"As a name, perhaps—I don't remember."

"Do you know Kitty Mock, the actress?"

"I've seen her act. Personally, I don't know her."

"How about Gene Cross?"

"I—well, yes! After a fashion, I know Gene Cross."

"Know his profession?"

"Yes, he's a private detective."

"What was he doing on Haviland's yacht the other night?"

"I don't know. It's what made me ask the questions I did about him, that night. I wondered who had brought the bounder on board."

"What opinion did you reach?"

"None, really. His presence puzzled me, that was all. I wondered, a bit vaguely, knowing him to be a detective, if he might possibly be shadowing your friend the doctor. I didn't see how or why—I just wondered."

"Or Miss Oliver?"

"The thought crossed my mind."

"Only Widdowson and I knew that the doctor and Miss Oliver were going to the party," said Blackwood dryly.

"Sure—it even crossed my mind that he might be working with *you*."

"He wasn't," said Blackwood.

"Then I'm still puzzled."

"Have your own relations with Cross—if any—been unpleasant?"

"Slightly, yes."

"No chance of his being on *your* tail, that night!"

Prentiss laughed. "I don't think so. No, I think not."

"It wasn't *you* who pushed him overboard on Tuesday night?"

"*What?*"

"That's one question you didn't expect?" queried Blackwood, grinning.

"Are you trying to be funny?"

"Not particularly. Cross claims to have been pushed overboard. If so, somebody pushed him. How about Holderness, the Englishman?"

"What about him? You mean that he may have push——?"

"I mean, what do *you* know about him?"

"Not a thing. Nice enough fellow. Aren't we getting a bit mixed?"

"Possibly," Blackwood agreed. A thought occurred to him. Since he was at it, he might as well run through the entire muster of names. "Do you know a man named Melton?"

"Yes, he was on the yacht, too. With his wife. I was with her, as it happens, when Cross went overboard. She heard the splash and screamed like a good fellow."

"It was Mrs. Melton that screamed?" *Well, well!* commented Blackwood inwardly.

"She let out quite a yelp. Others did, too, I believe. Hers, being partly in my ear, sounded rather notable. But if you think now that she pushed Cross overboard, you're crazy. She was beside me at the time. I don't know where Cross was."

Was it possible, Blackwood wondered, that the lady had been waiting for a splash? That she had had prior knowledge of its impendence?

He shrugged. "Trample has disappeared," he said briefly. "The police are looking for him."

"The doctor? I'm sorry," said Prentiss. "Is it as bad as that? I didn't think he was concerned in it."

"Keep on thinking so," said Blackwood. "Of course, you've answered the question that you think you haven't! So long."

"Go to hell, will you?" invited Prentiss pleasantly.

10.

So PRENTISS had spent the night at the Granada. Monday night! Blackwood was as sure of it as if he had seen the architect's name upon the register. The only alternative was that Prentiss had spent the night at the Jamaica. Either way, it had to be confessed that his alibi—if it were to be brought forward—would do him more harm than good. Prentiss was no fool. No wonder he preferred to reserve his defense.

However, Blackwood was almost ready now to absolve the architect from stain of sin. As he viewed the situation, after his interview with Prentiss, it was Prentiss's realization of the suspicious nature of his alibi that kept him silent, rather than a consciousness of guilt. He had no wish to be involved in any whisper of murder, and if he told the truth he *would* be. So looked the case to Blackwood at the moment.

Nevertheless, he reflected, it would be enlightening and satisfying to know precisely what it was that Prentiss had been doing at the Granada—or the Jamaica—on Monday night. Was he too the possessor of some guilty secret that might reflect on someone else? At any rate, the hotel registers ought to be checked at once.

It was, of course, quite on the cards that it was Prentiss himself, no less, who had chucked Gene Cross into the lake. He had frankly confessed to a knowledge of—and a dislike for—the tough detective. No particular reason to fall for Cross's tale of an international crook. Substitute Prentiss for Holderness in the set-up, as the object of the detective's interest, and what followed? Blackwood wasn't precisely sure. It seemed that whenever a new idea struck him the problem somehow became a little harder.

He went at once to the Jamaica, made a plausible enough statement at the desk, and glanced over a number of pages of the register. There was no record of Harry Prentiss, and Blackwood did not push the inquiry.

So Prentiss had stayed at the Granada, had he? But at the Granada, likewise, there was no faintest indication of the presence of the dapper architect on the night in question. Or any other night, for that matter.

"Stalemate!" said Blackwood, faintly annoyed.

"Unless he stayed with someone else," contributed White, the hotel watchdog.

Blackwood looked at him with admiring eye. "Joseph," he chirruped, "you have earned your salary for this week by that suggestion. Look into it, will you?"

So much for Harry Prentiss, he told himself with satisfaction. The architect could now be left to White. He was probably un-important, anyway.

A depressing thought of Horace Trample crossed his mind. What, if anything, he wondered, had the police discovered with reference to Trample? Presumably the doctor was still missing. It occurred to Blackwood, with a sense of reproach, that he had been hasty in washing his hands of Horace Trample.

He reached for a telephone and made swift inquiry.

Nothing!

But police investigations were notoriously slow—stupid, at any rate. He had no doubt that he could himself, if he were so minded, get wind of Trample. If the doctor was simply keeping out of sight, to escape annoyance—a bit of a euphemism, that!—

he was being aided, certainly, by some one of his confrères. It stood to reason that someone was helping him lie doggo.

If only he—Blackwood—now could get in touch with him. Find out what had alarmed him—what information he was concealing that might reflect upon another, eh? He smiled. This business of chivalrous concealment in protection of "another" was rather getting on his brain! Still, there might be something in it.

And it was always possible, of course, that Trample was in trouble.

Under his breath he whistled a few staves of the *Habanera;* its staccato melody pleased him. Then he went forth and took a taxi to the Fair Grounds.

Outside the door of the auditorium, in the Hall of Science, he paused and read the notices posted on a bulletin board. Amazing! All over the city, it appeared, were programs of deep interest to the profession. Clinical programs in the various hospitals; scientific programs in any number of auditoriums. . . . An appalling list! The beggars had saved up their most difficult and showy cases, apparently, for this Roman holiday; this carnival of reconstruction and elocution.

CLINICAL PROGRAM

OPERATIONS: GASTRIC CASES—*Dr. R. W. McNulty.*
    DEMONSTRATIONS: 1. Splenectomy.
                                2. Phlebarteriectasia.
OPERATIONS—*Dr. Philip Kretschmeier.*
                                1. Malunion of humerus with radial neurolysis.
                                2. Semilunar cartilage removal.
                                3. Whitman reconstruction operation.
    DEMONSTRATIONS: 1. Arthoplasty of the jaw.

2. Nicoli operation.
3. Fracture of the neck of the femur.
4. New method of knee joint arthrodesis.

DEMONSTRATIONS—*Dr. O. M. Hamilton.*

1. Reconstruction of Poupart's ligament.
2. Carcinoma of the large bowel.
3. Osteochondritis dissecans.

The case reports included "postoperative ileus," a discussion of postoperative peptic ulcer, an abdominal aneurism, and a mixed tumor of the soft palate: there were two cases of this latter. The astounded investigator read down the catalogue of entertainments offered, to its final line, which was "Luncheon will be served at 12:30 p.m. on the Roof Garden."

"Good God!" said Blackwood. "*Luncheon!*"

So this was the way doctors spent their time, on holiday, when they were not drinking with strangers; when they were not consenting to exchange rooms with sentimental travelers revisiting the scenes of early marriage.

There was a secretary, or something, just inside the door. He entered and made tentative—almost fearful—inquiry for Horace Trample. But the secretary shook his head and shrugged, indicating the congested auditorium, thick with the smoke of many cigars and cigarettes.

Every seat was filled; and on the rostrum, behind a pulpit, a venerable individual with white hair and spectacles was saying:

"The one person who can cope successfully with the suicide problem, gentlemen, is the doctor. He alone recognizes the hypochondriasis and melancholy of the potential suicide as a form of mental aberration or maladjustment requiring treatment, and his experience has taught him not to take lightly threats of self-destruction. By an analysis of one hundred cases of suicidal attempt, at Albert Finch Psychiatric Clinic, Seattle, I have shown that more than one third of the patients had already given a definite indication of danger by previous attempts at self-destruction. Approximately another third had threatened beforehand to take their lives. This clear evidence of warnings may perhaps raise the hope that here is something on which dependence may be placed as a help in the prevention of suicide. It is generally believed that threats of suicide are dramatic and do not result in the act. In my experience this is not true. A large percentage of those who commit suicide . . ."

Blackwood realized that it was probably going to be difficult.

He wondered vaguely if Cottingham ever had threatened to commit suicide. If so, and if he had subsequently done it, the threat had been no mere dramatic gesture. But Cottingham had been murdered, and by someone who wished the deed to *look* like suicide. However, if someone had known that Cottingham had once——

The secretary behind the little desk was saying: "As soon as the speaker is finished I'll have an announcement made, if you like. If Dr. Trample is in the audience——"

"I don't believe he's in the audience," said Blackwood hopelessly. Then he brightened. "All right, but make it clear, please, that it is Mr. Blackwood who is asking for Dr. Trample—or for tidings of him. I'm very anxious to get in touch with him as soon as possible."

It was an interminable address that the suicide specialist made; but it came to an end at last, and Blackwood saw the secretary's note carried forward to the chairman on the rostrum. In another minute it was being read. He listened anxiously.

There was no immediate response from the assembled doctors; then a man rose, in the middle of the audience, and pushed his way into the aisle. As he approached, Blackwood saw with surprise that he was Dr. Harold Marcus, the Granada's resident physician.

"Glad to see you, Mr. Blackwood," said the doctor, shaking hands. "Trample isn't here, of course; but I think I've got a line on him. Let's get outside, where we can talk."

He led the way into the corridor.

"You're on the right track, anyway," he continued briskly, when they stood outside the door in the afternoon sunlight; "and I'm certain the police aren't onto it, yet. Trample *was* here yesterday morning, whatever the police may think. I met a doctor here this morning who had seen him. I came here myself right after the inquest today, and stayed on for the afternoon session." The physician shrugged and grinned. "No use paying two admissions, after all!" he added.

"You mean you were looking for Trample on your own?" asked Blackwood curiously.

"Not at all. I came for the convention; but I happened to run across this doctor I was telling you about, and he was another poison specialist. It occurred to me that he might know Trample, since they were in the same line; and he did. He said he saw him here, at the meeting, yesterday morning. Also, he saw him *after* the meeting, outside the gates. Trample was just getting into a taxicab with somebody."

"The deuce he was!"

"So he says. No reason to disbelieve him, I imagine. He didn't know anything about the police wanting the doctor, of course. All that's been kept out of the papers—even the exchange of rooms. I just pretended I was interested in meeting Trample, and he told me what he could."

Blackwood was thoughtful. "It isn't much," he said at last, a bit ungraciously.

Marcus agreed. "Perhaps not," he said; "but it's something."

"Your doctor friend didn't see the fellow who was *with* Trample?"

"Saw him, I suppose, but nothing registered. No reason why it should."

"No clue to him whatever?"

"Not a thing. He just casually remembered that he'd seen the doctor getting into a cab and that there was someone with him."

"What kind of a cab was it?"

"A Purple. I asked that! Not much help, of course: the city's full of them."

"He had no conversation with Trample, yesterday?"

"Just 'Hello, how are you!' when they met in the auditorium. Didn't speak to him at all, when he saw him later, outside. No chance, even if he'd wanted to."

"Damn!" said Blackwood. "Who is this other doctor?"

"Fellow named Church—Brooklyn man, I think."

"He didn't see Trample at the afternoon session?"

"No. Thinks he wasn't there."

"I think so too," said Blackwood. "Hell of a lot of good it does me!"

"Well, that's all I know," said Marcus. "I thought I'd better pass it on. I'd have told you tonight, if you hadn't come here this afternoon."

Blackwood was tardily gracious. "Right," he smiled. "All thanks, anyway. As you say, it's something. When was the meeting over yesterday morning?"

"A little after twelve, I think."

"It marks the hour when Trample disappeared, at any rate," said Blackwood. "If it's of interest to anybody!"

He returned to the hotel, where he had a dinner date with Widdowson. There was time for a shower and a drink, and a trifle over for relaxation and reflection. All of these things he felt that he needed and had earned. But at the door of his own temporary establishment—the miniature gopher hole donated by Widdowson, for use when necessary—a thought stayed him.

Why not have it over with?

After all, he had been pretty lenient with Kitty Mock. He had given her every opportunity to tell her story. He had been, in point of fact, fairly lax in the matter of Kitty's duplicity. A certain sympathy for the attractive female had dictated his attitude; but it was principally his own vanity that had stood in the way of a showdown. He had set out to solve the mystery in his own way; and his own way had been, of course, the way of the cerebral story-book and stage detective. The time had come, it occurred to him, for a full-dress row, if necessary.

Why had not the police—Roach, that able exponent of the third degree—descended upon Kitty and blasted the truth out of her? Surely they must have suspicions. Were they too waiting for her in some manner to betray herself? Even to Roach, it must be obvious that she had not been altogether frank.

Was it possible that Roach would really permit her to leave the city, as undoubtedly she was planning to do? Would he not, in fact, crack down upon her at the first move in the direction of a railroad station—his hand forced by her determination to escape?

And if Paddy Roach anticipated Riley Blackwood in any matter of importance, it would be difficult for Riley Blackwood to forgive himself.

Well, well! Kitty Mock must tell the truth at long last. The truth, the whole truth, and nothing but the truth, so help her. No one knew more about it. Four persons had known, or knew, who the third man was in Kitty's room on Monday night: Cottingham, who was dead; Cross, who had disappeared; Kitty, and the elusive gentleman himself. Of them all, only Kitty now was available.

He descended to the street again and crossed to the Jamaica with a certain decision.

In the lobby of the other hotel, as luck would have it, he encountered Holabird, the manager. On his earlier visits of the day he had been successful in avoiding Holabird.

An oily smile sat upon the manager's lips. "Just a minute—er—Mr. Blackwood," he purred, with just a shade of emphasis on the name. "You weren't going to pass me without speaking, were you?"

"Sorry," said Blackwood. "I was in a hurry, and I didn't immediately recognize you. I have an appointment with Miss Mock."

Mr. Holabird too was sorry. "I'm afraid she's walked out on you, then," he observed. "She's already left the hotel. An hour ago!"

"Not really," said Blackwood. "She's—checked out, you mean?"

"An hour ago. In somewhat of a hurry. We were all very busy, for a little while."

There was something in the fellow's voice that was objectionable. Blackwood didn't like him. "H'm," he said. "That's ditching the company with a vengeance! We don't know anything about it, at the theater. You're sure she's really gone? She's not still in her room? I think I'd better have a look."

"She's gone," said Holabird. "I'm not sorry. The whole incident has been deplorable." He hesitated. "Ah—by the way—Mr. Blackwood—are you working under cover? I took the liberty of calling up the theater yesterday, after you had left. They assured me that no one of your name was working there."

Damn! Blackwood cursed inwardly. What the devil was the matter with Steep and Halpin, anyway? But he supposed he should have warned them. No doubt this infernal manager had got no farther than a switchboard operator. It was fairly annoying.

"My name is really Blackwood," said Riley Blackwood amiably. "I am investigating a serious matter in which Miss Mock appears to be concerned. I'm sorry if I am putting you to any trouble. As for Miss Mock, I saw her here this morning. Her decision to decamp must have been taken suddenly." He hesitated, then went on: "Perhaps you are telling me the truth about her. If you are not, I am bound to warn you that it may be awkward for you, if you try to protect her."

He took a tone that was still firmer. "Is she or is she not upstairs, at this minute?"

The manager shrugged. "You may go up, if you insist."

"Very well, I insist."

Blackwood spun on his heel and stalked away toward the elevators. After a moment he quickened his steps, for he was now quite certain that Holabird would instantly jump for a telephone and warn the actress of his coming.

It was unfortunate that the elevator had to stop so often; but after an interminable ascent it reached the eighth-floor level. Blackwood sped along the corridor like a sprinter. Without hesitation he seized the door handle of room 827 and entered.

The room was empty.

Two bags, however, were still waiting to be carried down. It looked like flight—almost like panic. The police, perhaps?

But had Kitty really gone, or was she even now hiding in another room?

A window curtain fluttered in the little alcove; and he crossed the room with swift strides, to peer inside.

Empty!

He glanced casually from the window. Damned if he hadn't forgotten to take in his handkerchief!

Then a quick step sounded beside him, almost lost in the pile of the carpet. He was aware of a presence just an instant too late to avoid the smashing blow that fell upon his head. And then there was another.

Very quietly Blackwood collapsed upon the carpeted floor, an awkward and ungainly tangle of arms and legs.

He lay precisely where he had fallen, when he returned to consciousness. Outside the light was waning; but less than an hour had passed. He was parched with thirst; and after a time it occurred to him that his head was aching wearily.

He rose painfully and staggered into the bathroom. He bathed his temples in cold water and looked at his reflection dimly in the mirror. Only his hat, it crossed his mind, had saved him from a very serious injury. It stuck a little, now, as he removed it.

At length he ventured on a light. He looked around him. The door of room 827 was closed but it was not locked. The bags were gone. No trace of Kitty Mock remained, unless it were a faint perfume that hung vaguely in some unknown dimension of space.

Blackwood was annoyed with Kitty. But was it a friend of Kitty's or some plug-ugly from downstairs who had cracked his valuable skull? Either way, it was Kitty who was to blame.

" 'You naughty Kitty,' " he quoted softly. " 'Now you shall have no pie!' "

The light, as he moved, picked out a dark spot on the carpet, and he dropped to one knee to view it at better range. A drop of his own blood, perhaps? A damned large drop! Who would have thought the old man to have had so much blood in him?

With infinite care, Blackwood inserted a fingernail beneath the little patch of darkness, then gently lifted it.

It was a good-sized patch of mud; and, as once before, upon an historic occasion, there was a cinder in its center.

Holabird was no longer in the lobby when he descended; and

after a moment of indecision Blackwood returned to the Granada. He found Marcus, the hotel physician, preparing to go out.

"Sorry to be a nuisance, Doctor," he apologized; "but I think I've got a nasty crack on the head. I wish you'd have a look at it."

He removed his hat and exposed a tangle of sticky hair.

"Great Scott, Mr. Blackwood!" exclaimed the physician. "What have you been doing with yourself?"

"To tell the truth," said Blackwood, "I was groping under a table, and I came up rather suddenly. I think I must have struck a protuberance."

"You look as if you had been hit with a hammer," said the physician. "Sit down there, over by the light, until I get some hot water."

He examined the wound with skillful eyes and fingers while bathing it with water. "It's a beauty, all right," he testified; "but I guess it isn't serious. Probably be painful for a time. I'll have to cut away a little of the hair. Better keep your hat on if you're going out to dinner," he grinned. "Must have had it on when all this happened."

"I did," said Blackwood.

His head was down; his eyes were fixed upon the floor.

Quite suddenly, with a curious thrill, he noted that the doctor was wearing a pair of brand-new shoes. They were a shrieking yellow, and almost certainly were not the shoes he had been wearing at the Exposition. He would have noticed them before.

Something inside was trying to tell him something. He moved sharply.

"Steady, boy," said the doctor, as if he were shoeing a horse. "Over in a minute now."

"I see you've bought yourself a pair of shoes," said Blackwood, in a voice that he did not recognize as his own.

Good God! Why had this not crossed his mind before? Another doctor—*Marcus!* Under his nose from the beginning! The man had actually testified as to his movements on Monday night. He had been out until one o'clock or after. That empty morphine tube—and Kitty's hypodermic! And the first small gob of mud had been beneath this fellow's chair, that morning in the dead man's room.

And why should not Kitty have known him intimately? It would not be the first time in the history of the world that an actress and a hotel doctor——!

Blackwood, with hanging head, regarded the yellow shoes with something like horror; with acute apprehension. He felt the physician's deft fingers moving in his hair, and his scalp prickled. What if——?

Marcus was a long time in replying, it occurred to him.

"Yes," said the doctor. "I stepped in a patch of mud outside the Fair Grounds. The others were a mess. There! That'll fix you up, I guess. Look in again tomorrow morning and I'll have another glance at it. Take a couple of aspirins, if you've got a headache, and tuck in early."

He stood back to admire his handiwork.

"Not at all, old man! Glad to have been of service. Good-night!"

11.

It could be! There was no doubt of that. It could be.

And what a simple explanation, if that were all of it! Simple and natural—and surprising. The good old formula. The sort of thing that lay concealed beneath the red-herring trickery of all good fictional problems, then bobbed up at the end to knock the cock-eyed reader cold with astonishment. And with dismay that he had not guessed it earlier.

"Elementary, my dear fellow! It has all been obvious from the beginning. It was the butler, of course!"

But if this were the explanation, what became of Cross? Charge off Holderness and Trample—Prentiss, Melton, and Miss Oliver—the whole ka-boodle—as just so much coincidence; just so many accidental crossings of a well-marked trail—and the problem of Gene Cross remained.

Possibly it was just as simple as *this* seemed to be. Had Cross been quietly eliminated? Why not? And if Cross, why not poor Trample also?

There was a hitch some place, however. Cross's life apparently had been attempted, once—on board the yacht—but it was not Marcus who had tumbled the detective into the lake that memorable Tuesday night. Marcus had not been on the yacht that night.

Possibly, after all, the Marcus assumption was a bit far-fetched. At one point, anyway, the doctor's good faith could be checked. This specialist named Church—from Brooklyn, wasn't he?—could no doubt be reached. If Horace Trample really had been seen on Wednesday, piling into a taxicab with some fellow who was not Harold Marcus, why, then, Marcus's new shoes might not wear so sinister an aspect.

It was always possible, of course, that Church belonged in the realm of the unicorn and roc; that the beggar didn't exist; and yet——

At any rate, Cross and Trample must be traced. Already too much time had been wasted on inquiries that only made the problem harder. And Kitty Mock must be run down and asked a leading question. One would be enough.

Blackwood found it difficult to sleep. Bursting with perspiration, he sat up and glanced at the illuminated dial of his clock.

Nine-thirty. And he had not been in bed before three for ages. His aunt might even burst in and ask for explanations, although he had sworn the China boy to secrecy.

Cursing the aspirin tablets he had so lavishly swallowed, he got up and bathed, keeping a towel around his wounded head. Then, wrapping himself in a robe of terrific pattern, he strolled into his living room and sat in darkness beside the open windows.

Out on the lake an excursion steamer was plodding into port, outlined in colored lights against the purple sky. The endless line of motorcars was coughing past, as always, in the street below. All the world was wagging merrily. He was appalled by his own isolation.

The wire, escaped from its own quarters, came and leaped upon his knee, ecstatically wagging everything behind its ears. Blackwood set the puppy firmly on the rug.

"Whisky, my son," he said, "go back to bed and don't wake up the household. Your papa is going out into the night."

He climbed into a Tuxedo and descended to the street; and a taxi took him swiftly to the hotel entrance. He ascended to the mezzanine in search of Widdowson. But Widdowson was missing from his smaller hideout. Undaunted, he ascended to the Blue Grotto in quest of his familiar.

There was a show in progress. An orchestra was playing lively music. With qualified apprehension, Blackwood viewed the half-naked figures of the professional dancers. Thelma, the principal, was doing something rhythmic and vulgar with her hips, abetted by her juniors. Under a rain of colored lights the girls were twisting joyously, always in unison, smiling their set little smiles of pleasure in the work that they were doing. Blackwood doubted that they really cared that much about it.

It was an early floor show, and it was drawing to a close. In a few minutes the rainbow sputtered and went out, the dancers vanished, and the customers piled out upon the floor for a waltz. A young man with audacious eyes appeared with a megaphone and made ready to sing the chorus.

Blackwood strolled easily among the tables, looking for Widdowson. There had been no sign of the proprietor when he heard himself hailed from the floor and, turning, saw Blaine Oliver and Harry Prentiss, twirling slowly with the waltzers. They stabbed with their fingers at an empty table which he had been upon the point of passing. Blackwood nodded and turned back.

In a few minutes they gave over their callisthenics and joined him. Blackwood nodded at a passing waiter.

"Is there any further word of Dr. Trample?" asked Blaine Oliver anxiously.

"Nothing," said Blackwood. "I'm sorry. What will you have to drink?"

"I'm buying this. Don't be silly, Blackwood," said Prentiss. "A highball?"

"Scotch," agreed Blackwood.

"Three Scotch highballs," said Blaine Oliver. "I've become a frightful sot since all this excitement started. My nerves require it. Isn't it dreadful about the doctor?"

"It's alarming," said Blackwood. He wondered if she was at her task of testing Prentiss's alibi and what she had discovered. "I'm going after him, before long," he added. "I'm fairly dissatisfied with everything that has developed, to date—even my own discoveries. Everybody with whom I talk seems to be protecting himself or some other fellow, and nobody gives a damn what has become of Trample."

Prentiss nodded his head in agreement. He seemed a trifle embarrassed. "Yes," he agreed, "Trample ought to be found. Where do you plan to look for him?"

"I don't know," admitted Blackwood. "I'm just hoping he isn't in the lake—or some place equally final."

"I'd help you, if I could," said Prentiss suddenly. "Miss Oliver and I have talked things over, to tell the truth. We don't blame you, really, for thinking that we have been a little less than frank."

Blackwood grinned. "Miss Oliver has been reasonably frank, I think."

"I know. So have I, generally speaking—but I suppose I can't expect you to believe me, unless I give you my confidence. In the beginning, to be honest, your amateur sleuthing rather amused me. Later it annoyed me. I can't say that I admire it, even now; but I'm willing to admit that you are a bloodhound on the trail. So, to save myself from further embarrassment, and God knows what else, and also because you appear honestly to be trying to save Trample from some sort of a frame-up, I'm willing to make a statement." Prentiss smiled to remove any suggestion of ill humor that his remarks might have seemed to contain.

"That's swell," said Blackwood, without emotion. "Are you going to tell me that you *did* stay at the Granada on Monday night?"

"Yes."

"I thought it could only be that. I'm sorry if——"

"Oh, it's nothing I'm ashamed of. But, my God! consider the circumstances! I met Miss Oliver in the lobby on Tuesday morning and helped her find the body. Accidental, of course—but who would believe me if I admitted I had spent the night in the hotel? When I saw the way things were stacking up, I decided to keep my mouth shut. Coincidences of the sort are constantly happening in life; but the police are pretty suspicious of them. For all I knew to the contrary, Blaine might have been a part of the conspiracy," grinned Harry Prentiss. "How could I be sure?"

"How indeed?" questioned Miss Oliver, a little satirically.

Prentiss laughed. "Sorry! But—self-preservation, you know! Then I met Trample, and liked him. I felt that he was an innocent victim of circumstance, and it seemed likely that he would be made the goat. But I couldn't see myself voluntarily stepping into his shoes."

The young man with the megaphone was crooning something so illiterate and so popular that everybody seemed to know it. The diners hummed it with him, and the dancers whispered it into the ears of their partners.

Prentiss raised his voice. "I stayed here, Monday night, with Frank Steele. We worked late on some plans, had some supper about midnight, and decided to stay in the Loop. And we had a room on the *ninth* floor! On the other side of the house from Trample, as it happens; but close enough to the whole episode to call forth some pretty nasty questions, after my Tuesday morning adventure. You see?"

Blackwood nodded. It was quite possibly true, he admitted to himself. To be sure, Frank Steele might have been a pretty girl, he reflected cynically; but the circumstance would not make a murderer out of Prentiss. In a pinch, the story could be checked. Meanwhile, he was prepared to accept it.

"And Cross?" he questioned. "You said you knew him. I think you said you had had an unpleasant experience with him."

Prentiss frowned. "That's true," he agreed. "Cross once thought he had caught me cheating on a contract with the city. He tried a little blackmail—offered to 'fix things' for me—and so on. I chucked him out of the office."

Sometimes Blackwood wished that again he was an innocent lad, thinking honorable thoughts about his fellow creatures. As a professional cynic he was bound to believe that Prentiss's experience with the tough detective in all probability had had something to do with a woman. He remembered the scattered papers in Cross's office; the sturdy little safe. Somewhere on the premises, no doubt, there was a dossier with Prentiss's name upon it. But the woman's name could make no difference unless she were Kitty Mock. Prentiss could not be expected to make confession of his misdeeds in front of Blaine Oliver. Blackwood was softly humming.

> " 'Two lovely black eyes—
> O what a surprise!
> Only for kissing another man's wife,
> I got two lovely black eyes.' "

A sweet song! He had not thought of it in years.

A surge of fellow feeling stirred in Riley Blackwood. "Well," he said, "don't let it happen again. I'm glad I ran across you here tonight; and I think these are our drinks approaching."

He was in a mood for confidences. Confidences background-ed by music. What he had needed for some time was somebody to talk to. Somebody who appreciated his efforts. Somebody who was sympathetic. Widdowson was not entirely satisfactory, even when he was available. More and more the hotel proprietor appeared to resent the continued investigation.

Over the highballs, while the music rose and fell, Blackwood poured out his troubles. He reviewed the case from its inception, realizing that much of it must still be unknown to his listeners. He dramatically concluded by brushing forward his long scalp lock and showing his honorable wound.

"You see," he shrugged, "I am rather obviously getting too *warm*, so to speak. Somebody is anxious to discourage me."

Blaine Oliver responded with a satisfying little cry of horror, while Prentiss made encouraging and slightly hypocritical noises over the rim of his glass.

"Just the same," said the architect, after a moment, "I can't help thinking that your latest theory is a trifle stagey, Blackwood. I mean what you call the 'Marcus assumption.' It's alluring and sensational—and surprising—but too much the sort of thing that happens in the last act, don't you think?"

"The butler?" questioned Blackwood. "I know—it crossed my mind."

"As for the fellow who hit you at the Jamaica, he *might*, of course, have been somebody connected with the hotel. You had made yourself rather unpopular, after all. You have a bit of a genius in that line, you know. However, I don't really think that. It seems to me that the fellow at the Jamaica was helping Miss Mock to get away. You came onto the scene unexpectedly, and he cracked you. Why? Because he didn't dare to have you recognize him. He was somebody that you knew—knew pretty darned well, I should say."

Blackwood nodded. "However, that would be true of everybody whom I have considered, even as a possibility."

"Look here," said Prentiss. "Face the probabilities. I hate to say it—but for the first time, really, I begin to suspect Trample. We all like him—sure—but do any of us really know him? He's disappeared in pretty mysterious circumstances, for an innocent man. There is testimony that he was seen, apparently in good health, as recently as Wednesday noon, getting into a taxicab. Suppose he has simply taken a room at the Jamaica and this damned manager—what's his name? Holabird!—is protecting him. He's helping your friend Kitty to escape when suddenly he is warned by Holabird that you are on your way upstairs. Right in the middle of the getaway! Well, he wouldn't be anxious per-haps to kill you; but he *would* feel called upon to put you out of the way before you got a glimpse of him."

Miss Oliver protested. "I don't believe it."

"It's infernally plausible," admitted Blackwood. "Who would be your alternative, Prentiss?"

"Cross, I suppose. He too has disappeared—and he's a bad baby. He wouldn't want to kill you, either. After all, you saved his life. But a small matter like a crack on the head———!"

"He was working for Cottingham," demurred Blackwood. "So, in a sense, am I."

"He *was*, yes! But if I know anything about Gene Cross—and I know a little—he wouldn't hesitate to change sides. Suppose he's working now for Kitty Mock. Blackmailing her too, per-haps; but still working for her! That tale he told Haviland sounds pretty fishy to me. He wasn't trailing Holderness. Holderness doesn't figure in the case: he just happened to be around while part of it was going on."

Blackwood thought it over. "Your point of view is a fresh one, and it's valuable," he confessed. "I've got them all so muddled in my mind that I can't separate the sheep from the goats. Still, in the case of Holderness, he was stopping with the Meltons, and Melton was a friend of Cottingham; he even identified Cotting-ham's body, officially, for the police. If, just for instance, Melton knew that Cottingham was in Chicago, masquerading as Chambers, and knew that he was in possible danger——"

"You mean, if Cottingham had told Melton that, for some unimaginable reason, Holderness was out to do him in, Melton would then somehow contrive to persuade Holderness to be his guest, so that—*what?* So that he could watch him? But he *didn't* watch him, supposing that to be the case."

"It should be easy enough to settle that," contributed Blaine Oliver suddenly. "Melton is here, somewhere, tonight. You know him, don't you, Harry?"

"So he is," cried Prentiss. "We danced past the Meltons, just a little while ago, and I nodded at them. I'd forgotten. Yes, I know them; well enough to speak to them, anyway. I only met them on the yacht, though."

Blackwood was elated. "Mrs. Melton too!" he said. "You told me it was Mrs. Melton who——"

"Who screamed in my ear when Cross went overboard," finished Prentiss. He rose to his feet. "Well, let's clear the decks a *little,* anyway. Let's get hold of the Meltons and give 'em the third degree!"

He moved quickly away among the tables and was lost to sight.

"Shall we dance?" asked Blackwood.

"If you like. You're sure it won't trouble your head?"

"Not unless we fall," he assured her. "We'll keep an eye on the table and stop when we see the others arrive."

The orchestra was playing some sort of a one-step. They were all alike to Blackwood, whatever they were called; but he was a good dancer, when he cared to perform.

They moved away among the swaying groups, with occasional backward glances at the table they had left. They circled about the edges of the floor, keeping their eyes alert for signs of Prentiss.

"So you persuaded Prentiss to reveal his alibi," said Blackwood, after a time. "Did he resent it?"

Miss Oliver frowned. "It was a hateful thing to do," she answered. "I didn't know how to go about it. You see, he had had an engagement with *me*, that night, and hadn't kept it! Finally, I told him you had been to see me, and that you were evidently troubled about both of us."

"What did he say to that?"

"Shall I tell you *exactly* what he said?"

"Please do!"

"Well, he said you were a 'damned nuisance.'"

"Oh, more than that, surely?" laughed Blackwood. "Surely he referred also to the quality of my sleuthing?"

"He said it was pretty juvenile," admitted Blaine Oliver reluctantly.

"Possibly it is," conceded Blackwood. "But I've made a lot of people uncomfortable. Anyway, he finally agreed!"

"He said that if I doubted him, he would tell *me*. I told him I *didn't* doubt him; but he told me anyway."

"He told you exactly what he told me, a few minutes ago?"

Blaine Oliver almost stopped dancing. There was a slight struggle, then she continued. "Of course! What are you suggesting, Mr. Blackwood?"

"Forgive me," grinned Riley Blackwood. "It was just another example of my juvenile detecting."

"You're such an awful brute," she told him. "Just as one is beginning to like you, all over again!"

"I'm horribly sorry. But I *want* you to like me, you know."

"You seemed doubtful about it, on the yacht."

He remembered their conversation and was amused that *she* remembered it.

"I've changed my mind," he said. "I have been slightly mad about you ever since that evening."

"Good heavens!"

"Fact!" said Mr. Blackwood. "Some day I'll do my card tricks for you. We discussed them, you remember."

"Don't," she begged. There was again the mocking quality in his voice and manner that she had resented on the yacht. Apparently his conversation was made up of the first things that entered his mind. Here they were dancing together. When he had placed an arm around her, earlier in the day, she had resented it; quite properly. Now it meant only that they were dancing—didn't it?

She felt that she was blushing. It was with a feeling of relief that, dancing nearer to their own table, she saw Prentiss and the Meltons looking around for them.

"Oh, there you are," said Harry Prentiss as they came up. He seemed to be displeased that they had gone away. "Mrs. Melton, may I present Mr. Riley Blackwood? You know his name, I'm sure. And Mr. Melton!"

Blackwood bowed and shook hands. It appeared that Blaine Oliver had met them casually, somewhere, after all. It was Mrs. Melton who remembered.

Fresh highballs were ordered, and for a time the conversation was general. Blackwood assumed that Prentiss had said nothing of the reason for the conclave. But it was inevitable that, sooner or later, the subject would come up naturally.

It came up fairly promptly in a burst of enthusiasm from Mrs. Melton, a large blond beauty who had gone West before it was the fashion. She was middle-aged but still attractive.

"Oh, Mr. Blackwood," she gurgled, "I want to tell you how thrilled I was by your magnificent exploit!"

Even Blackwood was a trifle bewildered for a moment. Which exploit, he wondered immodestly, did she have in mind?

"Magnificent exploit?" he echoed.

"When you rescued that awful man on Mr. Haviland's yacht."

"Oh, that!" said Blackwood. He added: "Well, somebody had to do it, I suppose. One does these things without thinking, you know. There's no heroism in them. Probably they're just foolish."

"I was literally frightened to death," she told him. "Mr. Prentiss was with me. I almost precipitated myself onto his bosom. Didn't I, Mr. Prentiss?"

"You *did* precipitate yourself," said Prentiss grimly. "You screamed lustily, right into my ear." He tenderly caressed the member he had mentioned.

Blackwood took the conversation in hand. It was obviously going to require a certain firmness.

"I've never heard how the dickens it actually happened," he remarked. "Where *was* the beggar, anyway? Perched on the rail?"

Mrs. Melton shuddered pleasurably. "I only heard that awful splash," she said. "My lips tried to frame the words 'Man overboard!' but no words would come. All I could do was scream."

Blackwood ventured to think that Mrs. Melton was a reader of lurid fiction; her descriptive phrases seemed to indicate it.

"Nobody seems to know what actually happened," said Melton. "He was just drunk, and he fell in, I imagine. I saw him a minute or two before the accident. I had just come up out of the cabin and was making my way forward. This Cross was in the little lane—or whatever they call it—that connects the front part and the back part of the yacht. You'll have to forgive my nautical phraseology! Anyway, it's fairly narrow; there's the wall of the cabin and the deck house on one side, and the rail on the other. He was making his way along, holding onto the rail, when I saw him: going forward, the same as I was. I passed him, and there was just about room for the two of us. The only other fellow I saw anywhere near was your friend the doctor—what's his name? The man who brought him round after you'd fished him out."

"Trample?" asked Prentiss quickly. "You mean, Dr. Trample?"

"That's the man. A big fellow—over six feet, with shoulders to match. Well, *he* was going back—aft—whatever the word is! He must have passed Cross, too. Anyway, in about a minute or so there was the uproar from the Duchess of Melton, and I gathered that somebody was overboard." He grinned at his wife. "The Duchess has remarkable lungs. I fancy they heard her over on the Fair Grounds."

"Remember that time I screamed when Josephine fell over the front porch rail, Porter?" Mrs. Melton laughed delightedly at the tardy recollection of *that* bit of screaming. Apparently it had been her masterpiece. "No great harm done," she added chattily. "She only sprained her wrist!"

The three conspirators were silent. They were considering, each in his own way, the shocking revelation they had heard of Trample's almost immediate presence on the scene.

Blackwood shook himself together first.

"Well, well," he observed, "I suppose it will remain a mystery. Not that it makes any difference, now. You didn't know the fellow, I suppose?" He looked at Melton.

The banker shook his head. "Barely exchanged a word with him. One meets some queer people at mixed parties. Holderness was interested in him, somewhat. Thought him an odd type of—'bounder,' I believe the word was."

"Speaking of Holderness," said Blackwood quickly. "Just who is he, Mr. Melton—if you don't mind?"

Melton was surprised. "I thought you met him; I thought everybody met him. He was the guest of honor."

"I did; but what's his line, I mean? Novels, exploration?"

"Oh! Yes, both of them. Principally travel books, however. He's a very distinguished fellow."

"So I gathered."

Damn it! thought Blackwood; he couldn't ask the question outright. Why didn't the man continue?

In a moment Melton continued. "Fact is," he said, not without some pride, "I'm helping to finance his new expedition."

"Really?"

"Yes, he's off to the Gobi Desert, now, as soon as he can get his party together."

Blackwood had to risk it. "By Jove!" he said, "isn't that the expedition that Jeffrey Cottingham was interested in?"

Again Melton was surprised. "Cottingham! I hadn't heard of it. No, no, I think you must be mistaken. I knew Cottingham—his recent death was a great shock to me; but while I didn't actually see him before his death, I'm sure I should have heard if he were interested. I can't imagine it. Cottingham didn't run much to that sort of philanthropy, I'm afraid."

"I merely thought I had seen something of it in the papers," lied Blackwood easily. "There's been so much about the poor devil in the papers recently!"

"His suicide was a great shock to me," said Melton soberly. "I couldn't believe it. And, speaking of mysteries, there *is* a mystery, Mr. Blackwood! What was Jeffrey Cottingham doing in Chicago, masquerading under another name? He had friends here—I was one of them, and I've run onto others since it happened. He let nobody know that he was here. The first I knew of his presence was when the papers announced that the body of a man named Chambers had been identified—provisionally—as that of Cottingham. I hurried over to the undertaker's place, where they had the body, and there he was. There's something very odd behind that case. And now it develops that his wife was here—an actress—and has come forward to claim his body! His first wife was an actress, I remember. Some men just can't let them alone."

Blackwood shook his head. "It *is* curious," he agreed. "You didn't know he had married this—what was her name—this Kitty Mock?"

"Hadn't the faintest," said Melton.

"We'd have been so glad to have them at the house," said Mrs. Melton, with regret. "I can't help thinking that actresses are fascinating, Mr. Blackwood."

Mr. Blackwood agreed, with reservations. "Fascinating, yes," he gestured; "but dangerous, Mrs. Melton—dangerous and—*ah*—unstable." He added virtuously, "They live their lives too violently, really, for those of us who try to preserve a certain calmness."

They got rid of the Meltons as rapidly as possible. Blackwood was faintly elated. Nothing had actually been proved, perhaps; but he had a feeling that Melton and Holderness were out of it.

The belated report of Trample's movements on the yacht dismayed him; but it was not final. More than ever, however, it made it imperative that the missing specialist should be found.

A curious thought entered his mind. Suppose Trample *had* pushed the drunken Cross overboard! What did it prove, anyway? That Trample also had been the assailant, so to speak, of Jeffrey Cottingham? Not by a large majority! Well, not necessarily, anyway. Cross might have made a highly offensive remark, there in the darkness of the passage; and Trample was a man of spirit.

The new thought shifted, and he looked at it from another angle. Suppose Trample to be following Cross, instead of vice versa, as he had once believed. Suppose Trample to have seen

Cross in the Granada on Monday night, and later to have drawn his own conclusions. Here, at any rate, decided Blackwood, was food for thought.

And he was still not satisfied that Harold Marcus was outside the picture. The idea was too striking to be laid aside.

"Look here," he said to his new confidants, "I think we're getting somewhere at last; but there are still a number of pockets to be explored. I want to see Widdowson tonight and talk to him about this damned doctor of his—this Marcus. After that, if nothing develops, I'm after Cross and Horace Trample tomorrow. Have breakfast with me, will you? About nine?"

Blaine Oliver and Prentiss were delighted.

"Cheers!" said Blackwood. "Nine o'clock."

He left them to their own devices and continued his long-delayed search for Widdowson.

The hotel proprietor was run to earth, at length, in his own quarters. He had left the Grotto early, he explained, with a touch of headache.

Blackwood snorted. Once more he told his dramatic story of his adventure and displayed his battered skull. "And you talk about a headache!" he concluded. "Well, listen, Tony—I'm not through yet."

He revealed his visit to the hotel doctor and his encounter with the yellow shoes.

"Nonsense!" said Widdowson heatedly. "You're crazy as a bedbug, Riley."

"Science has yet to demonstrate that bedbugs are actually crazy," responded Blackwood. "There are two schools of thought upon the subject, I believe. One group holds that——"

"You're just plain lunatic," continued Widdowson. "Everybody around here knows where Marcus spends his evenings. He's got a girl. Moffat could have told you that days ago."

"All right," said Blackwood. "But it's another little job for White, in my opinion. Have him look into it, will you?"

"There are mud and cinders all over Chicago," argued his friend complainingly. "I stepped in some myself, the other night. As a matter of fact, I believe there's some out back of the hotel at this minute. You might as well be suspicious of *me* as of Marcus."

Riley Blackwood grinned. "But you wouldn't hit me, would you, Tony?" he inquired.

"Wouldn't I?" said Widdowson. "Boy! I'm just waiting for a good chance."

12.

STILL FEELING pretty cocky, Riley Blackwood spent a busy Friday morning, or what was left of it when he arose. He had stayed the night at the hotel. It began with a visit from Joseph White, the chief of the hotel's detective staff, who got him out of his bath with tidings of no importance.

"Sorry about that Marcus hunch of yours, Mr. Blackwood," said Joseph White. "I'll look into it, if I can; but I ain't expecting much. The police asked Marcus a lot of questions on Tuesday morning, you know, after you'd gone away. Put every one of us on the spot; even old Moffat. They wouldn't be likely to overlook anything."

Blackwood thought it extremely likely that they would overlook a great deal. He said so.

"Well," said White, "I'll have a scout around and see what I can find out. About that Prentiss fellow, though, Mr. Blackwood: I can't get a line on him at all."

"He was here on Monday night," said Blackwood, glad of a chance to score. "He stopped with a bird named Steele—Fred Steele—or was it Frank? Anyway, Steele. So he says! I'm inclined to believe him. But look up Steele on the register and be sure that he was really at the hotel."

"You mean—he's *in* on this?" The detective was surprised and impressed.

"I mean he probably *isn't*. Don't try to understand it, Joe; it's very confusing. Just check up on Steele, that's all."

When the door had closed behind the detective, Blackwood finished drying himself, wrapped himself warmly in a robe, and had a drink. Immediately the telephone rang.

"Hello," roared Blackwood. "Yes—speaking! Oh, hello, Steep! It's you, is it? I was just wondering when you'd get around to calling me."

In point of fact, he had almost forgotten the manager of the *Uncle Claude* company; but he was faintly excited by the call.

He listened and then spoke. "Nothing definite, eh? Nobody saw the man? And that was over a week ago? It's principally Monday night I'm interested in. Kitty was in the cast that night, wasn't she?"

He listened again.

"Well, it isn't much; but it may help. Yes, I've got it. Thanks, old man. I won't forget it, you know. So long!"

He replaced the receiver. Damn Steep! He had probably bungled his part of the job. A big blue automobile might belong to anybody, these days. They were cheap enough. They gave them away with tins of tobacco.

He glanced at his watch, finished his dressing, and went down to join Miss Oliver and Prentiss, who were already in the breakfast room.

"Well, the Marcus hunch may yet turn out to be a flop," he greeted them. "He has a girl, it seems, with whom he keeps late hours. Presumably they are known to the night staff of the Granada. Also, I've heard from the theater. A couple of times, more than a week ago, Kitty was seen to step into a big blue automobile, a block away. Monogram or something on the sides—

nobody remembers what. And nobody saw anybody at all on Monday night."

"You can't run down the automobile?" asked Prentiss, with interest.

"Probably not. Only significant thing is that it met her a block away from the theater. That looks like caution, anyway. Well, well!"

They seated themselves and prepared to order breakfast. At once, however, a boy appeared with a telegram for Blackwood. He laid it beside his plate while he studied the bill of fare.

"If only Dr. Trample would come back and explain himself," said Blaine Oliver, "I don't think I would care any more *who* murdered poor Mr. Cottingham. I think I'll have the eggs, please. Does that sound very brutal?"

"Not at all," said Blackwood gallantly. "And do have toast and coffee with them. Prentiss and I are quite broad-minded."

She giggled. "I meant my sentiments, of course. Yes, toast and coffee, please."

Prentiss had already breakfasted, it appeared. "I came for the discussion only," he smiled. "A pot of coffee for me, that's all. Aren't you going to open your telegram, Blackwood? It may be important."

But breakfast with Blackwood was a rite; he ordered it slowly, with a due sense of its solemnity.

"Telegrams are important only to their senders," he replied. "This one is probably to announce the impending advent of Miss Winsome Whosit, for a personal appearance in the three-a-day."

He tore it open leisurely, glanced quickly at the signature, and frowned. After these preliminaries he read the message and made a loud remark. "Well, I'll be jiggered!" cried Mr. Blackwood.

He started to hand the yellow paper to Prentiss, then gave

it to Blaine Oliver. Prentiss rose and read the message over her shoulder. From the same position Blackwood read it over again.

HAVE TRACED DOCTOR TO THIS PLACE STOP
IN HIDING STOP NEED ASSISTANCE STOP
CAN YOU COME QUESTION

The place indicated apparently was Davidsons, a town in Wisconsin. The signature was a single letter—X.

"*Cross!*" ejaculated Harry Prentiss.

"Undoubtedly," said Blackwood. "Smart, isn't he? Conceals his name, knowing I will understand the significance of X. But why, in heaven's name, to *me?*"

"Mmm," said Prentiss, after a pause. "But why not, after all? Who else could he ask but the police? He knows you're working on the case."

"How the dickens could he? I didn't leave my card in his office."

"Well, what's your own opinion?"

Blackwood was still suspicious. "And why the dickens should he need assistance? If he's been after Trample and now has run him to earth, why doesn't he bring him back? He's man enough for that. Cross is a tough hombre."

"So is Trample, I imagine, in a scrap," said Prentiss.

Miss Oliver had turned a little pale. "Oh no! I can't believe it," she protested.

"I suppose it *could* be a trap," said Blackwood cheerily. "How very jolly! Yesterday's adventure wasn't exactly reassuring. I must be a very dangerous man! Still, if Cross is in Wisconsin now, he could hardly have been in Chicago yesterday evening— unless he flew. He *does* fly, come to think of it." He had suddenly remembered the military photograph in the detective's office.

"I've heard of this Davidsons place, I think," mused Prentiss.

"So have I. It's way up north, near the top of the state. It's a place where tourists detrain on their way to the smaller lakes. Tony and I have fished that region."

Their breakfasts arrived, and they looked at them without enthusiasm. The sudden summons had given them something else to think about. However, they managed to clear their plates.

"How about calling in the police?" asked Prentiss suddenly. "But I suppose that wouldn't appeal to you!"

Blackwood shook his head. "No, this is still my party," he replied. "I couldn't look a mirror in the face again if I asked assistance from Paddy Roach. No, I'm going to Wisconsin. After all, it isn't certain that this thing is from Cross. We're simply being bright. It's our infernal cleverness that interprets the signature in that way. Why, doggone it, it might be from Trample himself! He certainly wouldn't care to sign his name, knowing the police to be after him. 'X' stands for anything we want it to, doesn't it? It's the unknown quantity."

Prentiss agreed. "You may be right," he said. "It hadn't struck me just that way. It may be Trample's way of telling you that he needs assistance."

"Well, I'm going."

"Hang it," said Prentiss, "I wish I could go with you. But I've got to go to St. Louis tonight for the firm."

Miss Oliver had an exciting idea. "Look here," she cried, "maybe I could drive you there! If Dr. Trample——"

Both men cried out in horror. It was unthinkable, they said. Blackwood, however, gave it a second thought. It might be very jolly! Very jolly indeed.

"I'd love it," he said; "but I'm afraid it's out of the question. Prentiss wouldn't like it; and you'd need so many things, up there in the woods! Stouter shoes and stockings, for one thing."

She flushed at his contemplation of her attractive legs. Prentiss looked annoyed, and Riley Blackwood laughed happily. He had often wondered what, if anything, she saw in Prentiss.

Her interest in the doctor was romantic, of course, but fairly remote.

"Well," he said, "I'll have to hustle. There are several things to do."

Among them, he reflected, when he had left them at the door, was a spot of conversation with Widdowson. And a call to his aunt, to say that he was leaving town. He had no notion of disappearing in the Wisconsin wilds, leaving no record of his departure. Already too many persons connected with this mystery had vanished up the capacious sleeve of God. If Prentiss planned to stay long in St. Louis, there would be no one but Blaine Oliver to wonder what had happened to him. Certainly he would have to have a talk with Widdowson. And borrow a car.

He began another search for Widdowson, who as usual could not be found. It seemed to Blackwood that he was *always* looking for Widdowson and failing to find him. The fellow had as many hangouts as a bootlegger.

But Widdowson was not upon the premises.

Blackwood canvassed the possibilities and decided to take Haviland further into his confidence. In a pinch, the yachtsman would be a fellow of some resource. Might even organize a rescue expedition.

He telephoned to Haviland, almost expecting that he too would be among the missing. However, Haviland was merely "in conference," a secretary said. Would Mr. Blackwood hold the wire?

Mr. Blackwood held the wire, with mounting impatience, for a number of minutes; then he was talking to the yachtsman with forceful earnestness.

"It's either that blackguard Cross again," he explained, "or Trample tipping me off to where he's hiding. Either way, I wouldn't miss it for a million. What I'm wanting is someone to know where I've gone, in case I turn up missing. Get it?"

Haviland got it perfectly. "Nevertheless, Blackwood, aren't you sticking your nose into a lot of possible trouble?" he inquired. "After all, there are quite a number of policemen doing nothing in particular."

"To hell with the police," responded Blackwood. "I think they're spinach. Anyway, the fellow who sent the message *may* be Trample, and I'm not sicking the police on *him*, this afternoon."

"Very well," the yachtsman answered. "It's your funeral, not mine. But if you need more help, just holler for it. Wire me for anything you need. How long do you want me to wait before I begin to worry?"

Blackwood thought it over. "I'll be up there by tonight, I suppose. Well, give me until tomorrow night, at least, to wire you. If you don't hear from me, get in touch with Widdowson and organize a search party. Better get in touch with Widdowson anyway, tonight, and let him know what's up. I couldn't find him."

A very workmanlike plan, he reflected as he hung up the receiver. At any rate, he would get a decent funeral! Now if only he could get a decent car.

He descended upon Widdowson's garage, where he was known, and selected a heavy roadster that he had driven before. In its side pocket, as he drove gayly northward, reposed an ugly blue-steel pistol that he had never had occasion to use. It had been given him by his friends, Drury and Howe, of the Detective Bureau, with instructions how to handle it in an emergency. Very often he had wished that an emergency might arise to call it from beneath his pillow. It rather looked, by Jove! as if at last it had arisen.

Well, cheerio!

> *"There lived a knight in the days of old,*
> *Sing hey-lo, dey-lo, dilly!*
> *Who was famed afar for his deeds so bold,*

Sing hey-lo, dey-lo, dilly!
He walked alone in a garden fair,
He'd no idea a woman was there—
But, Lord, sir! women is everywhere,
Sing hey-lo, dey-lo, dilly!"

On the outskirts of Milwaukee he refilled his tanks, a matter he had neglected before leaving Chicago. At Hanbridge he paused for refreshments. At Guilders Green he blew a tire and cursed copiously, to the admiration of a group of the local citizenry. At Simmons Woods he failed utterly to miss a squawking chicken. At Tophole, he began—or so he told himself—to smell the fragrance of the lakes and forests, "the murmuring pines and the hemlocks," although he scarcely knew one tree from another.

At Harrisburg it suddenly occurred to him that he was being followed.

The idea, although not without its allure, shocked him. It froze the song upon his lips.

A big black car of expensive design seemed to be the pursuer. Or was it blue? It was difficult to be sure. Twice before, it occurred to him, he had noticed the thing, loafing along just out of hailing distance behind him. The last time had been an hour agone, on a fairly bumpy country turnpike that he had deliberately chosen because it appeared to be a short cut. Now he was back on the main road, and here again was the big black car—*was* it black?—strolling along with its hands in its pockets, having no difficulty at all in keeping just the right distance in the rear. There seemed to be two persons in the front seats; but it was hard to be certain.

Blackwood slowed up imperceptibly and endeavored to diminish the distance between the cars before his tactics should be discovered. He loosened the flap of the side pocket that contained his pistol. He didn't really want to shoot anybody, he decided; and, after all, the thing might be only a coincidence. But he did want a look at the driver of the other car.

His subtlety was quickly discovered, and the pace of the pursuing car fell off. In a few minutes the distance between the two again had widened. Well, there was no doubt of it! The other fellow was certainly on the trail. The murderer, he supposed. The fellow who had hit him from behind in Kitty Mock's apartment. How *very* jolly! So the telegram *had* been a trap, after all!

Yet apparently it had come from the Wisconsin tourist stop, still some hours distant to the northward. Had this relentless pursuer waited somewhere along the road to see him pass, then quietly fallen in behind? He tried to remember when it was he had first vaguely noticed the big dark car. And whether it really had been black.

Cross, perhaps, himself—or Cross and the mysterious third person of the trinity!

Blackwood spoke aloud. "Well," he observed, to test the quality of his voice, "if it's a race he wants, I'll give him one."

He stepped on the gas. The gleaming countryside of Wisconsin began to flow southward past the roadster like a rapidly manipulated motion picture. He missed a lumbering farmer's truck by an eyelash and dashed through a country village at terrifying speed. A dog ran out at him from the last farmhouse, barking, and for a few instants paralleled his flight; then it gave over the unequal race. A flash of red he took to be a filling station.

Over against the northern tree-tops the sky was pearly gray. Across the harvest fields dark forest patches loomed and vanished, dwarfed by speed and distance: vignettes of mystery and isolation, illustrations for a legend by Dunsany. The sun was halfway down the sky. The air was keen and clear. The road dipped like a roller coaster.

Three further villages were bisected and left behind, and a sweeping turn beset him on the right; behind the rustic fence that bordered it he glimpsed the headstones of a country church-yard. Stoke Poges, by the living Jingo! The ploughman home-ward plods his weary way, and leaves the world unto the poet Gray. Now fades the glimmering landscape on the sight . . .

"Easy, boy!" said Mr. Blackwood to the roadster. "Don't slice into the cemetery!"

At Easterling he drew rein and again lifted his eye to the little mirror that showed the road behind; but for some time there had been no sign of the pursuing auto. He had left it behind him like a decrepit baby carriage.

Relaxing, Blackwood lighted a cigarette and pushed forward without exertion along a road that paralleled the lake. He daw-dled through Petersham and Colville and Alta Vista, and avoid-ed the last big town that lay between him and the entrance to the lake country. The light was still excellent; there was yet some time to sundown. The fragrance of orchards was in his nostrils, and something sharper that was the smell of pines. At pleasant intervals the lake whispered or broke in little smothers of foam along the shore.

Would Cross be waiting him at Davidsons? Or was Cross behind him in a big blue car?

In the subdued light of early evening he entered Sturgeon Bay and once more filled up his tanks for the final dash to David-sons. There was no sign of the car that he still believed to have been pursuing him. Beyond the city the roads were lined with trees that leaned over until they almost met. For a time he drove through green cathedral arches and viewed with approbation the miniature dwellings tucked away in groves of autumn color. Then he swung into a highway leading along the curving shore of the bay and emerged again into late afternoon sunlight, with the water on his left and a tangle of uncleared forest on his right.

Some miles ahead, he had ascertained, lay the turning for Da-vidsons, a relatively narrow trail leading away by imperceptible degrees from the road he was immediately following. It would be necessary to look sharp, perhaps. He slowed the roadster to an easy saunter and turned his gaze inland. The air intoxicated him, and a high sense of elation flowed in his veins. New and frightful songs ran in his mind, including a bawdy bit about a certain Yonson who came from Wisconsin, the state name being pronounced with a jovial V. Mr. Yonson worked in a lumber camp.

Mr. Blackwood was working up the second stanza of this original contribution to national folklore when he glanced into his mirror for the first time, consciously, since he had left the tourist city behind him. He jerked in his seat.

A big black car—or was it blue?—was rolling along behind the roadster at a distance of possibly half a mile. It was not speeding. It was merely keeping the roadster within view.

A prickle of apprehension made the circumference of Blackwood's scalp and another trickled up his spine.

It was a lovely spot of earth for a murder. Isolated. Lonely. Away across the bay an ore boat was loitering along, miles beyond hearing; its smokestack gave forth thick skeins of smoky wool. In the woods to starboard the leaves whispered and birds called from the branches. A chipmunk scuttled across the path and vanished in the undergrowth.

Blackwood pushed his foot down on the accelerator and rushed northward across the state of Wisconsin.

The miles dropped behind; but the big blue car did not. If only he could be sure it *wasn't* blue!

More miles slipped past; and then, quite suddenly, he glimpsed the turning for which he sought, half hidden in the ragged landscape. He had just whirled headlong around a promontory of trees and shrubs, and for the moment the pursuing car was out of sight.

Blackwood wrenched at the wheel and sent the roadster crashing across a stretch of stubbled turf that was half a ditch and half an entrance to the opening in the forest. The car reeled and righted, skidded against a stump—then darted like a squirrel into the narrower track that pierced the dimness of the surrounding wood. He drove the roadster between two sentinel pines, a natural doorway, into the center of the tangle, and stopped it with a jerk. Then, in a moment, he was out upon the path and running back in the direction of the main road.

Pistol in hand, a sufficiently dashing figure, he hurried toward the turning from the road, and concealed himself behind a patch of leafy shrub.

He was barely in time.

The sounds of the pursuing car drew nearer; then for a swift moment it appeared in the openings between the trees.

With eyes that seemed to be bursting from their sockets, Blackwood saw the heads of Harry Prentiss and Blaine Oliver go jouncing past, behind the windows of a great blue car that missed the opening completely and went spinning northward along the peninsula toward whatever lay beyond.

13.

RILEY BLACKWOOD went on his way to Davidsons. He was vastly disturbed. That Harry Prentiss should have shown himself a liar and a traitor was, of course, distressing; but that Blaine Oliver should have been a party to the betrayal, as appeared to be the case, was a circumstance that profoundly discouraged him. He had looked for better things from her. He had even contemplated offering her his second seat on opening nights—an aperture usually reserved for a male companion or for his overcoat, when overcoats were in season. He had rather looked forward to adding a particularly charming telephone number to that selected group of numbers which he kept in a small red book.

And now—*this!*

Precisely what it meant he had no very clear idea. Whatever tentative conclusions he might have been upon the point of reaching, he told himself, were now shot to pieces. He was back at the beginning of things, nursing his early suspicions of the man who had, in a sense, at least, directed the discovery of Cottingham's body. And if Prentiss was the guilty man, Blaine Oliver in some fashion must be involved. In that case, there seemed to be only one plausible solution of their present movements. Unless they were hand-in-glove with Cross, they were planning to interrupt the scheduled meeting between Cross and Riley Blackwood.

Why?

Obviously because Trample, now run to earth by Cross, *did* know more than he had ever told about the murder, and might— if reached—be prevailed upon to tell it. And that telling would play the deuce with Prentiss and Blaine Oliver. It probably had been an error to show them his telegram.

Or was the alternative just as plausible? If they were co-conspirators with Cross, then the object of all three would be the closing of Trample's mouth before he could communicate with Riley Blackwood. In that case, the telegram had been from Trample, not from Cross, and Riley Blackwood certainly *had* been a chump to show the thing to Prentiss.

If the telegram had been from Cross, and he and Prentiss were in league together, then Prentiss must have had previous knowledge of the message; had known what it contained as soon as it was delivered at the breakfast table. As a matter of fact, hadn't he urged with some impatience that it be opened? In that case, the message was a trap.

But Miss Oliver, as usual, had defended the doctor.

"Damn!" said Blackwood. The whole thing was a headache. It was confused beyond hope of mental solution. The police probably had the right idea, after all. Third degree! Get somebody onto the carpet and give him the works!

A great deal, at any rate, depended upon Cross—whether he was an ally or an enemy. It was a problem shortly to be tested. Assuming, of course, that Cross had sent the telegram and was in the neighborhood. It had been Prentiss, by the by, who had first interpreted the signature.

Blackwood switched on his headlights as the sun sank over the water, beyond the trees. Driving as rapidly as the road permitted, he pushed on toward his destination. Sooner or later, the big blue car would learn that it had missed the roadster and would be back in a whirl of dust. Prentiss, he assumed, was unfamiliar with the geography of the region. They were now upon the peninsula, a long and narrow arm of the state reaching northward for many miles. On the immediate left was the wide body of water known as Green Bay; some miles to the eastward lay the main waters of Lake Michigan. But assuming that Prentiss ran the entire length of the peninsula before discovering his mistake, it would be only a few hours before he would reach land's end and come hurrying back.

Darkness had fallen when the roadster entered Davidsons. Blackwood drove slowly past the miniature railroad station, heartily glad to be away from the gloomy miles of trees for a time; although even now they hedged the little tourist city like a besieging army.

Suddenly he heard himself hailed, and in the darkness a man came striding toward him from the station platform. He recognized the stocky figure of Gene Cross; the figure of the man he had last seen sprawled upon a bunk in the cabin of the *Flying Fish*, recovering from his curious accident.

"That you, Mr. Blackwood?" called Cross again. He came closer to the roadster and peered in, a friendly grin upon his face. "Thought I'd pick you up about here, whether you drove or took a train. Sort of expected a wire from you, care of the telegraph office here."

They shook hands in the fashion of men who are warily sizing each other up.

"I gathered from your signature that you weren't calling attention to yourself," said Blackwood. He leaned out of the window, the better to converse. The evening air was cold; he was glad there was an overcoat in the rumble.

"Oh, that was for the people at the other end. I knew *you'd* 'get' it—but I didn't know who else might see it."

Blackwood decided to say nothing, for the moment, about the others who had seen it.

"What's up?" he asked abruptly. "If I understand your wire correctly, you think you've got something on the doctor."

"*Think!*" said Cross. "Boy! I've got them both exactly where I want them! Darned decent of you to come. I wasn't sure you would. I've never even thanked you for pulling me out of the lake."

Blackwood was puzzled. "Both?" he questioned. "What do you mean, Cross? Who is with the doctor?"

"Who do you think? Kitty Mock, of course! She joined him this morning. That's why I wired. Up to then I couldn't be positive I had the goods on them."

"The devil!" said Blackwood. His mind whirled. He hung over the edge of the window, staring at the man in the road beside him. This was the most bewildering blow his theories had yet received. What now became of his suspicions of Blaine Oliver and Harry Prentiss? Were they leagued with the doctor in a conspiracy to protect him against discovery?

He heard the amused voice of Cross continuing its explanation. "She got here by train this morning. Took a train out of Chicago, last night, I figure, and spent the night at Green Bay. This line is just a spur. Yep, her and the doctor! All by their little lonesome. Living in sin, that's what the preachers call it." Mr. Cross chuckled appreciatively. "Well, they couldn't find a nicer place for it," he added reflectively.

Blackwood couldn't believe it. "Where are they?" he feebly asked.

"Few miles from here. Just a short run out of town in a car. They've got a big stone house in the middle of a tract of virgin forest. *Virgin!* That's good, ain't it? Right on the water. I mean the land is right on the water. The house is back about a hundred yards or two, with a path down to the beach. I was there when the lady arrived."

"In the house?" asked Blackwood incredulously.

"No, hanging around. There's a little shack right down on the water—unoccupied. I slept there last night."

"Well," said Blackwood, "it beats *me*, Cross!"

Gene Cross smiled without exultation. "Easy as falling off a chair, Mr. Blackwood. Running people down is my line, you know. Maybe you didn't know!"

"I—*ah*—yes, I knew," said Riley Blackwood. "But how the devil did you find all this out, Cross?" he demanded.

"I'll tell you about that as we go along. I want to confront 'em tonight. So do you, don't you? Look here, you'd better park this car of yours in a garage until you want it again. I've got an old Ford that I'm using; that's it there, over against the station. And I know the way. We don't want *two* cars charging along through the woods. One makes noise enough."

"All right," said Blackwood. There was nothing for it now but to see it through. And he wanted to get away from Cross for just a minute—long enough to get his pistol out of the car pocket and into his own. God alone knew what was going to develop! "There's a sign up there a piece, across the road," he added. "I'll join you shortly."

Still considerably shaken by the revelations of the detective, he drove off to the garage. On the way he transferred the pistol to his side pocket and smiled a little grimly. After all, Cross was not exactly a trustworthy animal. On the other hand, there was an infernal plausibility about his story that was dismaying. It solved everything in the easiest way possible. Incidentally, it made a sap of Riley Blackwood. What it made of Harry Prentiss and Blaine Oliver, he could not imagine.

At the garage he made arrangements to leave the roadster until he called for it, removed his overcoat from the rumble, and tramped back toward the railroad station, his mind still rioting. He switched the pistol from his jacket pocket to the right-hand pocket of his overcoat and decided that he was ready for what might come.

"All set?" asked Cross, as he approached the Ford. "Climb in, and we'll get going. I've got provisions in the back seat, in case we have to make a night of it."

"Precisely what do you intend to do?" asked Blackwood, when they were started. "Even supposing that you've got the goods on Trample, you don't expect him to break down and confess, do you?"

Cross removed both hands from the wheel recklessly and lighted a cigarette. The spurt of flame in the darkness lighted up his hard face and the ironic smile around his mouth.

"Why not?" he retorted, tossing the match overboard. "Catching 'em together is as good as confession. They'll know that. Oh, they'll talk! I'll see to that. But I needed a witness with me when it happened, see? I don't want any talk of rough stuff later on."

It occurred to Blackwood that catching them together *was* practically equivalent to confession, at that. Each had unequivocally denied knowledge of the other. He persisted, however, in his cross-examination.

"What is your own interest in all this, Cross?" he demanded abruptly. "I don't quite see where you come in. For whom are you working?"

Cross chuckled in the darkness. "Kitty Mock'll know," he answered. "I'm still working for her husband. Oh, yes, he's dead! But what's the diff? He hired me to do a job for him, and I'm no quitter. There ain't any mystery about this case, Mr. Blackwood; there hasn't been any from the beginning. It's an open-and-shut case. The doctor was playing around with Kitty Mock, and Cottingham got wise to it. It's the good old recipe for murder. He was a jealous bird—always worried about his wife when she was away on tour. Fellows like that oughtn't to marry actresses; but somehow they always do. Anyway, he hired me to get the goods on them, and I got it. *We* got it—Cottingham and me together. That night—Monday night. I suppose you know that I was in Kitty's room that night, don't you?"

Blackwood laughed. "Yes," he admitted, "I did discover that. I knew you and Cottingham were both there; and somebody else too."

"Sure—and that somebody else was the doctor. He was there first. We knew he was there. I saw him go upstairs, and Cottingham spotted him in the room with a pair of binoculars that he'd brought along. There wasn't any doubt about it. We scooted across the street, took an elevator, and crashed the party." Gene Cross laughed appreciatively at the recollection. "They was a bit surprised," he added gently.

"Cottingham knew the man was Trample, all the time?" asked Blackwood. "When he met him first, in the Granada?"

"He was pretty sure, yes. So was I. I'd been working on the case for some time. Trample didn't come to Chicago that day or the day before. He came right after Kitty Mock came with her company. He was at another hotel for a time, that's all. I knew where he was."

The plausibility of it all was undeniable, Blackwood admitted to himself. "What happened at the Jamaica that night?" he questioned.

"Well, we bust in on them, as I say, and like to turned the doctor's hair gray. Kitty didn't give a damn at first. Told Cottingham to go to hell and get his divorce, if he wanted it. But the doctor wasn't pleased at all. He had a reputation to think about, I suppose. First thing he did was deny there was anything between them. He said everybody knew it was all right for a doctor to be in a room with one of his patients. We just gave him the grand razzberry. Later he tried to talk us around. Kitty telephoned for liquor, but we didn't wait. Cottingham had seen enough, and so had I. He said he *would* get his divorce, and we walked out on them."

It all checked very beautifully with what Blackwood had himself discovered. After all, Jamieson might well have believed Cottingham and Cross to be "excited."

"And you suggest that later Trample followed Cottingham back to the Granada and murdered him—put morphine in his liquor?"

"It was easy enough," said Cross. "Kitty's a dope, you know—not a violent one; but she takes the stuff occasionally. Trample was getting it for her. He had some in his pocket, I suppose. He left Kitty and followed Cottingham back to the hotel, had another interview with him, and dropped the stuff in the whisky glass when Cottingham wasn't looking. It would look like suicide, he figured—and it damn near did!"

"You weren't there yourself during the interview?"

"No, I'd left Cottingham outside the Jamaica. But later I thought of something I wanted to ask him, and I went back. It was a little after one o'clock—and Trample was just coming out of Cottingham's room. He didn't see me. He was hanging a card on Cottingham's door handle."

"Good God!" said Blackwood. "You saw that, and yet you didn't——"

"Butt in? No, and I'll tell you why. Of course, I wished later I had. I was suspicious as hell, even then; but there wasn't any proof that anything was wrong. I was afraid Trample would see me; so I turned and beat it downstairs. Then I called Cottingham on the telephone—and got him. He sounded a bit thick, and he admitted he'd been drinking; but he seemed to be all right. He told me he'd just got rid of Trample, who'd been trying to buy him off, and that he was going to bed. There it was, you see! What could I think? It seemed funny, his asking the doctor to hang out that ticket; but he must have done it."

"I see," said Blackwood thoughtfully. He was trying desperately to find some flaw in the detective's statement. What an idiot he had been, himself, not to inquire of the switchboard about calls to Cottingham's room in the early morning hours! "The exchange of rooms went through just as Trample told us, I suppose?" he continued.

Cross shrugged. "I don't know exactly *what* Trample told you," he replied; "but they certainly did exchange rooms. That was earlier, of course. Trample didn't know Cottingham by sight, and he fell for the story Cottingham told him. It was a fairly lousy one; but the doctor's something of an ass, after all."

Blackwood chanced a shot in the dark. "Do Harry Prentiss or Miss Blaine Oliver know anything about all this?" he asked suddenly.

But Cross's voice was blank. "I don't know them," he answered. "Where do they come in, Mr. Blackwood?"

"Damned if I know," said Blackwood a bit hopelessly. "Anyway, it's easy to see why you're on the trail. Where did you pick the doctor up?"

"Well, as soon as Cottingham's body had been found I knew who had killed him," said Cross easily; "but, of course, I couldn't prove it on his front teeth. I thought the police would get Trample and drag it out of him, as a matter of fact—his story was such a wild one—about that exchange of rooms, and so on. When they didn't, I knew it was up to me. I picked him up on Wednesday, after his damn convention, and I've followed him ever since."

"Then it was *you* that got into a cab with him a little after noon on Wednesday."

Cross's harsh chuckle grated against the darkness again. "So you know about that, do you? It was me, all right. He knew me, of course—and of course he got the idea that I was after him. That's what made him duck, I suppose. We rode into the Loop together, and he tried to pump me about what I knew or suspected. Pretended to be cut up about Cottingham's 'suicide,' as he called it; and blamed himself for being the cause of it. Very frank and open on the surface, you know. Naturally, I wasn't telling him anything. Well, after I left him—as *he* thought—he took another cab and lit out for a railway station. I followed him, and—here we are!"

"So it was Trample you were trailing on the yacht!"

"Sure it was. And I'll solve another little mystery for you, in case it's troubling you. It was your friend Trample who pushed me into the lake. If it hadn't been for you, I might be there yet. I owe you one for that."

"Don't think of it," said Blackwood politely.

Damn the fellow! He rather wished he had not bothered to pull him out that night!

They left the little city behind them and swung out into the open country. Immediately the trees resumed their solemn march on either side, very much—it seemed to Blackwood—as if they were files of soldiers on perpetual guard. He was ardently sick of trees, in spite of an early-morning notion that dwellers in the city were oafs and half-wits. Trees hemmed one in. They weighed mysteriously on the senses. He hoped that he would never *see* another adjectival *tree*. The poet who could sing of *trees* was full of bats and mice and *fleas*. Riley Blackwood, jiggling along a country road in northern Wisconsin, would have given up a dollar and a half for just one glimpse of a sputtering white electric sign in Clark Street.

For several miles the car rattled and bumped along the uneven surface, and the trees as they approached the denser darkness of the forest became taller and more numerous. The Ford rounded the corner of a darkened farmhouse and clattered westward; then again it turned to the north and entered ultimately into a patch of woodland that was heavy with the scent of pines. The moon was up. At times it seemed tangled in the tops of the tallest firs and pines; but its light was pale and ghostly among the trees. The stars, cold and hard, were little points of ice in the sky.

Blackwood was at his old task of thinking—reviewing everything that Cross had told him and checking it against his own experience. Somewhere, he had a feeling, there was a hitch; something that didn't exactly click. For one thing, Cross had lied about Harry Prentiss; he had said he didn't know him. That had not been Prentiss's story. Or was Prentiss lying?

Cross stirred and spoke. "We're coming to the entrance to his land before long, now. It isn't really his, I suppose. I don't know how he came to find the place; that's something we've got to find out. It's black as hell inside the woods, but the road ain't so bad. I've got a place where I leave the car, about a mile inside the grounds. Then there's another couple of miles on foot, and the road twists and turns like a snake; but the general direction is northwest all the time, until you hit the water."

"I should imagine it all belongs to some friend of his," said Blackwood. "He must have known about it before he took a train."

"He knew about it, all right," said Cross. "He headed for it like a homing pigeon. It's a wonder Kitty ever found the place."

"How *did* she find it?" Blackwood was suddenly curious.

"Fellow at the station drove her up. She must have had directions. I suppose it has a name. I haven't asked any questions in the town, yet." Cross peered ahead of him in the light thrown by the headlights of the car. "Right about in here, I think," he added.

He was now peering off to the left. "Yep, that's the place," said Cross; and Blackwood was able faintly to see a trail that led inward among the trees—a trail that vanished in a darkness that seemed comparable to no other darkness that he had ever known.

In a moment, however, the lamps were lighting it for progress. The Ford bumped over some fallen branches, lurched for an instant into a rut, and popped into the opening among the trees. Blackness surrounded them immediately, save where the headlights shone on bole and branch. Among the darker stems of beech and pine slim birches gleamed for an instant, as they passed, then vanished like swaying ghosts. They were the only trees that Blackwood knew by sight, or could be certain of, saving only the interminable pines and firs with which he was, by now, all too familiar. He had always thought that birches, in the Chicago parks, were rather pretty. These were distinctly eerie.

Cross was looking for the little clearing among the trees where he had found a parking spot. In the reflected glow of his cigarette, Blackwood saw the hard lines of the detective's mouth and jaw. He noted that Cross was freshly shaven.

"How did you know that Trample was going to be on board the yacht?" he snapped. "He didn't know it himself until an hour or so before he went."

The Ford stopped with a jerk.

"Here we are," said Cross, without emotion. "Hop out, Mr. Blackwood. I'm going to douse the lights in a minute."

Blackwood opened the door beside him and stepped out upon the earth. The leaves and twigs crackled under his feet. Cross ran the car into the clearing and himself dismounted.

"Another thing," said Blackwood. "How the devil did you know I was working on this case, Cross?"

"I went back to my office on Wednesday," answered the detective. "After you'd been there and turned my papers upside down. That's one way I knew. You just weren't smart enough."

"I was in your office on Wednesday afternoon," said Blackwood. "It was fairly late. At that time, if I understand your earlier statement, you were following the doctor."

The situation had come up suddenly. He realized that he had forced the issue. It occurred to Blackwood that this had been a very courageous thing to do, in view of the fact that very shortly, in all probability, he would be murdered.

"The two stories *don't* exactly click," admitted Cross. The headlights still burned upon the tree trunks. In the semi-darkness there was an evil grin on the detective's face. "Why, you son of a bitch," he added, "do you think I asked you up here for a picnic in the woods?"

They faced each other at a distance of six feet or less. The stocky tough stepped forward.

"Look here, Blackwood," he said. "There's one way out of this, if you'll listen to reason." He came in closer. "It's this!"

His right fist came up from somewhere near his knees.

Blackwood stepped back and watched him totter with the force of his wasted effort. Then, as the detective straightened, he stepped swiftly forward and kicked him accurately in the stomach. A foul blow. Considerably below the belt.

Cross wilted and collapsed on the ground, writhing and groaning. It seemed to Blackwood that there was a look of shocked surprise on the detective's face, in addition to his expression of great pain. But it seemed to him also that Cross was reaching for his pocket.

He brought out his own pistol and smashed the detective across the eyes and forehead with its heavy butt.

When it was certain that Cross was quite motionless, he strode to the decrepit Ford and hunted furiously among the odds and ends that littered the back seat. As he had hoped, he found a length of very decent rope, and with it tied the detective, hand and foot, in what he trusted was a competent and workmanlike security.

Nothing, he supposed, that Cross had told him was now to

be believed. He stood alone, in the heart of a Wisconsin forest, and considered his position. What would happen when Harry Prentiss and the jolly little Oliver came cantering back along the highway, to resume the trail?

Very softly, Blackwood whistled a bar or two of the *Habanera*—a grand melody—while he made up his mind.

He stooped to Cross's body and frisked it. An old police revolver, but a good one, came out of the back pocket of the trousers. Obviously the detective had not cared to fire it, or by this time Riley Blackwood might have been a dead man. The inference was that there were people in the neighborhood who might hear a shot. Cross had reached for his weapon only in an emergency.

There was nothing else of interest in the pockets: a disappointing circumstance.

He returned to the car and rummaged further in the back-seat bazaar. Cheers! This was what he needed—an electric torch! He had been a chump not to bring one along himself. But Cross had lied about the provisions—an awkward situation. Even a bar of chocolate would have helped. Did they send dogs out into the forest, he wondered, with little kegs of brandy tied beneath their chins?

"Here, doggie, doggie!"

Well, Cross wasn't dead, anyway. His heart was still pumping. He probably weighed plenty; but it would be a Christian act to get him into the car before turning him over to the authorities.

Mr. Blackwood tugged and swore and copiously perspired. At length, after great toil, he hauled and boosted the unconscious detective into the Ford and covered him with a blanket. He reached into the front seat and snapped off the staring lamps.

The night was black as the devil's riding boots. Queer noises sounded around him in the darkness: the groaning and sighing of the trees and the leaves, and stranger sounds that he could not interpret.

He snapped down the button of his electric torch and strode boldly along the twisting trail that led, he had been incredibly informed, to an old stone house in the middle of a forest.

14.

TREES THAT ARE only trees by daylight are many and various other things at night. They are lurking, impossible monsters of the animal world or crouching human ruffians, of ferocious aspect and intent, depending upon their shape, size, color, distance from the beholder, and general state of well-being or decay. One's own well-being has some bearing on the matter. Strong nerves are needed to walk among them in the darkness.

In the city, Blackwood's nerves were sufficient to their purpose, backgrounded as they were by a superb insolence and that sense of security which springs from a connection with a powerful morning newspaper. Something of this carried over, now, in the Wisconsin jungle; but he had a number of bad moments. Once he nearly shot an inoffensive stump that sprang at him without warning.

The old stone house, Cross had said, lay yet another two miles along the twisting auto road. It seemed imperative to ascertain whether it really existed. If it did not, the babes in the wood had nothing on Riley Blackwood, that metropolitan man of letters gloomily reflected.

The borrowed torch picked out the irregularities of the trail with fair precision. Its narrow beam skipped on ahead, revealing sudden stones and branches, pine cones and fallen acorns and startling growths of fungus, patches of green moss, and now and then a stagnant pool of water, still standing after the most recent rain. Once a tiny snake wriggled from the roadside into a nest of fallen leaves. There was no sign of moon or star above; the tree-tops met and interlaced. The road wound in and out among the great stems, apparently without rhyme or reason, yet with a certain rhythm.

A quality of nightmare informed the episode, and Blackwood could think of several things he would rather have been doing.

> *Come down to Kew in lilac time,*
> *In lilac time, in lilac time!*
> *Come down to Kew in lilac time——*

For half an hour he cautiously progressed, cursing each twig that crackled under foot. Then it seemed to him that in the distance he could hear the sound of long waves rolling on a pebbled beach. He glanced upward and beheld a star. In a moment there was another. The trees were thinning out; patches of sky were visible between their tops. Blackwood snapped off his torch and faintly saw the trail beneath his feet. Somewhere ahead there was a clearing, flooded with starlight. If Cross had lied about the house, he might even emerge upon the beach.

He pushed forward with greater caution and came almost suddenly upon the house.

The trees stopped abruptly at the edge of the clearing. They began again some fifty yards beyond. Overhead he beheld once more the panorama of the planets. The stars were sprinkled with a liberal hand; the moon shone silverly upon the house and grounds and on the outer rims of the encircling trees. It was a setting romantic and mysterious for a horror drama by O'Neill. For a moment Blackwood was tempted to adolescent applause.

The house was ugly and misshapen, and there was a jail-like quality about it that eluded definition. Two stories in height, for the most part, it fronted on a terraced lawn that ended in a grove of young trees, beyond which—at some little distance—he sensed the presence of the water. At front and back a wide stone porch was screened with heavy wire. A single turret, square and hideous, presumably looked out across the tree-tops to the bay.

Blackwood made a stealthy circuit of the house and grounds, keeping inside the fringe of trees. In an upper room, at the front of the house, a light burned dimly. The blind was only half drawn, and a curtain stirred in the light breeze of evening. By climbing to the top of the stone porch, it occurred to Blackwood that he might be able to see within; but the prospect of this activity filled him with no enthusiasm. The living room presumably was immediately below. He crept closer; then, with a little rush, crossed the lighted lawn and concealed himself in the shrubbery that lay beneath the windows. Above him, something gleamed upon the windowpane, and he assumed an open fireplace on the far side of the chamber. He dragged himself up the stonework of the porch and, leaning outward, looked through the lower window into the living room beyond.

There was an open fire, as he had cleverly deduced, and sitting before it was a woman. Apparently she was alone. Most of the room, however, was in shadow.

The woman's back was toward him, but it was a back that he was confident he had embraced. The outline of her head, too, was familiar. He had no doubt whatever that she was Kitty Mock. And in a moment, as if to confirm his opinion, she turned her head, and he was enabled to see her profile.

The woman was Kitty Mock.

Blackwood scuttled back to the relative security of the trees, for this was something he had to think about. Cross, in this one particular, at any rate, had told the truth. It was a sufficiently disturbing reflection—for when a man blends truth and falsehood skillfully in one comprehensive statement, it is difficult to tell the veracities from the fibs.

The immediate question was easy: Was Trample also in the house? It was reasonable to suppose that he would be with Kitty, assuming Cross's statement of their relationship to be correct. To be sure, he might be in another part of the house, on any little errand. The simplest way to ascertain would be to knock at the door and ask.

That would be also the most dangerous way, if matters were not precisely as Cross had suggested.

"The Emperor Napoleon used to say that attack was the best form of defense," mused Mr. Blackwood, rather as if he were speaking of an old friend.

But in spite of the Emperor Napoleon, he decided against any move too rashly suicidal. He sneaked away among the trees and once more bent his footsteps toward the water. It was at least conceivable that the doctor was a prisoner in the house, if nothing else; and there were points in the story told by Cross that could still be checked. There had been some mention of a shack down near the water where the detective had pretended he had spent the night. Trample, if he were a prisoner, might even be hidden in the shack.

But why the devil *should* he be a prisoner? It was a new idea, with attractions of its own; but if Trample was a prisoner, who the devil was his captor? Cross alone? Prentiss? Prentiss and Cross together? And what part was Blaine Oliver playing in a drama that starred also the ampler dimensions of Kitty Mock?

It seemed to Blackwood that there should be another figure in the tale—a shadowy figure in the background of all this mystery—a sort of directing genius in the wings, who gave the cues. The cast as it existed seemed somehow a little trumpery. Of them all, only Trample possessed the personality and glamour for the part of heavy; and Trample he was still unwilling to believe a murderer.

Cross's story had been somewhat of a masterpiece. Suppose he had told the truth in all relevant particulars, save only in his naming of the culprit! In other words, take Trample from the narrative and substitute the figure of another. Who must that other be? Who else fulfilled all necessary conditions?

Something inside of Blackwood again seemed to be trying to tell him something. But the message stopped somewhere just short of articulate thought. He shrugged and decided to risk a cigarette.

At a safe distance he brought forth his torch and studied his position. He was in a grove of trees less dense than that through which he had journeyed to the house, and a few paces to the right there was a curving trail that led apparently to the water.

He reverted to darkness, pocketed the torch, and stepped out into the path.

At every step the hiss and murmur of the waves were clearer, and when he had passed beyond the last fringe of trees he saw the dark expanse of water. Some distance to the north, against the white shine of the beach, a roomy cabin squatted. He stepped back again into the shadows of the trees to study it.

No light shone from the windows of the shack; there seemed to be no movement anywhere. If nothing happened, he decided, in a few minutes he would go forward and investigate. Cross, at any rate, would not be there to spring upon him.

Cross. It had been an hour, at least, since he had tied the detective with his own rope and left him in the decrepit Ford. There was small likelihood, he fancied, that the fellow would be discovered—even by Prentiss, if miraculously he ever found the trail. By this time possibly Cross had recovered consciousness. If so, he would be thinking dark thoughts of Riley Blackwood. Riley Blackwood was just a bit complacent.

The distance to the cabin was not to be accomplished in a sudden sprint, such as he had made across the garden. It was close to a hundred yards, he figured. He had never made that celebrated dash in ten flat, and he never expected to. The stretch of turf that he must cross was literally bathed in starlight. What a target he would present to anybody of a homicidal turn of mind!

There was only one way to do it: light a cigarette and stroll down there as if, at least, he had been born upon the place.

But with the cigarette halfway to his lips he paused and listened. Through the trees that lay between him and the big stone house had sounded faintly the accents of a motor—the unmistakable suggestion of an arriving car. More faintly still, he thought he heard the sound of voices.

He retraced his steps along the curving path by which he had descended to the water. In the distance a tiny light was moving through the trees.

Again he caught the faint echo of voices—men's voices, he was certain. But neither light nor voices came from the precise direction of the big stone house. They were farther to the north. The light was moving slowly. He pushed forward at what speed he dared and almost instantly fell headlong into a patch of creepers.

At the same instant, it seemed to Blackwood, a shot rang out ahead, at a distance that he could not guess. He scrambled to his feet and stared wildly into the darkness. The light was stationary now, and lower down. Apparently it had been set upon the ground. The voices had ceased. Blackwood swore bitterly and stumbled forward among the trees. He had lost the trail, he realized, some minutes before. In the circumstances he dared not risk his torch.

But as he groped toward it, the distant spot of light took wings. It rose from the earth to about the level of a man's dangling hand and continued on its course—in the direction of the house. With sudden philosophy Blackwood leaned against a tree and watched it go.

For ten minutes he stood in blackness, listening; then quietly he moved forward again among the trees. The light had vanished. There was now no sound of car or voices. The rustle of the tree-tops and the whisper of the water were a part of the silence of the night. Twice he ventured a quick spurt of guidance from the torch, then pushed on doggedly. What had been the meaning of the shot that he had heard? Was it Prentiss who had arrived by car, just before he had heard the voices?

The moonlight, after a time, was brighter; he was approaching another and smaller clearing. Vaguely he sensed a small white structure of wood. It was a garage, of course. There was certain to be a garage. A car had arrived, and two men had come from the garage, carrying a light.

He stumbled into a narrow road of earth and stone, faintly outlined in the moonlight. As he did so his foot struck into something solid that lay across the path. Solid yet yielding. Something repulsive and obscene.

A shudder shook him.

There was no possible question what the object was: it was a human body.

For a crawling instant Blackwood stood very still and listened to the hammer of his heart. Then he pushed down the button of his torch and looked.

It was the body of a man, face downward among the sharp, white stones. The body of Gene Cross. There was a bullet hole in the center of his back, from which a little flow of blood still oozed, staining the light gray jacket that he wore.

Blackwood turned the body over, with horror and reluctance. The battered face looked up at him. He had made no mistake. This was Gene Cross, and he was quite, quite dead.

In sudden panic Blackwood retreated to the beach. It was

clear that somewhere in the grounds a murderer was at large. He crossed the stretch of lighted turf with shaky strides, his pistol in his hand. But it seemed unlikely now that there was anyone lurking in the cabin. It seemed to Blackwood that Cross's murder still further bore out the story he had told, and that the place was really deserted.

The cabin was quite empty.

It was a dusty place, two rooms in depth, with another room at one side, overlooking the water. His investigation was rapid. Littered with old newspapers and magazines and old fishing tackle, with here and there an ancient hat, the shack was without clue of any sort. The hats were simply old sun-straws, purchased, he fancied, in the neighboring township. There was no record in the dust of Cross's earlier occupation.

Blackwood left the musty place in haste.

On all sides the cabin was bordered by a shingle-covered veranda, falling to decay; the flooring was of pine boards laid flat against the earth. At one corner stood an antique deck chair, from which it was possible to command a view of the opening among the trees that marked the pathway to the house. Blackwood fell into it with relief. At least, he reflected, he could not be taken unawares.

He was more weary than he had realized. Small wonder, as he came to think about it! The trip itself had been a grind.

The murder of Cross had shaken him more than he was willing to admit. But it was a step forward toward solution. He would think things out a bit before returning to the house. Surely by this time all the threads were in his hands. All that was necessary was a touch of genius in weaving them together.

Blackwood marshaled his suspects and his arguments and passed them in review before him. Trample, from the constabulary point of view, was still the favorite. He fulfilled all conditions; he was the perfect solution. Poor old Trample! Prentiss, in view of his most recent conduct, was a problem without an answer; but a very likely candidate for handcuffs, either as principal or associate. Prentiss was being just a little too smart.

Cross was in many ways the key piece to the puzzle, and Cross was dead. But Cross, who at the beginning had represented Cottingham, at the end had represented someone else. This was significant.

It seemed to Blackwood that he was overlooking something vital. A hell of a detective he had been! Prentiss and Marcus, at any rate, were still in the running. And Melton had never really been a suspect. For that matter, had Holderness? The fellow had a certain color, and Cross had once pretended to be interested in him.

"Damn!"

He marshaled his clues and found them surprisingly inadequate. There were no fingerprints of any further interest, according to the police; and according to Moffat, by way of Widdowson, the occupants of rooms adjoining Cottingham's had passed serene and uneventful nights, in their several chambers, while Kitty's husband was being made ready for the coroner.

The binoculars had served their turn. He had been rather clever about the binoculars, reflected Riley Blackwood; but he had been much less clever since. There remained to him only the memory of a hypodermic syringe and a miserable patch of mud. That patch of mud! The more he thought about it the more ridiculous it seemed. As for the second patch, so curiously similar, which had seemed to lend such high significance to the first, it was probably an 18-karat dud. Good Lord! He might have left it on the floor of Kitty's room himself. What man can be certain there is not a small wafer of earth upon his sole, concealed in the angle of the heel?

Discouraged, Blackwood peered at the illuminated dial on his wrist. In spite of everything, it was not yet quite ten o'clock.

Around him lay a singing silence, a silence made up of the myriad small sounds of night and lapping water. It was a soothing melody. He lay back in his chair and in five minutes was asleep.

Why had Cross been killed?

The question was in his mind as he awoke. Something else had awakened him, however. He sat up stiffly. His pistol, of course. It had slipped from his lap to the veranda. Blackwood recovered it with alacrity and stood up, wide awake.

If Cross had told the truth about Kitty and the doctor, then it seemed probable that it was Trample who had killed him. Who else, save Kitty, could there be? In that case, the car he had heard had been not Cross's but the doctor's. He had found the detective in the woods, released him, and brought him up to the house to murder him. It seemed to Blackwood an unnecessary journey.

But if Cross had lied about the doctor, there was only one reasonable explanation. It was very simple. Cross had been killed because he had failed to murder Riley Blackwood. Cross, part of the plot that had lured Riley Blackwood to Wisconsin, had freed himself and driven to the house, and he had paid the penalty of his bungling.

Blackwood felt confident that it was something of the sort. This was what he had been groping for, he told himself; and it pointed the way to solution. For it was obvious that Gene Cross, in any case, knew far too much for somebody's peace of mind.

Once more he peered at his watch in the semi-darkness. He had been asleep not quite an hour. To sleep at all had been a criminal offense, however. It was almost eleven.

He stepped from the veranda to the turf, then stopped in amazement. A chime of bells was ringing across the water.

Ship's bells! But there was no vessel on the water. No light save that of a distant lighthouse, winking from the mainland, miles away across the bay.

Something labored in his brain. Eleven o'clock—and a set

of bells had just struck six. It reminded him of something else. Somewhere, recently, this had happened before. Then his mind functioned, and he recalled the circumstance of which he had been reminded. The little clock in Kitty's chamber at the Jamaica—the morning he had stood outside her door and knocked. It had struck six when his watch informed him it was actually eleven. He had wondered how she ever got to the theater.

Something even then had puzzled him, but he had not stopped to tease it out. At the moment it had been unimportant. And when he had got inside the room he had not noticed it.

The secret of Kitty's clock was now explained. It was a clock that struck a ship's bells instead of ordinary hours. The coincidence was interesting. *Damned* interesting!

"Oh! Oh! Oh!" said Riley Blackwood aloud.

Once more his brain functioned, this time at incredible speed; and with a shock of dismay he saw his case spread out before him. It took his breath away. What an inconceivable idiot he had been!

Little matters that had troubled him fell into place with clicking sounds that he could almost hear. His mind raced. Prentiss? Cross? No wonder Cross had been murdered! No wonder the doctor had been kidnaped! He must actually have *seen* that first attempt. Melton's testimony had placed him squarely in the passage at the time that Cross went overboard. Prentiss too must have suspected something—tardily. But Prentiss was in no danger unless he reached the house before Riley Blackwood could get back. It was possible that Prentiss was not himself suspected.

He strained his eyes across the waters of the bay. There was no vessel within sight or sound. To the southward, and close at hand, a long dark promontory of wooded land jutted out into the water, concealing the shoreline beyond. Behind that barrier, he had easily assumed, lay miles and yet more miles of fir and pine and barren, rocky beach.

With long strides Blackwood set off across the flat; after a few minutes he began to run. But in a little time he entered into trees again and had to pick his way with caution. For several hundred feet he struggled through patches of alternating light and darkness, guided only by the vague sound of the water and his own sense of direction. Then he was on the long ridge of the promontory, looking through the last barrier of trees at the scene which lay beneath him.

It was a miniature harbor, complete with dock and pier, and at the landward extremity lay a smart new boathouse. Moored at the dock was something long and white that gleamed in the moonlight, marked by a little light that danced and dipped with every movement of the waves.

There was no other moving object within view.

Blackwood laid his hand against a tree and breathed heavily. For a moment he almost babbled. "What the—what—what the devil is the meaning of this?" he cried.

He scrambled down the intervening hillside with fear in his heart and emerged upon the dock. New revelations were clamoring in his mind. But even from the ridge his eyes had not deceived him.

The motor launch was trim and graceful, and saucy as the young woman for whom she had been named. Her hull, in the shimmering starlight, was white with a broad band of black. The curve of her stern and prow was as familiar to Blackwood as the lobby of a theater. He had sailed upon her many times.

She was the *Charming Sally*, out of Belmont Harbor, Chicago, and Tony Widdowson was her owner.

15.

BUT HURRYING STEALTHILY toward the big stone house, by the new path that he had discovered, Blackwood again was easy in his mind. For a number of terrifying moments the shock of his original revelation had been overwhelmed by the greater impact of that sudden sight of Widdowson's launch. Now he was coldly angry.

No doubt, with a little ingenuity, he could invent a case against his friend that would appear as damning as the case against the doctor. Certainly Widdowson had had the opportunity to murder Cottingham; and motives are easily imagined. Even the thought, however, was arrant nonsense. It was almost comic. And Widdowson had no wild estate in primitive Wisconsin.

No, the case was solved; it had been solved by that silver chime of bells across the water. Odd how little it required, at the last, to oil the wheels of intellect, reflected Riley Blackwood, a trifle immodestly. And it was ironic that the ultimate clue should be a clock on Tony's launch.

As if to clinch his solution, there came back to Blackwood a casual sentence dropped by Widdowson, in conversation, some weeks before. They had taken the *Sally* to the Fair Grounds for a look at the new splendors. "There's only one man in Chicago with whom I'd trust her," Widdowson had said, meaning the launch and not a woman.

This was a reckless business on which he had now embarked, thought Blackwood. He might be shot while crossing to the house. There could be no doubt that some watch was being kept for his appearance. The miracle was that he had not been trapped and murdered, down there beside the water.

Kitty was in it pretty deeply, he supposed. And Trample—what of Trample? Already murdered, perhaps, and buried in this wilderness of trees! It had been Cross who had done the job, of course—Cross who was now dead and damned himself. It had been Cross who had kidnaped Trample at the Fair Grounds and hurried him, on some pretext or other, to the harbor. Almost any story would have done. It had been Cross whom Marcus's friend had seen with Trample, stepping into the cab.

That telephone call? A relay! A smart trick, that. The murderer, of course, was already in Wisconsin. And he—Riley Blackwood—had blindly held the wire! It sickened him to realize how the fellow had lied to him, and how he had fallen for all his lies.

Oh, yes! it was all simple enough now. The invitation to the party—a ruse to find out what, if anything, was suspected. And again the irony of things, that Trample should have gone along. Even the patch of mud now found its little aperture in the completed picture. The grounds around the harbor were full of it—and cinders too.

When had Prentiss begun to suspect? And how? To be sure, he too had been upon the yacht, the night that Cross went overboard. A tardy memory of something he had heard or seen? It had struck him suddenly, at any rate, and obviously just after Riley Blackwood—that energetic sleuth!—had left Chicago. And *hard* enough to call off a trip of some importance.

Blackwood hurried through the last patch of trees and halted at the margin of the lawn. No feeling of nervousness now bothered him; his pistol—still a virgin—lay loosely in his grasp. It occurred to him to wonder if it kicked.

The firelight still leaped upon the pane. Upstairs the bedroom light still burned. And cool as was the night, Riley Blackwood's overcoat was beginning to discommode him. He slipped it off and left it among the trees.

Then, very quietly, for fear his knees should crack, he lowered his long body to the earth. It was undignified, he felt—like crawling to his seat along a theater aisle—but less dangerous than walking upright.

> *The stage is set;*
> *The lights are low.*
> *Ring up the curtain—*
> *Start the show!*

"Poem," murmured Mr. Blackwood, "by me."

But at the very instant that he began his crawl a faint sound struck upon his ear. It was as if it had been carried in telegraphic waves along the earth against which he lay. Somewhere he had heard or read that such things happened. He laid his ear along the ground and waited.

Nothing!

The sound was repeated, and this time he raised his head and heard it without difficulty. A faint, metallic sort of sound, somewhere over among the trees to his left. Near the garage, perhaps. Near Cross's body. Such a sound, perhaps, as a spade might make, striking against a stone, when it was plunged into the earth.

A shocking thought.

Blackwood rose painfully to his feet. With excessive caution he moved in the direction of the sound. The moonlight, as he reached the trail that led to the garage, lighted the broken stone with which the earth was salted. He crept forward on the border of the grass and reached a turning, around which he seemed to sense a brighter radiance.

Some fifty yards beyond, a lantern sat at the edge of the path, and in a miniature clearing, in the shadows of the trees, a man was digging a grave.

The body of Gene Cross still lay where it had fallen.

Blackwood turned softly and retreated toward the house. Now, he reflected, was his time—or never.

He crossed the lawn with rapid strides but without sound and mounted to the porch. The doorknob turned easily beneath his hand. He closed the door behind him. In a darkness lighted only by the leaping flames upon the hearth he looked at Kitty Mock. Her eyes were wide with stupefied amazement; her knuckles were at her mouth.

"One yip out of that beautiful mouth of yours," said Blackwood in a pleasant, low-pitched voice, "and I'll knock you for a row of ash cans, Kitty. Where is Dr. Trample?"

Her reply surprised him. "Thank God you've come!" said Kitty Mock. "I thought——" She stepped forward and laid a hand on his arm.

"What?"

"I thought you had been killed."

With a cynical smile he reassured her. "That shot, you mean? I see! No—that was Cross, passing to his reward. He is now in process of being buried."

"Dead?" she whispered.

Blackwood's smile broadened. "That's why he's being buried." It was an old joke but a good one. He snapped again, "Where is Dr. Trample?"

"Upstairs," she answered. "I've been—I've been nursing him."

"Oh yes?" said Blackwood. "I'll look into that in just a minute." But he was relieved by her reply. She might be lying, of course. There was something curious in the situation—and time was passing.

"He was hurt," she told him. "When he was brought here."

"How does it happen he wasn't killed?" he asked her brutally. "Are you lying to me, Kitty? I warn you—I've had enough of that."

She shook her head. "Don't be a fool! I'm telling you the truth. I'm glad you've come. I didn't think anyone would ever find us. I thought I could see it through alone—but I can't. My own life is in danger. I feel it! Don't you see? I suspected too! I've been trying to get proof."

Her words were now tumbling out and piling up on top of one another like the letters of a typewriter.

He shrugged skeptically. "You might have saved yourself a lot of agony if you'd taken me into your confidence."

"You wouldn't have believed me. You were so sure that I was guilty too. I was sorry to have to lie to you so much."

There was some truth in the reproach, he inwardly admitted. But he was sure that she was guilty now, for that matter. She was still a very creditable actress.

"You came up here with Cross and Trample——"

"And with *him* too," she interrupted. "He borrowed Mr. Widdowson's boat because it was fast; nobody suspected him but me. I didn't know the doctor had been injured; I didn't know he was in the boat until I saw him. I thought we were just going some place till things blew over. I wanted proof."

"Why did you think Trample was being kidnaped?"

"I know why he was kidnaped. That night—in my room at the Jamaica—Jeffrey Cottingham, my husband, swore he had told Dr. Trample all about it."

"About your affair with Haviland?"

The actress did not falter. "Yes!"

That was it, of course. Cottingham had lied in self-protection. Trample had known nothing at any time. But it was a miracle that the doctor was still living—if he really was.

Blackwood glanced swiftly to the window. How long, he wondered, did it take to dig a grave?

"All right," he said. "I'm going up."

He blundered to the staircase, looming dimly at one side, and clattered upward into darkness. It was possible that Kitty was telling the truth at last, he reflected; but there were still a lot of things requiring explanation.

The gravedigger might return at any instant. A touch of *Hamlet* in the wilderness! He felt his side pocket in which his pistol lay ready. The corridor, at the front, was thinly lighted by the low gleam in Trample's chamber. He tiptoed to the door and peered inside.

"Who's that?" a voice asked swiftly—with sudden fear.

Blackwood could have wept. That the arrogant, courageous doctor should have been brought to this!

"It's Blackwood, Trample—don't get excited." He strode quickly to the bedside.

"Good God!" The doctor's head rose from the pillow; the bed creaked sharply. "I almost shot you!"

Blackwood was astonished. "You've got a pistol?"

"A little thing." The doctor was apologetic. "It isn't a pistol. Miss Mock's, I think. She gave it to me tonight. That girl's all right. By George, Blackwood, but I'm glad to see you! What the devil——?"

"I'm afraid there's not much time for talk," said Blackwood swiftly. "Haviland is just outside. He's digging a grave for Cross—perhaps for all of us. He didn't see me. I could have killed him."

"He's murdered Cross?"

"Shot him in the back," said Blackwood crisply. "Look here, Trample! Can you move?"

Horace Trample sat upright in his bed. "Of course I can move. We've been fooling him, you know. He thinks I'm going to die. It's all that kept him from murdering me when we arrived this morning. They carried me to the house."

"Saving himself another murder," said Blackwood thoughtfully. "My God, what a situation for a man of Haviland's reputation! The public thought he was a saint. It was that that drove him to it, of course. He didn't *want* to murder anybody in the first place, I suppose. What's the matter with you, Trample?"

"Just a crack on the head. We've been pretending that I've got a concussion. I've learned to be quite an actor."

Blackwood walked over to the window and peered out into the night. Over among the trees he could just see the twinkling spot of light from the murderer's lantern. He came back to the bed.

"You'd better get into your clothes—if you're sure that you can make it. We'll want to get away from here. I may have to kill Haviland. You saw him push Cross overboard, didn't you?"

"Yes, I saw him." The doctor, a little shaky, was endeavoring to put on a pair of trousers. Blackwood steadied him. "That's one reason that I'm here," continued Trample. "Also, he thinks that poor devil Cottingham told me a lot of stuff the night we changed our rooms. He was afraid I'd talk and he would be accused of the murder. He still insists that it was suicide." The doctor sat down, and Blackwood handed him his shoes. "I can only say that he took a queer way of persuading me."

"It couldn't have been suicide, of course?" said Blackwood. "We can prove it on him, can't we?"

"Oh, it could have been, all right—but it wasn't! Cross had the goods on him. Pity he's dead; but I've picked up enough to know the situation. Cross was blackmailing him. Saw him come out of Cottingham's room, that night and hang that damned card on the door. Of course, he says Cottingham asked him to."

Blackwood nodded. "I think we've got him, between the three of us," he agreed. It pleased him to know that he had been correct in his own diagnosis of the ingenious tale spun by the detective in the woods.

He gravitated to the window again, and flung a question over his shoulder. "You're sure of Kitty, are you?"

"She's on the square—now, at any rate. She's sure he killed Cottingham, and she hates him. She came up here to prove it on him, when she thought no one else suspected."

"His whole course is a confession," said Blackwood. "He hired Cross to kidnap you, and later to murder me. That didn't come off, and so he murdered Cross himself. I've no doubt you and Kitty would have followed." He shrugged. "He'd have done better to stand the gaff in the beginning. He has children, of course—but what the hell! It's better to be a co-respondent than a corpse. And he's either got to die up here or 'burn.'"

The doctor was walking softly about the room, a trifle groggy. "My head swings a bit," he said; "but I think I'm all right, Blackwood. What do we do now?"

"Keep that popgun handy and back me up in case I need assistance."

The doctor twirled it on his little finger. "And what do *you* do next?"

"Damned if I know, exactly," admitted Riley Blackwood.

For the last time he moved to the window and looked out into the darkness. The little light among the trees had vanished.

A moment later his question had been answered for him.

From the stairfoot came a cry from Kitty Mock: "Look out! He's coming!" and at the same instant Blackwood, standing beside the window, heard the sound of footsteps on the stone porch below. The door was opening.

They tiptoed from the bedroom to the corridor and listened. The voice of Cope Haviland came up the dark stairpit from the living room. It was brisk and almost cheerful.

"Well, that's the end of Eugene Cross," the yachtsman said. "One down and two to go. Oh, don't be scared! I had to kill him, Kitty, or we could never have gone back. That crazy devil Blackwood is still somewhere in the woods. I hope he breaks his neck. What bothers me is, I'm afraid he may have gone for help. Look here, Kitty—I want to get away from here tonight! Good God! I thought we'd have some privacy up here." He laughed harshly. "Privacy!"

They heard her little cry of protest. "Tonight?"

"Sorry," said Haviland, "but it can't be helped. The launch is ready. I've just been down there. What about the doctor? Isn't he ever going to die?"

"He's—holding his own yet, I think," said Kitty Mock. She was acting superbly. Blackwood felt a little like applauding. "Shall I go up, again?" she asked.

It was too good to last.

A board creaked under Trample's foot; and Blackwood moved swiftly to the stairhead. Haviland's voice had changed.

"Who's that?" he asked. "You bitch, have you been fooling me?" He started for the stairs, and she attempted to intercept him; but he threw her roughly to one side.

Blackwood moved slowly down to meet him. "Get back, Haviland," he ordered easily. His voice, in the darkness, he noted with surprise, was firm and even courteous. He raised it slightly. "Get back, damn you! Stay exactly where you are. I've got a pistol on you—and you can't see me. Put your hands over your head and walk out into the room."

A roar of laughter swept up the stairpit.

"By the great hornspoon, it's old Riley, himself!" cried the yachtsman boisterously. "I might have guessed it. But how the devil, Riley, can I stay exactly where I am and still move into the center of the room?"

Blackwood was annoyed. "If you don't put up your hands and start," he answered viciously, "I'll shoot you dead as hell, Haviland. I mean it!"

The yachtsman slowly raised his hands until they were on a level with his ears and moved into the firelight. "All right, all right," he protested good-humoredly; "but I don't know what it's all about. What next, old man?"

Blackwood finished his descent, closely followed by the doctor. At sight of Trample, the yachtsman's brows pushed upward. He shot a savage glance at Kitty Mock.

"Yes," she said serenely, "I fooled you about the doctor too." She walked to Horace Trample's side and took the little weapon from his hand. "I'll help you keep an eye on this murderer, Mr. Blackwood," she finished easily.

"May I sit down?" asked Haviland. The question was abrupt. Without waiting for permission he dropped into a chair. "Of course, I know what all this means," he added, in conversational tones. "You think you've got me for the murder of Jeffrey Cottingham—Kitty's husband. You're crazy, all of you. Cottingham committed suicide. I went to him, that night, it's true, and tried to talk him out of bringing suit. It would have ruined me—with the reputation I've had as a reformer and philanthropist! He was courteous—he understood my point of view—we even had a drink together. But I couldn't move him. He wanted a divorce, and that was that. I went away, and next morning he was found dead. He probably finished the bottle, after I left him, and decided that suicide was the easiest way out for everybody."

The yachtsman spread his hands and looked about him with an appearance of great frankness.

"He finished the bottle, all right; we noticed that. I am willing to believe that the morphine was in the bottle, instead of in his glass." Blackwood was speaking quietly. "Did your husband ever use morphine, Kitty?" he asked.

She shook her head. "Never! It was I. I hate it, but—sometimes I have to have it. He used to get it for me. Haviland, I mean. That's how I knew that it was he who——"

"That's simply nonsense," interrupted the yachtsman impatiently. "He had the stuff himself, that night. It's easy enough to get when you know how. To tell the truth, I thought he got it from Dr. Trample. He'd often thought of suicide—he told me so. I think he tried to implicate Kitty; that's why he chose morphine. He was pretty mad at her, you know. He blamed her more than he did me."

Blackwood shrugged. "And because you thought you might be accused of murder, if it were known that you were in his room, you were willing to let suspicion fall on Dr. Trample? *Pretty!* But Cross knew all about it; and you were paying him to keep his mouth shut. He had a bigger hold on you than ever, after you'd thrown him overboard. You paid him to kidnap Trample and to murder me. After you'd failed yourself! Or did you try to kill me yesterday afternoon, in Kitty's room, when you were making ready to escape? I give you the benefit of the doubt. But it was you that hit me."

He caught the actress's little gasp and realized that she had not known of the episode in her apartment. She had been hiding, probably, in another room, after the manager had given the alarm. Ah, yes! That manager. He must have a little talk with Holabird when he returned to Chicago.

He continued with his charge. "At any rate, it was you that murdered Cross, and that would have murdered the doctor—if you hadn't thought that he was dying anyway. You would have murdered Kitty, too, after you'd got rid of all the rest of us!"

He finished his indictment with sparkling eyes. "Well, it was a large order, and an ambitious one; but you haven't got away with it. I'm almost sorry for you, Haviland—*but, baby, you're going to the chair!*"

Suddenly he smiled. "It may interest you to know that it was the sound of that little clock of Kitty's—the one you gave her, I believe?—that put me on your trail."

Haviland rose and yawned.

"I have no doubt that you've been very clever, Blackwood," he sneered. "Two and two make five! But, as it happens, I can prove everything that I've said. I have a paper here——"

He reached a hand into his inner pocket, and Kitty Mock screamed loudly.

Her ridiculous .32 cracked just an instant before Haviland's larger weapon, and the heavier lead plowed a furrow in the baseboard. Haviland's arm dropped helplessly at his side; his pistol thudded to the floor. The yachtsman clutched at his wounded arm—then, almost before they were aware of his intention, he bounded for the door. The next moment he was outside and clattering down the stone steps to the lawn.

Kitty Mock was staring at her weapon in astonishment; she was suddenly aware that it had been discharged. Her accurate shooting might have been regarded as miraculous if she had had any notion that she had pulled the trigger.

Blackwood, still clutching his pistol and cursing wildly, was hurrying across the lawn in hot pursuit of the escaping murderer, followed at some distance by the heavier Trample. But Haviland was already out of sight among the trees. Somewhere ahead they could hear the disturbance of his running. He was racing down the dim trail toward the water.

The drama critic of the *Morning Chronicle* emerged upon the dock in time to see the white arrow that was the *Charming Sally* shoot out into the bay, with motors roaring. She was headed eastward into the mystery of black and silver waters. Dimly, in her stern, by the somewhat confusing radiance of the moon and stars, he thought he saw a dark figure crouched behind her engines. The trail of the little launch upon the water was foaming white, a vivid spectacle. The staccato uproar of her motors persisted long after she had passed from sight.

It was some minutes later that Horace Trample came pounding down the pier. He had been delayed among the trees. He found his friend and rescuer lost in meditation.

"Good Lord, Blackwood," cried the doctor. "Did the fellow get away?"

But Blackwood only shrugged.

"I don't suppose it really makes any difference," he replied, at length. "He can't go any place in safety, once the telephones get busy. I was just wondering if he wanted to."

After a time he said complainingly: "Confound it, Trample! Do you suppose I ever *will* learn how to use this god damn gun?"

16.

"FUNNY THING about Miss Oliver and Prentiss," said Widdowson, a few days later. He spread a fragment of toast with marmalade, looked at it with appreciation, and popped it into his mouth. "I should think they'd have looked us up—at least to say hello."

Riley Blackwood's newspaper was propped against a sugar bowl. He had been reading a brief notice, written by himself, about an English company of Shakespearean actors that would shortly descend upon Chicago. His opinion of the company was not high, and a headline for his first review was beginning to form in his mind: "Hams Across the Sea—" and possibly something about a barbecue.

"Oh, no," he answered after a little silence; "they've seen enough of us, I fancy, to last them for a lifetime. They were fairly disgusted with *me* by the time we met them in Davidsons on Saturday morning. They'd been hunting for me half the night—trying to rescue me—and were almost annoyed when I showed up safe and sound." He laughed. "Prentiss's sudden hunch that Haviland was the trouble-maker was a daisy! It almost converts one to a belief in the futility of cerebral detection. Simply because Cross had been on Haviland's yacht and he didn't like Cross! *My God!*"

"It was decent of him to set out after you," said Widdowson.

"In a big blue car? He scared me half to death! Why the devil couldn't he have hired a white one, if his own was blue? Why the devil didn't he catch up with me and tell me what was on his mind? But no—he just wanted to keep an eye on me! Didn't want to alarm me, in case he might be wrong! Alarm me! That's all he *did* do!"

Widdowson laughed. "I'm sorry my boat was involved," he said. "It wasn't exactly theft—I'd told Haviland, time and again, he could have it when he wanted it; but I'd no idea it was missing. Where the dickens do you suppose he had the doctor hidden until Thursday evening? Trample was certainly kidnaped on Wednesday."

"On his own boat, of course. He simply brought your launch alongside and made the transfer. Cross was in charge. None of them reached Wisconsin until Friday morning, when Cross sent his telegram. When I telephoned Haviland on Friday— like a blinking idiot—he was already up there. I held the wire while somebody in his office relayed the call. I don't know whether I'm proud of myself or not, Tony. At any rate, you'll get the launch back. Even if Haviland has gone overboard, somebody'll pick it up."

"I saw Trample last night, for just a minute, by the way," said Tony Widdowson. "He isn't going back to New York immediately. Kitty's shipped her husband's body on, and I suspect she and the doctor will go back together. Now what do you think of that?"

"Good Lord!" said Blackwood. "Not really?" He considered the information for a minute. It might be quite a decent thing for both of them. Trample could cure the lady's appetite for drugs, perhaps—and if he couldn't, he could get them for her. As for Trample, he really needed some sophisticated person to look after him.

"It's not a bad idea, Tony," he continued aloud. "I'm really very fond of both of them. I hope you're right."

"Oh, I'm right enough," said Tony Widdowson.

For a few moments, Riley Blackwood continued to think about it; then he returned to the fascinating pages of the *Morning Chronicle*. Quite suddenly he sat erect and stared.

"Well, I'll be jiggered," he said, "if Prentiss and Blaine Oliver aren't going to do it, too! Her picture's in the paper."

"Get married?" asked Widdowson. "Well, I suppose that was inevitable. They've been thrown together in some curious circumstances. And people *will* get married."

Mr. Blackwood continued to look musingly upon the pictured features of Blaine Oliver. She had been a nice little thing. He had really liked her quite a lot. Once he had thought he would be able to add her telephone number to his little notebook. He had been vaguely thinking about giving her a ring, that evening— simply to ask if she were well and happy after her adventures.

There was a pencil beside his plate. He picked it up and idly drew a number of patterns on the margin of his paper. He flattened the paper out upon the table and wrote his name a number of times across the text. One signature that was particularly good, he shaded with little strokes until it stood out somewhat like a bas-relief.

It was a yellow pencil, with lead that was soft and black.

He placed the point against Miss Oliver's curving lip, beneath her attractive nose, and with careful industry gave her a sweeping and luxuriant mustache.

THE END

DISCUSSION QUESTIONS

- Were you able to predict any part of the solution to the case?

- Aside from the solution, did anything about the book surprise you? If so, what?

- Did any aspects of the plot date the story? If so, which ones?

- Would the story be different if it were set in the present day? If so, how?

- What role did the setting play in the narrative?

- If you were one of the main characters, would you have acted differently at any point in the story?

- Did you identify with any of the characters? If so, who?

- Did this novel remind you of anything else you've read? If so, what?

- What were some particular qualities that made Riley Blackwood an effective investigator? Were there any?

AMERICAN MYSTERY CLASSICS *from*

AMERICAN MYSTERY CLASSICS *from*

*Available now
in hardcover and paperback:*

And More to Come!

Visit penzlerpublishers.com, email info@penzlerpublishers.com for
more information, or find us on social media at @penzlerpub

John Dickson Carr
The Crooked Hinge

Introduction by Charles Todd

*An inheritance hangs in the balance in a case of
stolen identities, imposters, and murder*

Banished from the idyllic English countryside he once called home, Sir John Farnleigh, black sheep of the wealthy Farnleigh clan, nearly perished in the sinking of the Titanic. Though he survived the catastrophe, his ties with his family did not, and he never returned to England until now, nearly 25 years later, when he comes to claim his inheritance. But another "Sir John" soon follows, an unexpected man who insists he has absolute proof of his identity and of his claim to the estate. Before the case can be settled, however, one of the two men is murdered, and Dr. Gideon Fell finds himself facing one of the most challenging cases of his career. He'll soon confront a series of bizarre and chilling phenomena, diving deep into the realm of the occult to solve a seemingly impossible crime.

JOHN DICKSON CARR (1906-1977) was one of the greatest writers of the American Golden Age mystery, and the only American author to be included in England's legendary Detection Club during his lifetime. Under his own name and various pseudonyms, he wrote more than seventy novels and numerous short stories, and is best known today for his locked-room mysteries.

> "An all-time classic by an author scrupulous
> about playing fair with his readers"
> —*Publishers Weekly* (Starred Review)

Paperback, $15.95 / ISBN 978-1-61316-130-2
Hardcover, $25.95 / ISBN 978-1-61316-129-6

Erle Stanley Gardner
The Case of the
Careless Kitten

Introduction by Otto Penzler

Perry Mason seeks the link between a poisoned kitten, a murdered man, and a mysterious voice from the past

Helen Kendal's woes begin when she receives a phone call from her vanished uncle Franklin, long presumed dead, who urges her to make contact with criminal defense attorney Perry Mason; soon after, she finds herself the main suspect in the murder of an unfamiliar man. Her kitten has just survived a poisoning attempt, as has her aunt Matilda, the woman who always maintained that Franklin was alive in spite of his disappearance. It's clear that all the occurrences are connected, and that their connection will prove her innocence, but the links in the case are too obscure to be recognized even by the attorney's brilliantly deductive mind. To solve the puzzle, he'll need the help of his secretary Della Street, his private eye Paul Drake, and the unlikely but invaluable aid of a careless but very clever kitten.

ERLE STANLEY GARDNER (1889-1970) was the best-selling American author of the 20th century, mainly due to the enormous success of his Perry Mason series, which numbered more than 80 novels and inspired a half-dozen motion pictures, radio programs, and a long-running television series that starred Raymond Burr.

> "One of the best of the Perry Mason tales."
> —*New York Times*

Paperback, $15.95 / ISBN 978-1-61316-116-6
Hardcover, $25.95 / ISBN 978-1-61316-115-9

Frances Noyes Hart
The Bellamy Trial

Introduction by
Hank Phillippi Ryan

A murder trial scandalizes the upper echelons of Long Island society, and the reader is on the jury...

The trial of Stephen Bellamy and Susan Ives, accused of murdering Bellamy's wife Madeleine, lasts eight days. That's eight days of witnesses (some reliable, some not), eight days of examination and cross-examination, and eight days of sensational courtroom theatrics lively enough to rouse the judge into frenzied calls for order. Ex-fiancés, houseworkers, and assorted family members are brought to the stand—a cross-section of this wealthy Long Island town—and each one only adds to the mystery of the case in all its sordid detail. A trial that seems straightforward at its outset grows increasingly confounding as it proceeds, and surprises abound; by the time the closing arguments are made, however, the reader, like the jury, is provided with all the evidence needed to pass judgement on the two defendants. Still, only the most astute among them will not be shocked by the verdict announced at the end.

FRANCES NOYES HART (1890-1943) was an American writer whose stories were published in *Scribner's*, *The Saturday Evening Post*, where *The Bellamy Trial* was first serialized, and *The Ladies' Home Journal*.

"An enthralling story."—*New York Times*

Paperback, $15.95 / ISBN 978-1-61316-144-9
Hardcover, $25.95 / ISBN 978-1-61316-143-2

OTTO PENZLER PRESENTS

=== AMERICAN MYSTERY CLASSICS ===

Dorothy B. Hughes
Dread Journey

Introduction by
Sarah Weinman

*A movie star fears for her life on a train journey from
Los Angeles to New York...*

Hollywood big-shot Vivien Spender has waited ages to produce the work
that will be his masterpiece: a film adaptation of Thomas Mann's The
Magic Mountain. He's spent years grooming young starlets for the lead
role, only to discard each one when a newer, fresher face enters his view.
Afterwards, these rejected women all immediately fall from grace; excised
from the world of pictures, they end up in rehab, or jail, or worse. But
Kitten Agnew, the most recent to encounter this impending doom, won't
be gotten rid of so easily—her contract simply doesn't allow for it. Accompanied by Mr. Spender on a train journey from Los Angeles to Chicago, she begins to fear that the producer might be considering a deadly
alternative. Either way, it's clear that something is going to happen before
they reach their destination, and as the train barrels through America's
heartland, the tension accelerates towards an inescapable finale.

DOROTHY B. HUGHES (1904–1993) was a mystery author and literary critic famous for her taut thrillers, many of which were made into films. While
best known for the noir classic *In a Lonely Place*, Hughes' writing successfully spanned a range of styles including espionage and domestic suspense.

**"The perfect in-flight read. The only thing that's dated is
the long-distance train."—*Kirkus***

Paperback, $15.95 / ISBN 978-1-61316-146-3
Hardcover, $25.95 / ISBN 978-1-61316-145-6

Stuart Palmer
The Puzzle of the Happy Hooligan

Introduction by Otto Penzler

After a screenwriter is murdered on a film set, a street-smart school teacher searches for the killer.

Hildegarde Withers is just your average school teacher—with above-average skills in the art of deduction. The New Yorker often finds herself investigating crimes led only by her own meddlesome curiosity, though her friends on the NYPD don't mind when she solves their cases for them. After plans for a grand tour of Europe are interrupted by Germany's invasion of Poland, Miss Withers heads to sunny Los Angeles instead, where her vacation finds her working as a technical advisor on the set of a film adaptation of the Lizzie Borden story. The producer has plans for an epic retelling of the historical killer's patricidal spree—plans which are derailed when a screenwriter turns up dead. While the local authorities quickly deem his death accidental, Withers suspects otherwise and calls up a detective back home for advice. The two soon team up to catch a wily killer.

STUART PALMER (1905–1968) was an American author of mysteries, most famous for his beloved Hildegarde Withers character. A master of intricate plotting, Palmer found success writing for Hollywood, where several of his books were adapted for the screen.

"Will keep you laughing and guessing from the first page to the last."—*New York Times*

Paperback, $15.95 / ISBN 978-1-61316-104-3
Hardcover, $25.95 / ISBN 978-1-61316-114-2

Ellery Queen
The Siamese Twin
Mystery

Introduction by Otto Penzler

Ellery Queen takes refuge from a wildfire at a remote mountain house — and arrives just before the owner is murdered...

When Ellery Queen and his father encounter a raging forest fire during a mountain drive, the only direction to go is up a winding dirt road that leads to an isolated hillside manor, inhabited by a secretive surgeon and his diverse cast of guests. Trapped by the fire, the Queens settle into the uneasy atmosphere of their surroundings. Then, the following morning, the doctor is discovered dead, apparently shot down while playing solitaire the night before.

The only clue is a torn six of spades. The suspects include a society beauty, a suspicious valet, and a pair of conjoined twins. When another murder follows, the killer inside the house becomes as threatening as the mortal flames outside its walls. Can Queen solve this whodunnit before the fire devours its subjects?

ELLERY QUEEN was a pen name created and shared by two cousins, Frederic Dannay (1905-1982) and Manfred B. Lee (1905-1971), as well as the name of their most famous detective.

"Queen at his best . . . a classic of brilliant
deduction under extreme circumstances."
—*Publishers Weekly* (Starred Review)

Paperback, $15.95 / ISBN 978-1-61316-155-5
Hardcover, $25.95 / ISBN 978-1-61316-154-8

Craig Rice
Home Sweet Homicide

Introduction by Otto Penzler

The children of a mystery writer play amateur sleuths and matchmakers

Unoccupied and unsupervised while mother is working, the children of widowed crime writer Marion Carstairs find diversion wherever they can. So when the kids hear gunshots at the house next door, they jump at the chance to launch their own amateur investigation—and after all, why shouldn't they? They know everything the cops do about crime scenes, having read about them in mother's novels. They know what her literary detectives would do in such a situation, how they would interpret the clues and handle witnesses. Plus, if the children solve the puzzle before the cops, it will do wonders for the sales of mother's novels. But this crime scene isn't a game at all; the murder is real and, when its details prove more twisted than anything in mother's fiction, they'll eventually have to enlist Marion's help to sort out the clues. Or is that just part of their plan to hook her up with the lead detective on the case?

CRAIG RICE (1908–1957), born Georgiana Ann Randolph Craig, was an American author of mystery novels, short stories, and screenplays. Rice's writing style was unique in its ability to mix gritty, hard-boiled writing with the entertainment of a screwball comedy.

"A genuine midcentury classic."—*Booklist*

Paperback, $15.95 / ISBN 978-1-61316-103-6
Hardcover, $25.95 / ISBN 978-1-61316-112-8

Mary Roberts Rinehart
Miss Pinkerton

Introduction by Carolyn Hart

*After a suspicious death at a mansion, a brave nurse
joins the household to see behind closed doors*

Miss Adams is a nurse, not a detective—at least, not technically speaking. But while working as a nurse, one does have the opportunity to see things police can't see and an observant set of eyes can be quite an asset when crimes happen behind closed doors. Sometimes Detective Inspector Patton rings Miss Adams when he needs an agent on the inside. And when he does, he calls her "Miss Pinkerton" after the famous detective agency.

Everyone involved seems to agree that mild-mannered Herbert Wynne wasn't the type to commit suicide but, after he is found shot dead, with the only other possible killer being his ailing, bedridden aunt, no other explanation makes sense. Now the elderly woman is left without a caretaker and Patton sees the perfect opportunity to employ Miss Pinkerton's abilities. But when she arrives at the isolated country mansion to ply her trade, she soon finds more intrigue than anyone outside could have imagined and—when she realizes a killer is on the loose—more terror as well.

MARY ROBERTS RINEHART (1876-1958) was the most beloved and best-selling mystery writer in America in the first half of the twentieth century.

"An entertaining puzzle mystery that stands the test of time."—*Publishers Weekly*

Paperback, $15.95 / ISBN 978-1-61316-269-9

Hardcover, $25.95 / ISBN 978-1-61316-138-8

Mary Roberts Rinehart

Rinehart

Miss Pinkerton

Introduction by Carolyn Hart

After a suspicious death in a mansion, a nurse plays
spy, the housekeeper, too, behind closed doors

"An entertaining puzzle-mystery that stands the
test of time." — Publishers Weekly